To my dear readers,

We all read differently, a

If you are the sort of reade............... and read till you get to the end of a book, then please dive in and enjoy the adventure of *Storm Horse*.

To my dyslexic readers, who are like me, and to those other young people who may find reading a challenge, I'd like you to dip in and enjoy small manageable chunks of this book at a time.

You will see that *Storm Horse* is actually broken up into sections and has lots of exciting letters from the past inserted into the story from my main character Daniel's great-great-grandfather, who watched the racehorse Seabiscuit win races during the Great Depression in 1930s America.

So remember, one manageable chunk at a time, and before you know it you will have reached the end of the adventure.

I hope you all enjoy meeting Daniel and his friends as they plot to keep one rather special horse a secret.

Jane Eisa

Also by Jane Elson

A Room Full of Chocolate
How to Fly with Broken Wings
Swimming to the Moon
Will You Catch Me?
Moon Dog

Storm
Horse

JANE ELSON

Hodder
Children's
Books

HODDER CHILDREN'S BOOKS

First published in Great Britain in 2021 by Hodder & Stoughton

1 3 5 7 9 10 8 6 4 2

A CIP catalogue record for this book
is available from the British Library.

ISBN 978 1 444 95569 9

Typeset in DIN Light by Avon DataSet Ltd, Arden Court, Alcester, Warwickshire

Printed and bound in Great Britain by Clays Ltd, Elcograf S.p.A.

The paper and board used in this book are made from
wood from responsible sources.

Hodder Children's Books
An imprint of Hachette Children's Group
Part of Hodder & Stoughton
Carmelite House
50 Victoria Embankment
London EC4Y 0DZ

An Hachette UK Company
www.hachette.co.uk

www.hachettechildrens.co.uk

For my hero, Seabiscuit, and for all those to whom he brought hope

And for my dear friend Christopher Ryan, whose grandfather, Roy F. Ryan, watched Seabiscuit's grandfather, Man O' War, race at Kenilworth Park Racetrack, Windsor, Ontario in 1920 when he was nine years old

'When I bestride him, I soar, I am a hawk: he trots the air; the earth sings when he touches it; the basest horn of his hoof is more musical than the pipe of Hermes.'

William Shakespeare, *Henry V*

In The Beginning

My great-great-grandad, Cuthbert H. Brown Junior, lived in a car. His ma slept in the front seat, his pa in the driving seat and Cuthbert H. Brown Junior, who was small like me, curled up on the back seat with his sister Dora and brother Frank – all higgledy-piggledy with their pots and pans and clothes.

When it was warm, they slept on the grass looking up at the night sky, sending the stars wishes that they could get rich and live in a house again.

Because, you see, my American ancestors – that's why I said ma and pa (like old-time American films) – well, they lost everything, along with thousands of people, in what they called the Great Depression, and they often went to sleep with rumbling bellies.

Sometimes it's a bit like that for me, Daniel Margate, and some of the other kids on the Beckham Estate where I live in north-west London. Two whole months and a week ago, Mum and me and my little brother Jackson went on one of our visits to the food bank 'cause Mum had nothing in her purse to feed us with. When we reached the bit of the table with the pasta, Jackson flung himself out of his buggy on to the floor and screamed loud enough to shatter windows and Mum couldn't make him stop and started crying too. I curled up in a ball in the corner with my fingers in my ears. Then a lady called Jackie gave me a hot chocolate and a Jammie Dodger biscuit and Mum a hug and everything was all right again for two and a half minutes till Jackson started screaming again.

Anyway, back to the story I was telling you about. One day Cuthbert H. Brown Junior's pa used their last bit of gasoline (what we call petrol) and drove the car that they lived in all the way to a racecourse, to see the horse Seabiscuit race the great War Admiral.

Cuthbert H. Brown Junior's pa, Cuthbert H. Brown Senior – who was my great-great-great-grandfather – lifted him high on to his shoulders to watch Seabiscuit win in the most exciting race ever and the crowd went wild and their hearts felt mended again and they had hope. You see, Seabiscuit was too small to be a racehorse. He had knobbly knees, stubby legs and walked funny, swinging a foreleg out as he went. He captured the hearts of all the broken people who had lost their money in the Great Depression, thinking maybe they could be winners too one day.

This true story of Seabiscuit the racehorse from long ago gives me hope. Sometimes when it's dark I go outside and look up and I imagine Seabiscuit riding across the night sky. After the screaming incident in the food bank, I sneaked out of my flat and I went all the way up to the eighteenth floor of the Beckham Estate and up, up on to the roof (where we are not allowed to go), so that I would be nearer the night sky and feel closer to Seabiscuit as he raced through the stars. I held up my hands to my hero horse and made a wish. I swear Seabiscuit heard 'cause the very next week my mum got a job at the Beckham Animal Rescue Centre.

I said thank you to Seabiscuit, and saved three weeks' pocket money and bought lots of packets of Jammie Dodgers to take down to Jackie at the food bank for the other hungry kids. 'Thank you for your kindness,' she said and her eyes watered up. I know that Molly-May from my Silver Reading Group at school is always starving. I've seen her come out of the food bank with her dad. I hope Jackie gives her lots of biscuits. Whenever I've got enough money in my pocket I buy a packet of Jammie Dodgers to keep in my school bag for emergencies.

I daydream about Seabiscuit a lot: the racehorse who was too small, ridden by Red Pollard, a jockey who was too tall. (A jockey is the person what rides a racehorse.) Red Pollard had red hair like me, he carried a bundle of treasured books wherever he went, and walked around quoting Shakespeare to the other jockeys, saying things like 'O for a horse with wings!'

Red Pollard could read really well, but as for me – well, I just can't. When I try to read, the words get all jumbled and move all over the place. This is 'cause I'm dyslexic.

I wish I was Red Pollard, not Daniel Margate.

Chapter 1

My jumbled brain is going to EXPLODE with all the noise in my flat – Number 33, 6th Floor, Beckham Estate. I swear it is. Instead of me, Daniel Margate, the skinny kid with red hair and knobbly knees, sitting on my bed trying to think my thoughts, there will be an explosion of blood and gooey bits everywhere. I wonder if anyone will even notice?

My mum has her favourite Sunday ZF3 radio show blaring out, and she's . . . singing (if you can call it that) along to the music. I don't know what's more annoying – Mum's singing or the sound of two dogs barking at each other outside. Sounds like they are going to fight.

There's another red-headed kid here too (a littler one), bawling his eyes out. Staring at me from the bed in the corner of my room – correction: in the corner of what *used* to be my room – is my three-and-a-half-year-old brother Jackson, A.K.A. *room invader and destroyer of all my possessions.*

Mum said that he's too old to still be sleeping in with her and that brothers should share a bedroom. I tried my best to be generous and not mind, 'cause at least I am not sharing the back seat of a car with him like Cuthbert H. Brown Junior had to with his little brother Frank.

But why is Jackson staring at me? What does he want now? He's always staring at me, that kid. I need to find a way to sneak out of the flat with my treasure and go to my den. I keep my treasure hidden under my bed, away from Jackson's crayons.

'DANIEL,' bellows Mum from the kitchen. 'PLAY WITH JACKSON. I AM TRYING TO SORT OUT THE CUPBOARDS. CAN'T FIND MY BLENDER. I NEED TO MAKE A CHOCOLATE CAKE . . .'

I groan. Mum always does her chocolate-cake baking when she gets her stresses – usually when it's time to pay the bills. So though life's difficult at least there's yummy cake to eat.

Mum's so happy at work. Matt the Vet, who runs

6

the Beckham Animal Rescue Centre, and a team of veterinary nurses have flown over to India to help with a street dog project, so Mum's been picking up lots of extra shifts at the rescue centre to help out while they're short-staffed. But she's been a bit grumpy at home 'cause Jackson keeps waking up at night. That must be why she's baking again.

At least we've got flour and sugar and ingredients now Mum's got a job.

'DANIEL! PLAY WITH JACKSON NOW!'

Why does everyone shout in this flat? Why can't people in my family just talk?

All this thunderous noise is getting in the way of my lightning-speed thoughts. Pictures flash across my brain.

The lady who gave me this test and told me I got dyslexia said picture-thinkers think thoughts way faster than word-thinkers, and dyslexic brains are wired differently. 'Different is good, Daniel,' she said. Then she told me to imagine all the dyslexics in the world standing underneath this huge umbrella in the rain and she said dyslexia will be slightly different for all of you and you are all unique individuals.

'DANIEL, ARE YOU LISTENING TO ME?'

'Right, Daniel,' I say to myself. 'Do what Miss Raquel tells you to do: *break life up into small manageable chunks and BREATHE, DANIEL, BREATHE.*'

Manageable chunk 1 – play with Jackson

I breathe and heave myself up and stump over to Jackson's bed in the corner, where he's lying on his tummy surrounded by toy cars, screaming.

As soon as I'm near, Jackson miraculously stops screaming, stands on his bed and flings himself at me.

I catch him before he goes crashing to the floor which, if you ask me, is astonishing, 'cause I never manage to catch the ball in PE at school, not ever. And Jackson's so heavy. He has a burst of red curls sprouting out of his head (like me) and a river of snot running down his face. (Not like me!) Gross! I hold him away, but he wriggles and flings his arms around me. I don't know why he likes me so much, 'cause I just think he's annoying.

'Dan-Dan, play racing,' he says. 'Me War Adeemal,' which is how Jackson says War Admiral. I always let him be War Admiral 'cause it means that I can be Seabiscuit.

About halfway up the wall, I have stuck a green strip of paper over the blue wallpaper. It runs all the way around the bedroom, starting just above the headboard of Jackson's bed in a circuit till it reaches his bed again. This is my racing track. I made two racehorses out of cardboard and threaded string through them and attached it to the race track. One is Seabiscuit the other is War Admiral. If you jiggle and pull the strings the racehorses move, and it's our most favourite game in the world. We've played it a thousand times before. I should be a kind older brother and let him win sometimes, but when I'm Seabiscuit I just can't. Seabiscuit has to win, because if he does there's a chance that school will be less rubbish and things will be OK.

'I'M DOING A PROPER GRAVY DINNER,' shouts Mum from the kitchen, 'and chocolate cake for afters.'

Sounds of the blender mixed with an old Spice Girls song blast from the kitchen. I hear Mum singing along to the 'zig-a-zig-ah' bits. She always pretends she's Posh Spice, only she ain't posh, not one bit.

I tell her she should really pretend to be Ginger Spice 'cause of her hair.

I can't hold Jackson a second longer.

'Time to race,' I say.

I hand him a string.

'Are you ready?'

He nods.

'On your marks, get set, go!'

And we're off. Only, I am not Daniel Margate, playing with snotty-nosed Jackson. I am Seabiscuit. I do know I'm not a little kid any more. I do know I'm in Year 8, but I just have to escape from my jumbled world and give my brain a break, racing in my dreams.

I jiggle-jiggle and pull my string and behind the wardrobe the horses go and out the other side and over my bed and – YES – I pass War Admiral and – yes! – Seabiscuit wins.

This is the only thing I'm ever first at and it's against a three-year-old kid. Jackson pulls War Admiral's string too hard, trying to catch up, puckering up a bit of the wallpaper that has become bubbly and loose.

'Jackson, CAREFUL,' I say. 'You're spoiling my racetrack.'

'I want ADEEMAL WIN,' he bellows.

'No, Jackson, Seabiscuit won. I was fastest and it's War Admiral not Adeemal. The Biscuit won fair and square.'

This was Seabiscuit's nickname and I like it. I wish I had a nickname.

Jackson opens his mouth and lets out a yowl and Mum's singing gets louder and more out of tune, and I just have to get out of this flat, with my treasure, before my brain really does explode.

Manageable chunk 2 – escape to my den

Jackson, who has now calmed down, is curled up on his bed and scratching away at another bit of bubbling wallpaper. (I bet I get the blame for that!) While he's in his own world, I creep across my bedroom, duck down and lie flat on my tummy to look under my bed.

A strange world of mountains of broken toys reaching up to the bedsprings, and pools of old socks and jumpers. A world of forgottenness.

I stretch my arm out behind a pile of old board

games, and feel for my bundle of treasure wrapped in my old school jumper with a hole in the elbow.

I wriggle out from under my bed and shove the bundle under my T-shirt. I don't want Mum to bother me with texts asking where I am, so I do my sneaky-trick and turn my ringtone up really loud and drop my phone on the carpet so it looks like it's fallen out of my pocket. That way, when Mum phones me to see where I am she will hear it and think that I left my phone at home by mistake.

Jackson is curled up in a ball, fast asleep. Mission accomplished. I creep out of my bedroom and along the hallway.

As I pass the kitchen, Mum has her back to me. She's spooning the chocolate-cake mix into a bowl. I nearly run into the kitchen and ask if I can lick the bowl out 'cause that is definitely up there with my favourite things, but I'm super strong and resist the temptation and creep past Mum.

I whisk my jacket off the peg in the hallway and close the door quietly behind me, stepping into the cold September day.

Manageable chunk 3 – start the adventure

I step out of the view of the kitchen window so Mum can't see me. I pull my precious bundle from underneath my T-shirt. I grip it between my knees and begin to wriggle into my jacket, but I have trouble getting one of my arms in the right place. Eventually, my hand appears out of the twisted sleeve and I hurry along, past the next few flats to the stairwell. Red Pollard could win races *and* read and understand Seabiscuit, who was a complicated horse. And me? Well, I can't even put on my jacket.

The sky darkens; it looks like it's going to rain. I hear muffled arguing coming from one of the flats, and the sounds of lots of televisions, then a baby crying and bass music beating from the flat at the end, but it's still quieter than it was in my flat. The dogs I heard earlier have stopped barking at each other. I dither over how to go down: lift, stairs, lift, stairs? I don't want to bump into any of the Beckham Street Boyz, the gang that rule our estate.

They're not the only gang I try to avoid, 'cause at my school, Heath Academy, there's also the Cinder

Street Boyz: Baz, Sol and Nico. I've been good at dodging them so far. They haven't noticed me yet but they have a habit of picking on certain kids and I don't plan to be one of them.

I hear some shouting coming from the stairwell. The Beckham Street Boyz like to sit in huddled groups on the stairs with their dogs. I press the button for the lift and jiggle from foot to foot till it comes.

I nearly fall off my own feet. I'm just not good at balancing. The lift doors open to a man with a pink Mohican standing in front of a poster stuck on the lift wall advertising the **BAM FESTIVAL** – which stands for Body and Mind. They've been banging on about it at school – and there are posters everywhere. The whole borough of Camden is taking part.

When the lift doors open at the bottom, I jump out and run across the nearly empty courtyard. I pass Michael who lives at number 5 – he's dressed in his usual bow-tie and silver jacket. Mum told me Michael's mum lives in Jamaica with her family, 'cause she's sick – that's why he lives with Aunty Lou. We catch eyes for a dot of a second as he pushes his hair-twists out of his face. The kids round here call him Prof M 'cause he's good at inventing things. He seems as if he would make an interesting friend, but I don't 'spect he would want to be friends with me. Although he's looking lost and lonely lately as his best friend Nell from our estate has gone to stay with her mum in Yorkshire.

My tummy rumbles.

I feel in my jacket pocket. There's two pounds.

'Jubilations!' I say out loud and then bite my tongue, 'cause 'jubilations' is not the kind of thing you say out loud in front of the kids on our estate. It's from this old black-and-white film about a boys' boarding school that I watched with Jackson. It made us laugh and we kept saying 'jubilations' to each other after that. Only, Jackson can't say it properly and says 'jubeeeealakrons'.

I look round to see if Michael heard. He's looking at me, laughing, as if he's going to say something but then his Aunty Lou appears at the doorway and calls, 'MICHAEL. IN. IT'S GOING TO RAIN, I CAN FEEL IT IN MY BONES.'

I hurry towards Bernie's Burger Bar 'cause I know he's got a £2 burger deal on. Napoleon the ginger cat is batting an empty burger box along the ground with his paw. People on my estate nicknamed him Napoleon 'cause he invades whichever flat he pleases. He springs towards me, winding his way round my legs, sending me flying.

As I gather my legs and arms up to stand, Nathan, one of the Beckham Street Boyz, passes me, carrying a bag of chips. His nose stud and gold teeth glint at me. I pluck up all my courage and say, 'Alright, Nate,' which is how everyone round here greets him. But it's like I haven't spoken. It's like I'm invisible.

'What can I get for you, Daniel?' says Bernie, smiling from behind the counter. There's a photograph of him with all his children on the wall behind him. That's most probably why he's good at remembering every kid's name on our estate. He's had a lot of practice with his own family. I'm rubbish at remembering names.

'I'd like a burger please, Bernie,' I say, putting my two pounds on the counter.

'I've got some fresh and hot coming right up. Ketchup?'

'No thanks,' I say. 'Ketchup looks like blood. I don't like blood.'

Bernie cracks up laughing.

'I'll tell you what,' he says. 'I'll throw in a bottle of lemonade.'

'Thanks, Bernie,' I say.

'What you got hidden there?' he says, nodding at my jacket.

'It's my treasure,' I say, clutching my bundle closer.

'Oh, treasure,' says Bernie, winking at me, placing the burger and bottle of lemonade in front of me and swooping up my two pounds from the counter.

I hurry out of the shop, towards the wasteland, which is what we call the scrubby grassland next to our estate. There's a breeze in the air, and I hurry on towards the Beckham Animal Rescue Centre where Mum works.

Buster the Staffie comes running out of the entrance. He scampers up to me and puts his paws on my knees.

'Hello, boy,' I say, patting his head. Everyone knows Buster. He likes to explore, and he makes it his business to escape through his kitchen window on the eleventh floor of our estate and to sneak into the rescue centre and visit the dogs. Mum's got Buster's owner, Finn, on speed dial.

'BUSTER,' shouts Finn, running up behind him. He

doesn't say hi, even though I smile at him.

On I go, past the rescue centre, but there's some kids from our school walking towards me.

They are getting nearer and nearer. Too late, I realise that it's Nico, Sol and Baz – A.K.A. the Cinder Street Boyz. THIS IS NOT A MANAGEABLE CHUNK. This is not manageable at all. Maybe they won't see me. No one else has today, apart from Bernie. And Michael, for a second. I stumble over a stone and when I look up they are pointing and laughing and I know that they've seen me all right and there is no escape.

Chapter 2

Baz bumps into me hard, sending me flying, and as my bum hits the ground my burger box flies out of my hands and my lemonade bottle rolls away. Nico, Baz and Sol crack up laughing. Some of my treasure digs into my leg as the bundle shifts, poking out beneath my jacket. I curl into a ball and shove it back; they must not see my secrets.

'Never saw you there,' says Baz, putting out his hand to haul me up.

'Thanks,' I say, grabbing it but he lets go halfway up and back down I fall. They laugh harder.

'You go to our school, innit,' says Baz.

I nod as I scramble up to standing. I spy my burger box on top of a small grassy mound and run over to get it, clutching my treasure under my jacket with one arm.

But Nico reaches my burger first. He snatches the box and holds it high up in the air out of my reach.

'You run funny,' says Baz and he starts running round in a circle, flinging his arms and legs in all different directions.

'Oi, bone boy,' says Nico. 'You're so thin we could use you as our goalpost.'

'Or we could kick you around like a football,' says Sol.

The Cinder Street Boyz laugh like it's the funniest thing ever. *Pretend you're Red Pollard*, I think to myself. *Be bold.*

I take a big breath. 'Please can I have my burger?' I say, but it comes out as a squeak.

'Let me think about it,' says Nico. 'Ummm, thought about it and the answer's NO. Come on, Cinder Street Boyz, we have food.'

And Nico passes the burger box to Sol because, as their leader, he is going to have first bite of the burger. My burger.

Sol rips the box open and grabs my burger and opens his big mouth—

'No, you don't.'

I swing round to find Melody Jackman, all-round superstar of Heath Academy from Year 11. She's head prefect and I bet you anything when she goes to Heath Academy Sixth Form she'll be head girl. There's nothing she's not good at – she's super brainy and good at sports and drama. She's even done modelling, she's so pretty. She played Mary Seacole in the school pageant for Black History Month and was in the newspapers and everything. She towers above me and flicks her braids behind her shoulders and glares at Sol. Next to her as always is her best friend, blonde, spiky-haired Polly Stainsby.

'Sol, give the burger back to the little kid, now,' says Melody.

The Cinder Street Boyz are staring at her like their brains have gone mushy and Sol shoves the burger box back in my hand.

'We was just messing.'

'The kid wasn't playing,' says Polly.

'My name is Daniel,' I say.

'Are you all right, Daniel?' says Melody. She's never actually spoken to me before.

'You must tell us if you're being bullied,' says Polly.

'We weren't doing no bullying,' says Nico.

'No, we was just having a laugh,' says Baz.

'Not very funny,' says Polly.

Melody walks towards me, smiling. 'We'll walk you where you're going, if you'd like – won't we, Pol.'

A panic ball bounces around in my chest 'cause I don't want anyone to know where I've made my den. 'I'll be OK, I—'

But before another sound can leave my lips, Sol is right in front blocking me.

I do a quick side dodge before he steps back on to my feet.

'Don't go with the little kid, come with us, 'cause we've got something of interest to tell you, as it goes. You do drama, innit, 'cause you want to be on the telly, right?' says Sol.

And I see this light of longing switch on behind Melody's eyes as she changes before me.

'Yes, I want to be a TV presenter,' says Melody, flicking her braids behind her shoulders again as the wind blows them in her face.

'Well, Melody,' says Sol, 'we might have some information for you, as it goes.'

'Yeah,' says Nico. 'We heard some things when we was made to stand outside the head's office.'

'Aren't you always outside Mr Lawson's office?' says Polly, rolling her eyes to the sky. 'You might as well sleep there.'

'We hadn't done nothing,' says Baz. 'We heard 'em talking—'

'Shut your words, Cinder Street Boyz. I'm doing the chatting,' says Sol.

'Our school's going to be on TV,' says Sol, puffing himself up like a big man.

'What?' says Melody, her eyes gleaming.

'Yeah, they said they're going to tell us in assembly tomorrow. They didn't know we was listening,' says Sol. 'That Carrie Crawford, off the *Seven Show*, is coming into our school with a film crew.'

'What?' says Melody. 'Why's she coming to Heath Academy? She's the best—'

'Yeah, well, you know our enrichment reading groups?' says Sol.

At the word *reading* my tummy drops with a thud to my toes.

Reading for pleasure is what Mr Lawson, our

headteacher, bangs on about all the time. Our whole school is divided into 'enrichment reading groups' and has to have sessions in the library with Mrs Johnson the librarian. Purple Group is the best which, of course, Melody and Polly are in, and I'm in Silver, which is the worst. For me, reading is not pleasure, it's torture! I used to really like our library reading sessions because it meant spending time with Wilbur the reading dog.

Wilbur the Staffie came in every week with his owner Marnie and he was the best to read to because, you see, Wilbur never judged me when the words jumbled up – not like people do. He would just snuggle into me, looking up with big eyes like he was treasuring the words as they started to come slowly from my lips. But Marnie has moved up to Scotland and taken Wilbur with her. I really miss him, and now the Silver Reading Group, if you ask me, is a disaster! I tune back in to Sol's words in case they concern me.

'What, all the reading groups are going to be put in a hat?' says Melody.

'No,' says Baz. 'Not—'

Sol glares at him and he shuts his mouth.

'Yeah, right, two groups are going to be picked and they're going to do this Big Read Off competition thingy and it's going to be on the telly.'

My lightning thoughts explode. *No, no, no, please, please, please no*. Supposing, just supposing, the Silver Reading Group are picked out of the hat. A Read Off sounds horrendous. The thought of me struggling to read in front of my whole school, let alone on the telly, makes me feel like I'm going to be sick.

'No,' says Baz, hopping from foot to foot, 'Silver Reading Group ain't going in the hat – remember Lawson said – 'cause they ain't up to it.'

'Yeah, 'cause they're too stupid,' laughs Nico.

I burn up but massive waves of relief swim over me, putting out the flames. 'THE SILVER READING GROUP ARE NOT IN THE HAT,' I want to shout up at the sky, but I don't. I just stand there looking down, feeling awkward, wanting to escape to my den.

'Oh, wow. If the Purple Group gets to perform, I'll be able to impress Carrie Crawford. It's my moment to get discovered. This could be my big break!' squeals Melody, jumping up and down.

'Yeah,' says Nico. 'Supposing our Green Group gets put on the telly.'

The Cinder Street Boyz all laugh and punch each other on the shoulders.

'What – you lot would want to *actually* read in front of the millions of people who watch the *Seven Show*?' says Polly.

The laughter stops.

The Green Reading Group, everyone knows, is for kids who mess about and disrupt other kids wanting to read their books.

'Oh,' says Melody, 'I do hope they pick the Purple Group.'

Nico struts up to Melody. 'You know what, I got a feeling they will.'

'Well, you've got a chance I suppose,' says Polly. 'I mean, not being funny, but it's good that the Silver Group are not in the hat. It wouldn't be kind.'

I want the grass to suck me into the earth right now so I disappear.

But no one looks at me. It's like this Year 8 kid standing right in front of them doesn't exist. They don't know or care that I'm in the Silver Group and as I watch them I'm not hearing their words any more, just noise as they start to relax and natter. I just see laughter, hair flicking and twinkly eyes.

Time to make your escape, I think, but I step back right on to my lemonade bottle lying hidden in the grass, lose my balance and fall hard on my bum. My jumper bundle falls out from beneath my jacket and my burger box goes flying.

They all turn.

I am no longer invisible.

'Up you get,' says Melody and as she grabs my arm to heave me to my feet I see Nico grab my jumper bundle.

'Don't touch it, give it back please,' I stutter. 'Please don't touch my treasure.'

'His treasure,' repeats Nico, and Baz and Sol crack up – all of them laughing at me, the joke.

Polly takes the bundle from him.

'What reading group are you in, Daniel?' asks Polly and I know she's trying to change the subject out of kindness.

'Silver,' I say.

'Oh,' says Polly. 'I didn't mean . . .'

'Ha,' snorts Nico.

She hands my treasure back to me. 'There you go, Daniel.'

'Come on, Pol, I want some chips,' says Melody.

'Yeah, I'm starving,' says Nico. 'Coming to Bernie's with us, girls? 'Cause I got some more information for you, as it goes. There's also gonna be this Get Britain Fit Race. The *Seven Show* thinks they can get boys away from computer games and into running,' he laughs. 'As if that's going to happen.'

'Yeah,' says Baz. 'They're going to film a race at our school.'

Running is my second worst thing after reading. Well, at least Mr Sugden, our PE teacher, won't pick me to run. I'm rubbish at sport. They all walk away and I breathe again. But then a strange sadness fills me. I'm glad they've gone, and I would have been fearful to go with them. But it would've been nice to have been asked, that's all. Just to be asked.

'JUBILATIONS,' I shout out, when there's no danger of them hearing me, just to show I don't care.

Only, I do care.

A thundercloud explodes and the rain drops from

the sky, bouncing off the grass.

Shoving my jumper bundle back under my jacket, I scoop up my lemonade and burger box and run through the pounding rain, towards my den. By the time I reach Apple Tree Wood I'm soaked. Through the trees I go and at last, the Old Shed appears. I grab the key that's kept hidden under a big stone by the door. I turn it in the lock and, struggling to lift the catch in the rain, I heave open the door, flick up the light switch and collapse on to a bale of straw and breathe.

I look around at my favourite place in the world. It's enormous. This is where all the extra food and other donations for the rescue centre are stored. Tins of dog and cat food are piled against the wall. An old rusty pitchfork leans against a wheelbarrow in the corner. There's a plastic bin and a pile of extra blankets for the dogs, but my favourite thing of all is the high mountain of straw bales. Loads of rabbits get abandoned and end up at the rescue centre. Camden Athletics Club held a sponsored Running for Rabbits Fun Run to buy hay and straw for them. They raised a lot of money, which is why the straw-bale mountain for their bedding is so high. I love to climb it to the top and hide from the world. There's also bales of sweet-smelling hay in the corner.

And the best thing of all is that while Matt is away, he said *I am in charge of the Old Shed* and it is my special duty to keep it tidy and to bring up anything they might need to the rescue centre. I am too young to be a proper volunteer with the animals at the Beckham Animal Rescue Centre and I know that I've basically just been left in charge of cans of dog and cat food. I also know full well it's 'cause no one has time to come down here at the moment, including the local vets who are all taking turns to cover Matt! But, still, it made me feel important . . . something I don't often feel. And 'cause no one has the time to come down here it's the perfect place to make my den.

Right now, I'm happy for a shelter from the rain. Water from my hair is dripping down the back of my neck and trickling down my nose. I balance my burger box and lemonade on the bottom hay bale that's jutting out and shake my hair like a dog, unzip my soaking jacket and take hold of my treasure bundle. The jumper feels damp – I clutch it and climb up the straw bales and sit cross-legged at the top. Slowly, I unwrap my jumper with the hole in the elbow and reveal my most sacred treasure: a scrapbook that belonged to my great-great-grandfather Cuthbert H. Brown Junior. I thank all of the clouds in the sky that it didn't get wet.

On the brown paper cover is stuck a newspaper picture of the Great Seabiscuit, head held high, posing for the camera. Underneath it, written in kid's writing, it says: *My Scrapbook, Cuthbert H. Brown Jr*. He would have kept this very scrapbook in the car that he lived in. I lift the brown-paper-covered scrapbook to my nose to breathe in the fusty, dusty smell of days that have vanished into the tick-tock of time along with Cuthbert H. Junior who lived in a car. I open its crackling pages one by one to reveal my greatest treasure of all: letters that Cuthbert H. Junior actually wrote to Seabiscuit.

I lift my scrapbook to my ears and gently move the pages, and in the crackles – just like when you lift a seashell to your ears to listen to the ocean waves – I am sure I hear the sounds of Cuthbert, his brother Frank and sister Dora, running, playing, laughing, before they curl up under the night stars in their car for the night.

Then I lift out my most sacred treasure of all my sacred and greatest treasures. *One of Seabiscuit's actual horseshoes that he wore on his very hoof.* I kiss the horseshoe and lay it on the straw bale next to my books.

My tummy rumbles. What I really want is . . . Mum's gravy dinner and the chocolate cake that will surely be ready now. But I'll have to make do with my burger.

I scramble down the straw bales and pick up the abandoned burger box. The bun is soggy and has come open, the burger and onions all higgledy-piggledy. I sigh and shove the burger back in between the wet bread. I take a bite. Gross! But I'm starving so I take another bite. Grosser. The bread feels all slithery in my mouth as I swallow it.

I put it in the plastic dustbin in the corner and open my lemonade. It fizzes up into my face. I'm so glad that the Cinder Street Boyz didn't see that! I take a few gulps to take the taste of soggy burger away and climb back up the bales.

A bolt of lightning strikes as I open my scrapbook. Mum read the letters to me every night when I was a kid, so even though the words *turn themselves inside out and upside down and trick me* they are, as I said, stamped on every bone in my body 'cause I've heard them through all the years of my life. Now that I'm twelve Mum doesn't read to me no more. I wish she did.

The letters are really old, so I barely touch them, hovering my finger just above the page.

> Cuthbert H. Brown Jr
> 3rd Car from the Gate,
> USA
> November 30th 1936
>
> Dear Seabiscuit,
>
> Today I saw your picture staring right at me from out of the newspaper.
>
> You are one handsome horse.
>
> I hope it is all right, Mr Seabiscuit, sir, if I tell you my troubles.

Thunder crashes. The light in the Old Shed flickers and there's a kick against the shed door. I jump right out of my bones. My breath stops as the wind whips at the windows, rattling them.

'Please, please don't let the Cinder Street Boyz be

outside,' I say over and over again, praying to the Great Seabiscuit up in the sky.

The wind halts and everything's still apart from the beating of the raindrops and the hammering of my heart. I breathe and go back to reading Cuthbert's letter.

Ma said that she could not think straight with Dora and Frank running round and round playing and screaming so I looked into her eyes and I knew that she needed

A stamping and a snorting come from outside.

I listen . . . .

Nothing.

I shake my head. The wind is playing tricks on me. I start to read again.

I knew that she needed to have a good weep and didn't want us children to see her. Pa had heard that there might be some labouring work going the other side of town and had left our automobile-home this morning before the birds started singing.

I grabbed a bundle of clothes from out of the back of the seat. I tried to find some clean and warmer clothes for us all to put on but, to be honest, everything was looking mighty raggedy.

I did my best because Ma likes us to keep ourselves nice but it's hard to keep yourself looking nice when you live in the back of an automobile.

After putting a clean pinafore and an old coat that was too small on Dora, who was wriggling so, I tried to put an extra sweater on Frank, who curled up in a tiny ball and would not let me put his arm through the right sleeve, so I left the sleeve dangling. I took firm hold of Dora and Frank's hands and marched them away quick, as I could see a tear trying to escape from Ma's eye.

We carried on marching over the grass, away from the automobile and down to the river to our old wooden bench. It's not really ours, Seabiscuit, but we like to think of it as ours, but there was a man curled up asleep on our bench — a battered trilby tilted over his face, holes in his boots and a cardboard sign saying: Please give me a job. Over him was a newspaper that he was using as a blanket. It was rustling in the wind.

I started a game of hide and seek to keep us warm, and I shuffled on to the small bit of bench that was left, with my hands over my eyes counting while Frank and Dora ran away screaming.

Seabiscuit, that man must have been fast, fast asleep because he didn't even wake but, you see, as I kept counting I was peeping between my fingers, so I could see where Frank and Dora ran to keep them safe.

It was then that I saw it, Seabiscuit — your handsome horse face staring out at me from the man's newspaper and it was like you knew what I was thinking. It's like you were my best friend in the world, so I stood up and bent right over the man, so I could get a good look. I could just make out that you had won a race called the Bay Bridge

Handicap. I could not read all of those words 'cause the sleeping man had his hand over them but it's like you galloped across the page of the newspaper and into my heart and stayed there. Thank you for being my friend.

Love from,

Cuthbert H. Brown Jr

A lightning flash lights up the window and there looking right at me, peeping through a forelock, is an eye and a flaring nostril. Scrambling down the straw bales, I run towards the door, but I trip over my feet and fall flat on my face. Is it what I think it is? Hauling myself up, I dash to grab the door handle. The wind blows it open in my hand, knocking me backwards.

Another flash of lightning and under the dark sky and thunder clouds, galloping away, I make out the most beautiful white horse just before it disappears through the apple trees and vanishes on to the wasteland.

'My Storm Horse,' I whisper.

What is a horse doing near the Beckham Estate?

Chapter 3

I dream that I am riding . . . Riding on the white horse, racing the wind under the stars and—

School trousers are dropped in my face. Mum's standing over me and Jackson's bouncing on top of me. It's Monday morning!

'Ten minutes, Daniel,' shouts Mum over her shoulder, on her way out of my bedroom. 'I want you washed and dressed. My alarm didn't go off, we're late. The hole in your trouser knee is mended and the rest of your uniform should be dry. It's still hanging on the clothes horse in the bathroom.'

'School, school, school, school,' shouts Jackson, doing an extra-big bounce and landing on my stomach.

'Ouch!' I sit up and grab hold of him before he does it again.

He giggles, slides off my bed, and starts running

round in circles like a dog chasing his tail.

The white horse! I must find him. Why was he running free and wild over the wasteland by the Beckham Estate?

'Mum, listen,' I say, jumping out of bed and landing on Jackson's crayons. (Double ouch!) I hobble over scribbled drawings, which have completely taken over my side of the bedroom.

'Mum.' I run into the kitchen and cough dramatically. 'I think getting caught in the storm has taken it out of me.' I do a most dramatic shiver and stagger across the kitchen, banging my knee on the cupboard. 'All that rain. I shouldn't go to school today. I need to rest.'

Mum looks up from pouring cornflakes into a bowl for Jackson and puts her hand on my forehead.

'You haven't got a temperature, Daniel. There's nothing wrong with you. And don't you ever go out like that and leave your phone behind again. Especially in a storm! Do you understand me?' I watch her mouth go up and down but I'm not listening to the words. I'm thinking of the white horse. I come to as she says . . . 'and you needn't think you can skive school.'

'Mum,' I try again. 'I know how hard you're working with Matt the Vet away. Well, I can help—'

'Nice try, Daniel. SCHOOL, NOW,' she yells as she cuts herself a big bit of chocolate cake for breakfast.

'Mum, have you got the stresses again?'

She just sighs and shrugs her shoulders.

'Get dressed, Daniel.'

And so the mission begins. I am no longer Daniel Margate, I am Red Pollard, famous jockey.

And I know kids in Year 8 shouldn't really make-believe like this, but I play this game with myself that Red has been kidnapped by his arch-enemy (today it's the Cinder Street Boyz) and is on a mission to reach the famous Seabiscuit before the race begins.

Draping my trousers round my shoulders like a cape, I run into the shark-infested waters (our bathroom, with Jackson's blow-up shark from the London Aquarium) and I reach with my almighty powers up to the top of the mountain (top rail of the clothes horse) and I tug down my navy blue jumper and my school shirt, and start to pull on my clothes. But that's when it starts to go horribly wrong, as the clothes are winning the battle and I end up entangled in a web of

40

jumper arms and trouser legs, sprawled on the bathroom floor.

'Daniel, GET A MOVE ON.' Mum bangs on the door.

I untangle myself and somehow manage to struggle into my clothes and then I am out of the bathroom and battling through a swamp (Jackson's crayon drawings). I spot a poisonous snake (my school tie wrapped round a chair leg). I know I have to kill it. I grab the end and pull but it's clinging on – I roll around the floor trying to get it free. I'm winning. I see two lions ready to pounce (Mum's furry slippers) and—

'Daniel, WHAT ARE YOU DOING?'

'Nothing,' I say, scrambling to my feet and re-entering my Monday morning world.

She grabs the tie and ties it for me. No matter how much I practise, I still can't seem to tie it. Then I run around looking for my pencil case, ruler and geography book.

'HAVEN'T YOU GONE YET?' shouts Mum from the kitchen.

I give up, and finally make it out of our flat – without my lost things –

And down to the courtyard of our estate.

'Michael, MICHAEL, MICHAEL.' It's Aunty Lou, standing on her doorstep waving a pair of football shorts and a shirt in the air. I see Michael in his school uniform, way ahead, looking up at the sky with his hands in his pockets, disappear into the Patels' shop across the courtyard.

I turn on my heels and walk up to Aunty Lou.

''Scuse me, ummm . . .' And my words disappear. I know everyone calls her Aunty Lou, but I've never really spoken to her before.

She looks at my stumbling mouth. 'You can call me Aunty Lou.' She smiles. 'Everyone does. It's Daniel isn't it – Amy-Beth's child?'

I nod, smiling. She actually knows my name! I'm not invisible to her.

'Aunty Lou, would you like me to try and catch Michael up and give his PE kit to him?'

'Oh, Daniel, would you? Thank you.' She hands the kit to me. 'Michael walks this life with his head in the clouds.'

I turn to run.

'Oh, and Daniel?'

I turn back.

'My good friend Mr Samuels is starting teaching today at Heath Academy. You make sure you're a good boy for him.'

'Yes, Aunty Lou. Promise.' I turn and run, splashing through the puddles, pretending to be Red Pollard on Seabiscuit, as I run towards the Patels' shop.

The hoot of a horn makes me jump. I didn't notice the white van driving past. I recognise the green woolly hat and black curls of Obo, a workman who's been working on our estate so long that all us kids know him. He gives me a wave as I dart around the van.

I'm puffing as I enter the shop and spy Michael standing by the crisps, his head in a magazine.

I take a breath. 'Michael,' I gasp.

He looks up startled, then grins and then the rest all comes out in a letter mash-up, 'YouforgotyourPEkit.' I hold out the clothes.

He laughs. 'Thanks.'

And we just stand, blinking at each other in the sudden ray of sunlight that spurts through the window between the newspaper stand and the fridge for fizzy drinks.

Talk to him, Daniel, talk to him . . . I tell myself in my head. 'My name's Daniel,' I finally say.

'I'm Michael.' He beams at me. 'I'm coming to your school later,' he says, ''cause I've been picked . . .'

And the last words escape my ears as a group of Beckham Street Boyz burst into the shop, walking through me like I'm not even here.

'Yo, Prof M . . . you reading again, innit,' says a boy with a gold tooth and a cut by his eye.

'You done any more inventions, Prof M?' says a boy with a purple bandana and a black hat pulled low over his head, and they all jump on Michael – play fighting and he's laughing and shouting along with them, and there are legs and arms everywhere and Mrs Patel is screaming over the top of them, 'Out, out of my shop, now, and Michael are you going to buy that *Young Scientist* magazine or not?'

I slip out of the shop without ever finding out what Michael's been picked for and why he's coming to my school. But at least he now knows my name.

I jump on the 342 bus and go upstairs so I can look out over the heath – it's a long shot, but maybe I'll spot the white horse from up here. Was he even real or was the lightning playing tricks on me? I know I *should* tell the Beckham Animal Rescue Centre there was a horse running free in the thunderstorm, but I make a reason list why not to tell any grown-ups about the white horse.

1. He may not be real and then I will just look foolish.
2. I don't want to, 'cause if they catch him they'll send him to somewhere like Pegasus Horse Sanctuary in the countryside and I would never see him again. But I want to see the white horse again with every breath in my body.

Pressing my face against the cold bus window and steaming it up, I whisper, 'Run free, run free, wherever you are.'

I look and look and I'm sure I see a flash of white shimmering in the distance. But then the bus turns and I can't see and— WAIT!

The bus is turning down the wrong street!

I stumble downstairs. 'Where are you going?' I say to the driver.

'Same route as always,' he says, 'this has been the

route of the 562 for as long as I've been a driver.'

562! I thought I was on the 342. I AM ON THE WRONG BUS.

I stagger off and start crossing the road to get the bus back in the other direction.

'WATCH OUT, DANIEL.'

I step out of the way just in time. Akin Ojo from my Silver Reading Group does a wheelie right past me, nearly knocking me flying.

I wave and shout, 'Hi, Akin!' but he doesn't reply. A red car pulls up in front of him and a tall man gets out. It's Mr Ojo, Akin's dad. I remember him from parents' evening. Akin wobbles on his bike and lands in a heap on the pavement. His dad grabs the blue bicycle, opens the boot of his car, shoves the bike in and slams it shut.

'Do not think you are getting your bicycle back . . . You should concentrate on books . . .' I am too far away to hear all of Mr Ojo's words, but a few extra-loud shouts reach my ears.

'You are late . . . When I was a boy I read every day before breakfast.'

How can anyone read every day before breakfast? I

doubt even Red Pollard could do that – he would be too busy riding Seabiscuit.

Akin is looking at the pavement shuffling his feet, shoulders hunched, looking oh-so sad.

'AKIN,' I shout as his dad gets in his car and drives off. 'YOU CAN GET THE BUS WITH ME IF YOU LIKE.' He turns round for a second. We lock eyes, but then he ignores me and scuffs off down the road. I wish he had come on the bus with me. It would feel special to have a friend to go to school with.

Chapter 4

By the time I get to school I'm so late.

It's not my fault that I read the bus numbers jumbled, is it? Some people have dyslexia with just letters, but I've got it with letters and numbers. 3 switches to 5, and 4 to 6, and 8 tricks me all the time, so getting on the right bus is a challenge. The good thing is that I don't have to avoid the Cinder Street Boyz as I walk across the empty playground.

As I enter the school building and walk down the corridor to the office, I walk past the sports trophy cabinet where there's a photograph of Akin with his best friend Ste. They both have medals round their necks – Ste's is gold, Akin's is silver. They're both laughing – Akin looking much happier than he did when I saw him earlier. And Ste looking happier than I've seen him in for ever. Ste was Heath Academy's champion runner till he had the car crash. He disappeared for most of Year 7 and the whisper was he nearly died. Now he's in the Silver Reading Group with Akin and me.

'Daniel Margate, late again,' says Miss Raquel and she pushes the late book towards me to sign and takes my phone off me and puts it in a box, which is a school rule.

Then, from her drawer Miss Raquel takes out a pencil case, ruler and geography book – all the things I lost last week!

'Yours, I believe.' She laughs.

'Thanks, Miss,' I say.

'Everyone's still in registration,' she says, 'and then the whole school are going to the hall for an exciting announcement about the Body and Mind festival.'

That will be about the *Seven Show*, I think to myself and imagine what it would feel like to stumble through a reading in front of my mum, the whole school and the trillions of people watching on television. I shudder.

'Daniel. Daniel . . . DANIEL.'

I snap from my dream.

'Daydreaming's good, Daniel, but now's not the time. Get to registration.'

'Miss, there's a rumour going round that there's going to be a reading competition. The Silver Reading Group can't be in it, Miss Raquel, they just can't.' I'm double-checking that Baz wasn't lying.

'Everyone has different strengths, Daniel,' she says, smiling.

'I don't think I have,' I say.

'You'll find it, Daniel. You'll find your strength.'

And I nearly tell her about the white horse, 'cause Miss Raquel is the type of person that makes words step out of your mouth without your brain telling them to, 'cause she's so kind. But instead I feel my mouth smiling back at her, even though I'm late again and in trouble.

As I go to leave Miss Raquel's office, Ste Gordon swings himself through the doorway on his crutches. He has a cage on his leg with pins going through it to mend the break. It must hurt.

I step out of his way.

'Hi, Ste,' I say, but he ignores me.

Five minutes later and I'm still roaming the school

corridors. The truth is, that even though I have been at Heath Academy for a year and I'm not some new Year 7 kid, I still get lost in this huge, enormous school. That's also 'cause of my dyslexia. I've taken a wrong turn again and have somehow ended up in the gym.

There are muffled words coming from behind the PE-equipment cupboard-door at the back wall of the gym. I turn on my heel, ready to hurry out . . . but Red Pollard would want to know what was going on, I think. He would never run away from hidden words.

I creep towards the door and put my eye to the crack.

Nico is sitting astride the gymnastics vault and Sol is leaning against it, holding the gigantic school top hat that Heath Academy uses for raffles. I spy Baz fiddling with a pile of hoops in the corner. Nico is emptying coloured counters out of the top hat, and spreading them over the top of the vault.

I realise that they are the colours of the different reading groups in Heath Academy: blue, green, yellow and purple.

Huge relief floods me, as I don't see silver. Baz was right.

'Get all of them green ones out,' says Sol. 'Cinder Street Boyz ain't doing no reading on TV.'

'I'd be good on TV, me,' says Baz, rolling a hoop in his hands.

'Shut up, Baz – you on the telly? Don't make me laugh,' says Nico, shaking the top hat upside down to make sure it's empty.

'Hide these, will you?' I spy him handing Baz the green, blue and yellow counters so only the purple ones are left. These he scoops back in the hat.

Baz hides the other colours behind a box of skipping ropes in the corner and goes back to the hoop, flicking it forwards and backwards.

'Yeah, that should get Melody on TV,' Nico mutters to Sol. 'Have you got them?'

Sol nods and pulls a tube of silver counters out of his pocket and the Cinder Street Boyz' shoulders start shaking with silent laughter.

Silver! I watch him add my reading group to the top hat.

There's just going to be purple and silver!

'We need to sneak back into class,' says Nico, swinging himself off the vault. Picking up his school bag, he swaggers towards the door followed by Sol. Baz lets go of the hoop and it goes crashing into the metal base of a hurdle.

'Baz, you fool,' hisses Sol, and he whacks the PE cupboard door open. I flatten myself against the wall, just in time, so I am hidden behind the open door.

I stay as still as the lions in Trafalgar Square till the Cinder Street Boyz have left the gym. Then I duck into the cupboard and grab the top hat. I've got to get those silver counters out.

Heavy footsteps.

I freeze.

The cupboard door swings open to reveal Mr Lawson, the headteacher.

I've been caught!

Chapter 5

Mr Lawson gives me that look that only headteachers do. Ice shoots through my bones and I just stare right back at him, the way that only a school kid caught in the act does.

'What?' splutters Mr Lawson. 'WHAT ARE YOU DOING HERE? You should be in registration . . . erm?'

'Daniel, sir,' I say. 'Daniel Margate . . .'

'Yes. Daniel.'

And then my words keep coming out of my mouth before my brain can stop them.

'I got on the wrong bus, sir, I got lost, sir, and then I got lost again in this school, sir, 'cause it's too big, sir, and . . .'

Mr Lawson smiles. 'Yes, it is rather big isn't it . . . Kept getting lost myself when I first started working here.'

I grab the top hat. 'Mr Lawson,' I say. 'Um, the counters, they . . .'

But the rest of my words just sizzle and die, 'cause if I grass on the Cinder Street Boyz they will do more to me than steal my burger.

Mr Lawson takes the top hat from me.

'What reading group are you in, Daniel?'

'Silver, sir . . .'

'Well, Daniel, you don't have to worry yourself about this hat.' And I know he said that 'cause he doesn't think we are in the hat, but we are. Lots and lots of times.

Mr Lawson marches me out of the cupboard, out of the gym and down some stairs and more corridors, and I wish I could tell him about the silver counters in the top hat but the words get stuck. I just can't, and I feel sick as sick can be. Then I hear the waspish buzz of many, many kids. We've reached the school hall and now it's too late.

The buzzing stops the minute Mr Lawson walks through the door, and as I stumble over legs and feet to reach an empty chair in the second row, my face burns. Everybody is staring at me.

Mr Lawson clunks up the steps by the blue velvet curtain, on to the stage and stands behind his wooden lectern. He balances the hat on top of it, next to a massive star-shaped trophy, with a small bronze book in the middle. He looks round at everyone, coughs and smiles.

'Heath Academy, I have some exciting news for you.' The sea of whispering rises. He holds up his hand to stop the tide.

'The *Seven Show* are going to be covering the BAM festival on TV, and several schools have been chosen to participate in their exciting broadcast. Carrie Crawford from the *Seven Show* will be coming to Heath Academy herself with a camera crew to film our school's activities. First, we will be participating in the Big Race Off to promote exercise and how it is good for your mental health. Five pupils will be chosen to run in a race which will be filmed simultaneously with other races up and down the country to create one big event.' The wave of excited chatter rises again and I look round at all the sports stars of Heath Academy, puffing themselves up, hoping to be the chosen ones. Akin is properly wiggling with eagerness, like he's going to explode. His chair is rocking as he raises his arms, pretending he is cheering to the crowds. All the kids around him laugh. Then I spy Ste sitting with the teachers, his crutches at his feet, his caged leg stretched out in front of him, looking so sad. My feelings hurt for him. Ste was the fastest runner in the school. Now he just sits on the side and watches.

'QUIET,' bellows Mr Lawson. The buzz stops.

'I shall be in consultation with Mr Sugden to decide who will be chosen to race. There will also be . . . wait for it, wait for it . . . a Big Read Off for the "Mind" part of the festival.'

I glance around me. I think everyone is gaping at him except for Baz, Sol and Nico in the back row, elbowing each other, and Polly, sitting with her eyes tight shut, clutching the hand of Melody, who is looking up to the ceiling murmuring what is most probably a prayer.

'Yes, this will be a competition between two of the reading groups at Heath Academy,' carries on Mr Lawson. 'It will take place on Sunday the first of November.'

First of November – that's the same date that Seabiscuit beat War Admiral all those years ago in 1938. I tune back in to Mr Lawson's words.

'The winner will be judged by Carrie Crawford and Miss Darwin, our drama teacher. Two school reading groups will be picked out of the hat to compete. Four members of each group will take part.'

Four, I think. Only four people and there are lots of people in the Silver Reading Group so maybe, just maybe, this Read Off thing won't touch me at all.

Mr Lawson shakes the hat and looks around. He gets everyone to do a drum roll, slapping their hands on their knees. And as each hand slaps, my heart kicks against my ribs trying to break free. *Please not me, not me, not me, not me,* I chant over and over.

Mr Lawson wiggles his fingers and pulls a purple counter out of the hat.

A second of relief that it hasn't happened yet. Not quite this second.

Melody and Polly jump up in the air, whooping. Mr Lawson laughs.

'As head prefect, Melody, you can be team leader. Would you like to come up on stage please and pick three other members for your team.'

Melody tosses her braids and struts on to the stage like a model.

'I pick Polly and Max,' she says. Max is this boy who is always in the lab doing experiments, even at break time. Polly and Max run on to the stage, while everyone claps.

'And the final member of my purple team is Alice.'

She is the girl in Year 11 who always helps Mrs Johnson in the library. Alice is very small with curly brown hair.

She runs on to the stage with people yelling, 'Yes, Alice! You show 'em, girl!'

'And they will be reading against . . .' The slapping of the drum roll starts and Mr Lawson waggles his fingers again and plunges his hand into the hat and my breath stops.

And he pulls out a purple counter. Mr Lawson coughs and looks embarrassed.

'Oh, I must have put more than one in by mistake . . . Drum roll again please.'

And his waggling fingers pull out and there it is shining in his hand, glinting with meanness. *A silver counter*.

The whole school goes quiet. Mr Lawson blinks, then blinks again, coughs then splutters, goes to speak then shuts his mouth again.

Someone snorts and then giggling starts which swells into a full belly-laugh until the whole school is laughing at us, the Silver Reading Group.

'WILL YOU BE QUIET,' roars Mr Lawson, then he looks around the hall and his eyes settle on me.

'No, no, no, no, no, please,' I whisper.

'Daniel Margate, you can be the silver team leader. Would you come on to the stage please.'

My trembling legs feel like someone else's as I put one foot in front of the other and wobble past all the knees of Year 8 and pass the row of teachers and Miss Raquel, who whispers, 'You can do this, Daniel.'

I wobble-step, wobble-step, wobble-step, up on to the stage.

'Daniel,' says Mr Lawson, trying to smile, 'pick your team.'

I swivel round on the spot and gape at all the sniggering kids staring back at me – all apart from the Silver Reading Group members, who are dotted around the hall, trying not to meet my gaze. Except

Molly-May, that is, who is sitting so straight, with her arms folded and her eyes goggling at me like she is going to spontaneously combust.

You are Red Pollard, I say to myself, *and you have just won a race on Seabiscuit*. I can almost hear him neighing. I pull my shoulders back and hold my head high and look over the kids' heads. Out of the window I can see far, far across the playing field and into the trees beyond the fence and my breath catches because I think I see a flash of white. I did – I saw it.

'Daniel, pick your team,' hisses Mr Lawson through gritted teeth.

I'm going to pick from my form, I think, *'cause older kids aren't going to listen to me as team leader, are they?*

Who would Red Pollard pick? *Be kind*, I hear a voice say in my head. And then I think, *I bet we get biscuits at The Big Read*.

'Molly-May,' I say.

She jumps up, her smile giant, her glasses wonky, her too-big uniform looking as if it belongs to a Year 11. She picks her way through the kids and up on to the stage. Alice gives her a hug. I think she is one of life's kind people.

My eyes rest on Ste Gordon. Red Pollard smashed his leg up once when he fell off a horse. *Pick Ste*, I hear Red whispering in my brain.

'Ste Gordon,' I say. He stares daggers at me.

'Ste, I would like you in my team,' I say again.

He folds his arms and looks up at the ceiling, like I haven't even spoken.

'Excellent choice. Ste, you can stay where you are,' says Mr Lawson. 'No need to come up.'

Ste ignores him and, grabbing his crutches, starts hobbling towards the stage.

'And your final team member, please, Daniel,' says Mr Lawson.

Red Pollard – always the centre of attention, always spinning a yarn – would've loved Akin Ojo, who makes people laugh and is always the centre of a group of kids and always, always in trouble with his dad. I wish I was more like Akin and less like Daniel Margate.

'Akin, please sir. I want Akin.'

'I'll kill you, Daniel,' mouths Akin and doesn't move.

'Akinkunmi Ojo,' bellows Mr Lawson. 'On to the stage now, please. Move it.'

Akin moves, receiving pats on the back as he starts to make his way up on to the stage, then bows. Everyone applauds.

'Well done, Silver Reading Group,' sparkles Melody in her head-prefect voice.

Polly grins at me. I try to grin back but my mouth won't work.

'So there you have it,' says Mr Lawson. 'The Purple and Silver Reading Group.'

Everyone bursts out laughing at the word 'silver'. Mr Lawson turns purple. 'QUIET.'

I walk over to stand next to Mr Lawson.

'Excuse me, sir,' I whisper, 'but could we have different team names? Everyone knows that Silver Group's the worst. I think it might stop them laughing at us?'

'An excellent idea, Daniel,' he booms. 'We can come up with better names than Purple and Silver. Melody, what would you like your team to be called?'

She goes into a huddle with her team and then says, 'The Shakespeares.' Everyone claps wildly.

'Daniel, would you name your team please.'

In my brain, food banks and Jammie Dodgers and Seabiscuit's nickname, the Biscuit, whirl round and round like a washing machine and out of my mouth bursts, 'The Biscuits.'

Everyone screeches with laughter except for Ste and Akin, who look like they want to kill me, and Molly-May, who is just standing there quietly smiling.

I feel dizzy with fear.

I spot Baz, Nico and Sol, who are bent double, slapping each other on the back. I hear in my head the thundering of hooves and something deep inside me snaps.

Seabiscuit was the horse who was too small to be a racehorse, ridden by Red Pollard, who was too tall to be a jockey.

Underdogs just like us, the Silver Reading Group, who struggle with words. Yet Seabiscuit won time and time again, so why shouldn't we be champions? I step forwards and words come out of my mouth before my brain can stop them.

'Go on, you can laugh all you want. We all know

that we, the Silver Group, are the worst readers in the school.'

The hall goes silent.

'But we, the *Biscuit Team* will prove you wrong.'

Molly-May steps up next to me, shoulder to shoulder.

'You tell 'em, Daniel,' she whispers in my ear.

With a whoop of, 'BISCUITS ON TV, INNIT,' Akin steps next to us, but I know he's just being a showman to the audience when he whispers in my ear, 'Daniel, I'll get you for this.'

Ste just droops on his crutches, glaring poison arrows at me.

'We will show you,' I say to my whole school. 'Just wait and see.'

And from the years gone by, Seabiscuit raises his head and stares me straight in the eye.

Chapter 6

I stand there, not quite believing what just came out of my mouth.

As the bell goes for the first lesson the assembly hall empties of pushing, shoving, jostling kids.

'Come with me, Shakespeares, for a little chat,' says Mr Lawson.

I bet it's to tell them that they have to be extra good to make up for the fact that we are so rubbish.

'Biscuits, Mrs Johnson will come and collect you to take you to the library,' says Mr Lawson.

When the hall is empty, Molly-May, Akin and Ste surround me. Ste pokes me in the chest with his crutch, a poke for each word as he says, 'Daniel man, the Biscuits is a dumb name, why did ya pick me? I ain't even been in school.'

'Ouch! Ste, that hurts,' I say.

'Stop it, Ste.' Molly-May pushes the crutch away so that Ste wobbles.

'I don't want to do no reading on no TV and that's a fact,' says Akin. 'The only thing I want to do on the *Seven Show* is ride my bike and show off my wheelies. Why did you have to go and pick me, Daniel?' And he picks up the top hat and plonks it on my head. As my world goes dark, I hear the counters clatter on to the stage and think about Mr Ojo's car driving away with the blue bicycle in the boot.

'Akin.' I pull the hat off. 'You won't be doing wheelies on the TV while your dad's confiscated your bike, will you? So don't you think if you actually do reading on the *Seven Show*, your dad might actually give it back to you?'

It's like a flicker of light goes on in Akin's eyes as he thinks this over. Slowly he holds up his fist and I bump it with mine. 'Nice one, Daniel,' he says. 'I think that might work.'

Bumping knuckle to knuckle feels good. No one ever does that with me.

'Oh, Akin,' says Molly-May, standing next to me with her arms folded. 'I knew your dad would take your bike away one day. I knew it, after you knocked into me dad and sent those shelves crashing when he done that bit of work for your dad in the summer.'

Akin shrugs his shoulders. 'I was on my last chance. I gotta get my bike back,' he says.

This is good, I think. I've got Molly-May and Akin sort of wanting to be in my team. Now I got to convince Ste. As Biscuit Team leader it's time to give my team a talk.

'I'll tell you why I picked you all,' I say, and I start to tell them about Seabiscuit.

'He was the greatest racehorse that ever lived. Only, he was too small to be a racehorse and he had knobbly knees and he walked funny.'

'What you saying?' says Ste, going to poke me in the chest again.

'Don't, Ste,' says Molly-May. 'Seabiscuit won races all the time, I seen the film with me dad.'

'Yes,' I say, 'and Red Pollard, his jockey, was way too tall really for a jockey and he fell off a horse and his leg got shattered and he was told he'd never ride again. But he did.'

I see a distant dream of hope slowly crawl across Ste's face. But then it's gone.

Akin has climbed on a chair and is resting his belly on top of the wooden lectern and is pretending to swim. The lectern topples over on its side and he comes crashing down in a heap. Molly-May collapses on the floor with giggles. A big belly laugh explodes from Ste and I can see just for the moment he's forgotten his troubles as he wobbles on his crutches and nearly ends up on top of Akin.

As I hold my arm out, Akin grabs it and pulls himself up.

'They realised,' I say, 'that Seabiscuit was fooling around, and could be fast if he wanted to,' I say, looking Akin straight in the eye.

'You can do this if you want to, Akin,' says Molly-May.

'I'm in,' says Akin, grinning as he gives me another fist bump.

'Don't you see, Ste?' I say. 'Seabiscuit won against all odds and if we really work hard, I reckon we can be winners too.'

But Ste still doesn't look convinced. And to try again to grab his interest, the white horse I saw last night nearly escapes from my mouth, but I chew the words back.

'The world will know about us if we do this,' says Akin.

'Well, don't go exaggerating, Akin, those watching the *Seven Show* will know about us,' says Molly May.

'I want to walk again . . .' Ste starts saying slowly. 'I want to run again and I want to read better than what I do.'

We are silent for a moment as we take in his words, and I wonder if the others are also thinking that it must be hard being Ste.

'So, you're in?' Akin says finally.

Ste shrugs a reluctant yes and Akin, me and Molly-May crowd around him cheering.

While we are huddled together, I look into everyone's eyes and I see the fear.

'I don't want the school laughing at our reading,' whispers Akin.

'I don't want to do this, not one little bit,' says Ste.

'I'm scared,' says Molly-May.

Chapter 7

'Right, Biscuits. We've got six weeks.' The four of us are spread across the bean-bags in the library, listening to Mrs Johnson. Today, she's wearing an orange head wrap, the colour of sunshine. Along with Miss Raquel, she's one of my favourite people at Heath Academy. She draws people to her library-wonderland of books with her dazzling warmth.

'You can say no to the challenge, in which case you will stay exactly where you are, or you can work really hard these next six weeks towards the Big Read Off and at the very least, you will improve. Even if it's just a bit. As they say, reach for the moon, and you'll land among the stars. But,' she says firmly, 'you are going to have to commit to practising every single day.'

'We will do it,' I say.

'Yep, I'm in,' says Akin.

'And me,' squeaks Molly-May.

'What about you, Ste?' says Mrs Johnson. 'I think this challenge will help you get your reading back on track.'

Ste just shrugs his shoulders and stares at the carpet.

'OK, let's start right now,' says Mrs Johnson.

I run my hands along the shelves and pick out an old book, *Black Beauty*. I stare at the beautiful black horse on the cover and wonder what the white horse I saw last night is doing right this moment? I hope he's safe.

I open the book and try and read the first sentence out loud, but the words and letters are moving, tricking me.

The fiSt

No, that's not right. I look again: 'first', it says 'first'. So:

The first PalaCe

So this book's about a horse that lives in a palace.

'Look again,' says Mrs Johnson, coming up behind me and holding her finger under the first sentence.

I read it again.

The first place that I can well remember was a large pheasant

'A pheasant's a bird, Miss, isn't it?'

'Try again, Daniel,' she says.

The first place that I well remember was a large pleasant

It says 'pleasant meadow' . . . I am only halfway through the first sentence and I am already exhausted. How am I ever going to read on TV?

I plonk myself back on the green bean-bag and stare at the first page and struggle through each letter. By the time I get to the end of the page I realise that because all my energy has gone into working out what the words actually were, I haven't grasped the story behind them. Plus, the white horse from last night won't stop galloping through my thoughts.

I look around at the others. Molly-May is now sitting on a chair next to Mrs Johnson, reading words slowly to her. Akin has made a pile of books so high I cannot see him, and Ste is asleep. We are never going to be good enough for the Big Read Off at this rate.

'Akin, get on with your reading,' says Mrs Johnson as his book tower totters over, on to the floor.

'I miss Wilbur,' says Akin. 'I'm missing our reading dog bad.'

'I liked reading to Wilbur,' I say.

'Me too,' says Molly-May.

Mrs Johnson looks sad.

'I wish Wilbur was here with all my heart, but he's not,' she says.

Ste lets out a spluttering snore. Akin and Molly-May explode with giggles.

'Shush,' says Mrs Johnson, 'his poor body has been through so much.'

I think of all the broken bones of all the jockeys who have fallen off horses through the years. That's a lot of bones.

'Now get back to your reading practice,' says Mrs Johnson. 'You're in here until break today.'

That means I'm missing maths – yes!

Concentrate, Daniel, take the words in, I say to myself as I read the first page again and again.

When the bell rings for break, Molly-May and Akin can't get out of the room quick enough. Ste wakes up and clatters after them on his crutches.

I carry on reading.

'Go and get some fresh air,' says Mrs Johnson.

'I need to practise, Miss,' I say.

'You need a break, Daniel,' says Mrs Johnson.

'I want to do well, Miss.'

'I know you do, Daniel, I know,' says Mrs Johnson as she beckons me out.

I wander into the playground – the overwhelming world of nudging, pointing, giggling kids – and I don't know which way to walk.

Akin is playing football but he actually looks over at me and waves.

My heart does a little leap as I wave back.

Molly-May runs over and links arms with me.

'I like being a Biscuit,' she whispers into my ear.

'Where's Ste?' I ask.

'Medical room,' says Molly-May.

'Oi, bone boy!' I look up to see Sol, Nico and Baz walking towards us. 'Get our ball back!' And my feet leave the ground as they pick me up and run with me past the big tree and up to the high wooden fence – and before I know it, I'm on the other side.

It's totally forbidden to go over the fence.

'It'll be somewhere in the trees,' shouts Nico from

the other side of the fence. 'I kicked it 'ard.'

I walk through the clumps of trees, over a clearing and deeper through tangles of bushes, looking for the ball.

The white horse is standing under an oak tree, his head is up and he is looking straight at me.

Chapter 8

The white horse is in the shadows of the trees. I don't know who saw who first.

My breath catches.

'Hello, boy,' I say, 'hello,' and walk oh so slowly towards him. He snorts and stamps his front hooves.

'It's OK, boy. I won't hurt you.' I put out my hand and slowly touch his soft muzzle. I think this is quite possibly the best moment of my life.

'Where have you come from eh, boy? What's your name?' I whisper.

The look in his eye is knowing and brave and as fearless as Seabiscuit himself.

Why shouldn't this white horse be called a name to honour Seabiscuit?

He needs to be named after some sort of biscuit. Custard Cream? No, Digestive? I can't call a horse

Digestive . . . Bourbon? That's quite good. My tummy rumbles and makes me think of the food bank that day I was really hungry and food-bank-lady Jackie gave me a . . . Jammie Dodger.

That's it! Jammie Dodger, in honour of Seabiscuit.

'Hello, Jammie Dodger,' I say. He nudges me with his nose. I think he likes his new name.

'They are my best biscuits,' I whisper to the horse as I stroke him. 'I always have spare ones in my school bag for emergencies, Jammie Dodger, and I reckon you are the best horse in the world.'

'OI! HAVE YOU GOT OUR BALL YET?' It's Baz, yelling like a fool, his voice echoing through the branches. A flock of birds rise as one up into the sky. Jammie Dodger's eyes flash wide and he whirls round and gallops off through the trees.

'Stay safe, Jammie Dodger,' I call after him.

Where has the white horse come from? Who does he belong to?

As I walk back towards the fence, I wonder if he ran away from his owner. Or maybe he has been abandoned?

I see the football perched on the top of a bush and

reach up and grab it and make my way back through the trees.

Jammie Dodger might go back to the wasteland, I think. There are apples to eat and shelter under the trees and if he was there last night, maybe it's one of his favourite places. I make up my mind to go back to the Old Shed and wait for him tonight.

Turning the wrong way a few times, I eventually see the fence through the trees but it seems like Baz, Nico and Sol have gone. The noise from the playground is getting quieter and quieter as it gradually empties.

The bell for next lesson must have rung.

'They put him over here, sir.' It's Molly-May's voice.

A teacher with grey hair, kind eyes and a crinkly smile pops his head over the fence.

'Hello, Daniel,' he says, 'I'm Mr Samuels.'

'You're friends with Aunty Lou, aren't you, sir. She told me to behave in your class.'

He smiles and it's like his whole face jumps alive.

'Right, Daniel, let's see if we can get you back on the right side of the fence, shall we? That looks a good place to get over,' he says, pointing to a fence post jutting out with a dent in the wood just above it, which a thousand kids must have used to climb back over to rescue a thousand lost balls.

I reckon Red Pollard would have just leapt over the fence on Seabiscuit, no problem, and I bet you anything Jammie Dodger could easily jump over, but me – Daniel Margate? Useless!

I toss the ball over the fence.

You are Red Pollard, I say in my head.

'Go on then,' says Mr Samuels, and he looks directly into my eyes like he's some sort of magician and I swear I feel I can do anything.

I put my foot up and it slips back down. I do it again and it slips again.

'You are Red, you are Red, you are Red Pollard,' I say. I put my foot up on the fence post, and this time it holds. I stretch to grab the top of the fence and pull myself up and put my foot in the dent in the wood, and I am over. I land on my bottom in a patch of long grass and scramble to my feet. I did it. I feel proud.

I feel good till I see the kids from my class pour into the playground dressed in their blue shorts and T-shirts. It's PE with Mr Sugden. My worst lesson.

'We got to go,' says Molly-May.

'You run along,' says Mr Samuels. 'I just want a word with Daniel.'

Molly-May disappears over the playing field.

'Who put you over the fence, Daniel?'

'I don't know, sir. It happened so quickly. They picked me up, ran with me and popped me over.'

I hate lying to Mr Samuels.

'Are you being bullied?'

'No,' I say.

I know it says on those posters that you should talk to someone, but I can't grass on the Cinder Street Boyz.

I try and change the subject.

'Did you have a nice weekend, sir?' I ask.

'I did, Daniel. I went horse riding.'

Mr Samuels knows about horses!

'Do you know about Seabiscuit, sir?' I ask.

'Yes, Daniel, I do. "The little horse that gave a nation hope",' he says.

My heart races as I think of all the questions I want to ask him. As we walk over the grass I try to find out what food is best for horses, how to groom them, how to get a horse to trust you . . .

I'm doing this partly because I'll do anything to delay PE.

But also because I need to know as much as possible about how best to look after Jammie Dodger, for when I see him again.

Please, I say up to the Great Seabiscuit in the sky, *let Jammie Dodger came back and see me tonight in the Old Shed.*

Chapter 9

I may be able to delay PE, but there's no way to get out of it. Believe me, I've tried. I really wish it was the end of the school day so that I can lie in wait for Jammie Dodger. I want to be with him now, stroking his nose, instead of here in the boys' changing room, feeling as if the whole world is standing on my shoulders.

Manageable chunks, Daniel, I hear Miss Raquel say in my head. *Manageable chunks.*

Manageable chunk 1 – put one foot in front of the other to get my PE kit from the locker

Manageable chunk 2 – find key for locker
Where is it? Where is it? Where is it?

Manageable chunk 3 – take out scrapbook and

**horseshoe carefully then tip bag upside down
to find key**

**Manageable chunk 4 – shake out all books in
case key stuck in pages**

**Manageable chunk 5 – pick out key from inside
maths book** (Not used today 'cause of extra reading
practice, ha ha.)

**Manageable chunk 6 – put key in locker and
pull out PE kit** (Pooh, it stinks. I forgot to take it
home for Mum to wash.)

**Manageable chunk 7 – change into PE kit, trying not
to put both feet through one of the shorts leg-holes**

This is a lot of manageable chunks, but the next one –
actually walking out on to the grass to join the rest of
my class – is not manageable, not manageable at all!

I sit on the bench in the boys' changing room. I wish
I was wearing the red-and-white jockey silks that
Red Pollard wore to ride Seabiscuit, instead of my

smelly blue shorts and T-shirt. I'm so late I might as well be even later.

I get this overwhelming need to read a letter in my scrapbook. I reason to myself that it's reading practice and I need as much of that as I can get.

So I sit down on the bench in the changing room, and open my scrapbook.

February 27th 1937

Dear Seabiscuit,

I can hardly believe that I am writing this, but today I actually saw you.

You wouldn't have known that your friend Cuthbert H. Brown Jr was one of the sixty thousand people that were cheering you on in the Santa Anita Handicap, but yes, sir, I was there, high up in a tree outside the track, watching.

You were a long way off, this little teeny horse, and sometimes I could see you and sometimes — well, I just couldn't, and I could only hear the faintest bits of the race announcer when it carried on the breeze, but still, watching Red Pollard riding you was the most exciting day of my whole life.

I hollered, 'Go on, Seabiscuit,' so loud I nearly fell out of the tree. My pa, who was on the branch below, reached up and grabbed hold of my ankle to hold me steady.

Your red racing hood and Red Pollard's distinctive red-and-white silks makes you mighty easy to pick out. You were in ninth place at first, and I was willing you so hard to gallop past those other horses.

Then I couldn't see you for a bit, no matter how hard I tried, so I climbed further up the tree, even though Pa yelled at me not to. And the next time I saw you, you were all alone at the front and I was hollering, 'Go on, Biscuit, go on, Biscuit, BISCUIT, GO ON!'

And then this horse, Rosemont, came right from the back, cutting in and out of horses and it made my heart uneasy to see it.

And for a moment I looked down and I could see the pain and joy in all those people in their shabby clothes, with holes in their boots, and they were all yelling for you, Seabiscuit, and I realised in that moment that you were running for us, for people like my pa who had lost his home and his job. You were giving us hope that we could be winners too.

People were roaring so loud I reckon the clouds and the sun in the sky could hear the cheers.

Then you darted left and it was like you and Red weren't so sure of yourselves any more. Rosemont was coming up behind, faster and faster, and then you were neck-and-neck over the finish line, but from the almighty cheer that went up, we were all sure that you had won.

But then there was this silence, like the world just stopped.

I climbed down the tree to stand next to my pa on his branch. I could see there was a horse's head carved into the tree trunk.

'They are not sure who won, Cuthbert. So we are waiting for the judges to take a look at a photograph of the finish,' Pa said. 'But it has to be Seabiscuit, I think. Why, he's the fastest horse in the world. Look.' And he pointed to a photograph whizzing down a wire that started at the photo booth overlooking the track and went over the crowds all the way down to the judge's platform.

I shut my eyes and reached out and ran my finger round and round the outline of the horse's head carved into the trunk, whilst whispering, 'Please win, please, please, please let Seabiscuit be the winner.'

Then there was this howl and I opened my eyes and Rosemont's name flashed up on the board as the winner. The howl got louder and louder — it was like the day was broken, and along with it our dreams. I looked down and my finger was dripping blood, bleeding, with a splinter sticking out of it. I yanked the splinter out but I didn't even feel the pain.

All I could think about was that I wanted to be able to run up to you so badly and give you the biggest hug, and say, 'It's all right, you did your best.' I know your heart must be hurting now, but don't you see — you nearly won, you nearly did, and you will win again.

Guess what? I have one of your actual horseshoes. A reporter who was walking away from the racetrack told us that Mr Howard, Seabiscuit's owner, gave it to him.

'Here you are, kid,' he said, 'keep it for luck.'

I think this is quite possibly the best day in my life.

Cuthbert H. Brown Jr

A shadow falls over my scrapbook. I look up. It's Mr Sugden. Brown gelled spiky hair, the whistle round his neck swinging and a sneer on his lips.

'Daniel Margate, get out on to the playing field this minute.'

Chapter 10

As I walk past the long-jump sandpit towards the kids in my class, I feel the cold, wet mud from yesterday's storm seeping through a thin patch in my left trainer. Sugden, who's marching ahead, blows his whistle, blasting my ears off.

'YOU SHOULD BE WARMING YOUR BODIES UP, NOT YOUR MOUTHS,' he yells to my class, who are just standing there chatting. There's a sudden silence as some kids start stretching, others jogging on the spot.

I can see that Mr Andrews, the TA, has got Ste organising the class into teams. He smiles over at me. I wish he was the teacher and Mr Sugden was the teaching assistant.

'Ste will put you in a team,' he says.

They like to keep Ste busy in PE so that he

doesn't feel too left out. Ste swings himself over to me on his crutches.

I smile and try again. 'All right, Ste?' But he ignores my smile.

'You're in Akin's team,' he says.

'Over here, Daniel,' yells Akin, and his shout warms me. It's like I belong, 'cause no one usually picks me.

Maybe this lesson won't be so bad, I hope, crossing my fingers.

The 400-metre race starts but I'm not watching them, instead I'm skimming my eyes across the woods, beyond the fence, for Jammie Dodger. I hope he's safe.

'Akin's team,' yells Mr Sugden and I trudge to the starting line.

The whistle blows and we're off. We have to run once round the whole track.

Akin shoots to the front. Everyone is ahead of me, even Molly-May, and she is not a fast runner at all.

And this time I am not Red Pollard. I am the horse himself. 'You're Seabiscuit,' I say to myself, 'the fastest horse in the world. Run!' And for a moment I feel strong. I feel fast. I will bring glory to those who cheer for me. I run for the men in the shabby clothes with holes in their boots. I run for my great-great-grandfather, who lived in a car. I run for everyone who ever went hungry. I hear the cheers in my head and I've almost caught Molly-May, I almost have. Akin is now way ahead but I feel good. I feel fine.

Something moves in the corner of my eye. Distracted, I look. Sol, Nico and Baz peep out from behind the big tree by the fence. They must be bunking off. Baz starts doing an impression of me running, his legs and arms going in all directions, and I don't feel good any more. I don't feel fine. I feel foolish. 'You are Seabiscuit,' I say, but I don't feel like Seabiscuit. I feel like Daniel Margate who runs funny. Then Akin stops in his tracks, turns round and runs backwards to Molly-May. What is he doing? I just stop myself bumping into Akin as he crouches down and Molly-May clambers on to his shoulders in a piggyback.

He then continues to run the race with Molly-May on his back and *still* passes everyone. Sugden, who is at the finishing line, opens his mouth into a roar, his face purple. Ste is next to him, bent double laughing, trying to balance on his crutches, and behind them I see Mr Lawson and Mr Samuels marching across the playing field towards us. I stumble. My legs give way and the grass is coming towards my face, closer and closer until, splat – cold, wet *darkness*. Seabiscuit didn't like running in mud either, it's a known fact. This is my last thought before I hear Mr Andrews' voice.

'Are you OK, Daniel? Let's get you up.' But I scramble up myself, mud dripping off my T-shirt and shorts.

Akin is sandwiched in between Mr Lawson and Mr Sugden, who are both talking at once. Mr Samuels is standing a little way off, watching.

Words like 'fooling around', 'dangerous', 'not working to the best of your ability' float around them. Molly-May is on the outside of the sandwich, trying to squeeze into the filling next to Akin.

Then Akin's voice, powerful and strong, cuts above all of them.

'But don't you see, I wanted Molly-May to know what it feels like to be first.'

The playing field falls completely silent apart from the birds calling to each other in the woods. Mr Samuels turns his head away and we lock eyes for a shorter time than it takes a blackbird to do a single call, but in that second I see he is moved to his very core by Akin's words, and he gets it. He totally gets it and he is like this honorary Biscuit, even though he is a teacher and would never be in Silver Reading Group.

'Daniel Margate, are you OK?' Mr Lawson calls over.

I nod.

'Good. No bones broken?'

'No, sir,' I call back, feeling my face burn and I know it's as red as my hair.

'Gather round, gather round,' says Mr Lawson. 'I have an announcement, but first let me introduce you to Mr Samuels, who is our new history teacher. Mr Samuels had a free period so I thought I would show him our sports facilities. Please give him a Heath Academy welcome.'

'Welcome to Heath Academy, sir,' everyone drones together.

'Now, as you know from assembly, we are taking part in the Big Race Off and the Big Read Off as part of the Body and Mind festival—'

'Yes, I have made a note in here' – Mr Sugden comes marching up to stand next to the headteacher – 'of who I think would be good candidates. I thought Akin and—'

'There's been a change of plan, Mr Sugden,' says

Mr Lawson. 'Since it's part of the campaign promoting that exercise is for everyone, the *Seven Show* have asked for us to ensure the race will include one of our fastest runners – so, Akin, I would like you to take part – but also to include those who find sport more of a challenge and also some whose *behaviour* is more of a challenge, shall we say . . .' He chuckles and then his face goes purple and he shouts, 'COME OUT FROM BEHIND THAT TREE, THIS MINUTE.'

Even the birds seem to stop singing as Nico, Sol and Baz emerge from behind the tree.

'Over here.'

The Cinder Street Boyz do the walk of dread to stand in front of the headteacher.

'Sir,' says Baz, 'we saw this white 'orse, galloping, he was.'

My heart leaps up to my throat, no no no. The Cinder Street Boyz must not go near my Jammie Dodger.

Gallop away, boy, I pray silently. *Be safe.*

'Yeah,' says Nico. 'Over there he was, in the woods.'

'Yeah, we wanted to make sure he was all right. He must've escaped.'

'A likely story, a horse. Come to my office after

school,' Mr Lawson splutters. 'You three are the perfect candidates for the Big Race Off. You will train for it and you shall focus on it. Now who else . . .' His eyes then settle on me and he is smiling . . . *No no no . . .*

'Ah, Daniel, perfect. Let's get you running, shall we? It will be good for you and nice for the *Seven Show* viewers to get to know you in the Big Read and Big Race Off. I think the producers will like that.' He is still smiling at me, but my mouth is stuck. I can't smile back.

This can't be happening. How have I, Daniel Margate, ended up in the Big Read Off *and* the Big Race Off in one day? I have gone from being invisible to getting into a situation where the whole nation will watch me. Twice.

'Please, sir, I can't . . .' But the headteacher has his back to me as he strides across the field towards his office.

This is turning out to be the longest day ever.

As we walk back to the changing rooms, Mr Sugden steps in line with me. Mr Samuels is with him.

'Daniel, I want you to take this race seriously. Somehow, you need to get from the beginning of the race to the end. Do you hear me?'

Mr Samuels smiles. 'I am sure he will do his best, won't you, Daniel?'

'Yes, sir,' I say. 'Somehow, I will get there.'

Chapter 11

When the bell rings at the end of the school day, I'm out of there. I hadn't been able to concentrate all afternoon. My mind was galloping around with Jammie Dodger, looking at the school clock, willing it to whizz round to 3:30.

I still think my best bet is to lie in wait in the Old Shed. If he went there last night, he might go there again. Maybe Apple Tree Wood is where he comes for shelter and apples to eat when it gets dark. In the day, he must roam between the wasteland and the heath and the woods behind our school.

'The woods behind our school is not a good place to be, Jammie Dodger,' I whisper under my breath. 'Not if the Cinder Street Boyz saw you.'

There's a sign on the school gate.

Camden BAM Science Club this way ↑

As I get caught up in the crowds pushing towards the bus stop, I see Michael trying to force his way through in the opposite direction.

'MICHAEL,' I shout, nearly busting my lungs.

He sees me, waves, then gets swept away with the tide of children.

I make sure I ask the driver that I'm on the right bus before climbing to the top deck. I spend the whole journey looking out of the window for Jammie Dodger. I think I see him once, something white in the distance, but when the white shape flies up in the air I realise it is a flock of seagulls.

I nearly fall down the stairs when it's my stop, and race across the wasteland to get to the Beckham Animal Rescue Centre. I meet Mum here every day, then we go back to the Beckham Estate together and get the lift up to the eighth floor to get Jackson from Lizzie, who minds him while Mum is at work.

Liam is on reception at the centre. I like him a lot. I hear a 'zig-a-zig-ah' coming from the laundry room.

'You can go through to her,' he says with a laugh as he lets me through. Mum always sings when she is washing the towels for the animals. I walk through the cattery, past mewing, purring cats and a big tabby in the corner, batting a toy mouse with his paw. Mum has her back to me, loading dirty towels into the machine.

'Mum,' I say. 'I've got some tricky homework, can I do it in the Old Shed before coming home? I can't concentrate with Jackson annoying me.'

'As long as you're not too late,' she says, not even looking up. 'Did you have a good day at school?'

I nearly tell her about me being in the BAM festival not once, but twice, but I'm desperate to get to Apple Tree Wood and my den in the shed. I decide not to tell her right now. Maybe I won't tell her at all. If she doesn't know, there's a tiny chance she won't watch the *Seven Show* that night to see me make a fool of myself. So I just say, 'It was all right.'

While she's got her back to me, I grab a towel and shove it in my school bag. *It's not stealing*, I reason to myself. They are for the animals and Jammie Dodger is most definitely an animal.

'Daniel, there's a sack of carrots someone's left outside the door of the Old Shed, donated for the rabbits. Very kind. Can you put them inside – tidy though, in a corner or something. We've been run off our feet all afternoon. Had an abandoned greyhound brought in. She was found tied to a park bench. She just looks so sad. Ever so gentle she is, like a lamb. I need to take her an extra blanket. Do you want to see her?'

'Yes please, Mum,' I say.

We make our way to the kennels. I'm greeted, like always, by a choir of barking dogs of all sizes. I see Jessica, one of my most favourite people who work with Mum, wearing a purple Beckham Animal Rescue Centre T-shirt, sitting on the floor of the kennel at the end, holding her hand out to a beautiful blue, long-legged greyhound.

She is holding a biscuit in the palm of her hand, but the dog stands in the corner, head bowed, not interested.

Jessica comes to the kennel door and takes the blue fleece blanket from Mum. 'Thanks, Amy-Beth,' she whispers. 'Hello, Daniel. We haven't named this one yet. What do you think?'

A sliver of silvery sunlight comes through the window, making the dog's coat glisten. 'Silver,' I say, 'without a shadow of a doubt.'

'Silver,' repeats Jessica. 'I like it.'

'So do I,' says Mum.

'I'm in Silver Reading Group at school and it is a known fact that Seabiscuit had his own guard dog who was called Silver.'

'You and your Seabiscuit,' says Jessica with a laugh. 'Silver it is, then.'

All the time I have been talking, the greyhound has been watching me, whining ever so quietly.

'Do you want to see if you can get her to eat something?' says Jessica. 'Come and sit next to me.'

I hand Mum my school bag and follow Jessica back in and sit with her on the floor.

She hands me the dog biscuit and I hold it out. The beautiful long-legged dog walks gracefully over to me and sniffs at my school jumper. Then takes the biscuit gently from my hand and eats it up.

'She likes you,' says Jessica.

Warmth pours through my bones as I stroke Silver. I may not be good at schoolwork, but I am good with this dog and Jammie Dodger let me stroke him too. Maybe today isn't all bad.

Silver lies down on the blue fleece blanket that Jessica has laid out for her.

'We should let her get some rest,' says Jessica. 'Thanks, Daniel.'

'Sleep tight, Silver,' I say.

Grabbing my school bag back from Mum, I hurry out of the rescue centre, through Apple Tree Woods and towards the Old Shed, looking left and right through the trees as I go. There's no sign of a horse.

I see the sack of carrots leaning against the door, get the key from under the stone and drag the heavy sack into the Old Shed.

I dump my school bag down in the corner and look around me. I could make this into a stable!

Hardly anyone ever comes down here. And even less now that I'm in charge of bringing food up to the rescue centre while Matt's away . . .

My first mission is to take enough animal food up to the rescue centre to make absolutely sure that none of the staff need to come down here.

I load the wheelbarrow with carrots (leaving enough for Jammie Dodger) and cabbages from a big bendy tub in the corner, and tins of dog and cat food, and wheel it through Apple Tree Wood and round to the back of the rescue centre, where I knock on the door.

Liam opens it. 'Brilliant, Daniel – this will keep us going.' We empty the wheelbarrow and then I push it back as quickly as I can, down to the Old Shed.

I decide to start making the Old Shed into a stable straight away. If Jammie Dodger comes again, maybe it will entice him in.

I look around me. The cubbyhole cut into the left wall is like a small walk-in office with its own door. There's nothing but a table in there at the moment.

I set to work, putting tools, the remaining tins of dog and cat food and anything that Jammie Dodger could hurt himself on, into the cubbyhole.

I also put the wheelbarrow and an old rusty pitchfork and the plastic bin in there as well and close the door. I drag the rest of the sack of carrots into the cubbyhole to keep them hidden from a certain horse who might want to eat the whole lot!

My arms ache and I'm boiling up. I tear my school jumper off and throw it on top of my school bag. I climb to the top of the straw-bale mountain and push six bales off the top and watch them crash to the ground. Next, I spy a pair of old pliers on the window ledge and cut the twine round each of the six bales, one at a time.

Then I shake the straw out and keep doing this till the floor is covered, to make a bed for Jammie Dodger. I put the pliers safely in the cubbyhole.

He'll need something to drink from. The bendy tub that the cabbages were in could be filled with water. I take it outside and shake off the dust; it gets into my mouth, my eyes, goes up my nose and I'm a coughing, sneezing, spluttering snot-machine. I run into the shed and wipe my face and nose on my school jumper. Mum would kill me if she could see, but she can't and what else am I meant to do?

There's a hose and a tap outside, attached to the side of the Old Shed, that Beckham Animal Rescue Centre uses to wash the dogs on hot summer days.

I run through the door and round to the tap, underneath the **BSB** graffiti where the Beckham Street Boyz have left their mark. Turning the water on, I drag the snaking hose out to the front and wash down the bendy tub. It's now purple – the colour of kings and fit for my Jammie Dodger to drink from.

But the voice inside my head says, *But he's not yours, Daniel. Who does he belong to? Who could have abandoned such a beautiful animal?*

I silence the voice. He's the horse of my dreams. I fill the purple tub, wind the hose away and drag the heavy water back into the Old Shed, splashing it everywhere. I'm properly soaked.

I then get some carrots from the cubbyhole and lay a trail of them into the Old Shed to tempt Jammie Dodger in. My arms shaking, my legs wobbly, I sink on to one of the bales that is jutting out at the bottom of the mountain and wait and watch through the open door. I feel so sleepy. It's been the longest day in school ever.

I fetch my scrapbook from my bag. If I read another letter, maybe I'll stay awake . . .

March 2nd, 1937

Dear Seabiscuit,

I thought I should tell you a bit about myself, so as we can get better acquainted like good friends should.

Well, my story starts way back before I was born. Pa was a tailor at Russo and Son in New York.

My pa stitched the gentlemen's suits and

my ma worked in the store, greeting the customers. Pa said Ma's smile put fresh spring daisies to shame and he decided then and there to marry her. Pa said the day they got hitched was the happiest day of his whole life. Then I was born in 1924. I had a very happy first few years of my life with Ma, Pa, my little brother Frank and then baby Dora, who came along and made our family complete. Then, on October 29th 1929, when I was five, the stock market in New York crashed, as you well know, Seabiscuit, and Russo and Sons was shut and men came and threw all the fine suits that Pa had stitched out on to the streets of New York, and all the people who had lost their homes and jobs were on their knees fighting over the cloth. Pa said that was the worst day of his whole life. Ma and Pa lost their home because they had no money to pay the rent and we had nothing left to live in but our automobile.

Pa made out to us it was this exciting adventure, living in the automobile, but I

could hear Ma crying at night, so I knew
the adventure was only pretend.

Pa is originally from California like you,
Mr Seabiscuit, sir, and my ma was born in
New York. When the stock market crashed,
Pa's dream was for us to head towards
California and Hollywood. He wanted to try
and get work in the costume department,
stitching clothes for the movie stars.

'Everyone loves the movies, Cuthbert,' he
says every day. 'People need dreams and
movie stars need clothes to act the dreams
out. We'll be fine once we are in Hollywood.'

Something nudges my dreams. I open my eyes.
My breath stops. His horse nose is against my cheek.
He snorts. I put my hand out slowly, slowly and stroke
the side of his face. He nudges me again, stamping
his hoof.

'Jammie Dodger,' I whisper. 'You came.'

Chapter 12

Very slowly, I swing my legs round so I'm facing him. I see my scrapbook where it's fallen on to the straw floor and slowly stretch to get it before it's stamped on by Jammie Dodger.

Straight away he has his nose in it, inquisitive, investigating.

'Careful, boy, those are letters my great-great-grandfather wrote to Seabiscuit, the greatest horse that ever lived – that is, apart from you, Jammie Dodger.'

I scoop the scrapbook up and balance it on a bale jutting out above my head, keeping it safe.

Jammie Dodger starts to walk around the space, sniffing, nudging. I think he likes it. I walk over to the purple water bucket, dipping my hand in.

'Look, Jammie Dodger – would you like a drink?'

He follows me over and dips his nose in. I remember

what Mr Samuels said about making a horse feel safe, and I stroke him over and over as he drinks and drinks like there's no tomorrow. Lifting his nose out of the tub, water droplets spray everywhere. I grab a handful of hay for him to munch on.

He lifts his tail and does a big steaming poo. I get the pitchfork from the cubbyhole and shovel it up and take it outside, dumping it behind a tree. When I go back in the shed, he's actually lying down with his legs folded underneath him, peeping out a bit to the side, but his head is still up. He looks so content to be there, as he takes in the stable I have made him. I sink to my knees next to Jammie Dodger and stroke his thick winter coat. At least that will keep him warm.

'Are you tired, boy? That's it, you have a rest. Would you like me to read you a bedtime story? I'm not too good at reading, Jammie Dodger, but I'll do my best.'

I reach high to the straw ledge for my scrapbook, sink down in the straw and snuggle up to the horse's warm belly.

'Let me find the place I got to. Ah, here we go, Jammie Dodger. Are you comfortable? This is a letter my great-great-grandfather wrote to Seabiscuit, the greatest racehorse of all time and who your name honours.'

I read the last bit I got to again:

'Everyone loves the movies, Cuthbert,' he says every day. 'People need dreams and movie stars need clothes to act the dreams out. We'll be fine once we are in Hollywood.'

But to be honest, we live here, there and everywhere — on the road, sometimes staying in places for weeks and months.

Something was happening . . . It was like I just knew that Jammie Dodger was not going to judge me. I still stumbled and the letters played tricks, but my fear of words had gone. It was just like it felt when I used to read to Wilbur at school. I carry on:

Ma says that Pa had the finest most delicate fingers from stitching cloth, but now they are rough and hard because Pa has to grab work where he can get it. A day here and a few days there — but it's not stitching cloth, it's building roads or digging tunnels and that's no work for fine hands used to stitching. When Pa manages to get a day's work, we eat, but sometimes we have to go to the soup kitchen.

Ma's mighty strict about our schooling, no matter how hungry we are, which is why I am able to write to you, Mr Seabiscuit, sir. Sometimes when we drive near the rail track and I see people running, clinging on to the outside of trains to take them some place — some of them boys not much older than me — I am glad we have our automobile.

Jammie Dodger is asleep. 'You rest, boy,' I whisper.

I know it's time to go. I decide to leave the stable door unlocked so that Jammie Dodger isn't trapped. He might want to eat some grass and apples. He might want to go for a midnight gallop under the stars.

'Thank you for listening to my reading,' I say to the sleeping horse. 'You don't care that I stumble over my words, just as long as I am talking to you.'

My brain starts to race. If Jammie Dodger can help *me* read, then maybe he could help the others. We used to have a reading dog. Why shouldn't the Biscuits have a reading horse?

Chapter 13

I wake up before the birds on Tuesday morning and creep out the flat before Mum or Jackson are awake.

The air's crisp as over the wasteland I go, through Apple Tree Wood, wondering if Jammie Dodger is in the Old Shed.

The door's open. Jammie Dodger's gone. Nothing but a patch of straw he weed on, piles of poo and the flattened straw where he lay to show he was ever here. He stayed all night, judging by the amount of poo he left!

Using the pitchfork, I lift the wet straw and poo into the wheelbarrow and scrape his flattened bed to one side, just in case one of the shelter staff come down here. I look around me. No one would ever guess that a horse slept here for the night.

My arms ache, and I think I must get strong like Red Pollard was.

By the time I'm finished, it's still early for school, but I decide to head there anyway so that I can get to the library and use the computer before class.

I lock the Old Shed door behind me and hurry to the bus stop. I don't have to wait long for the 342 bus, and I climb up to sit on the empty top deck, looking left and right for glimpses of Jammie Dodger. I know it's a long shot, but from this height I have a good view of the heath.

'Stay safe, Jammie Dodger, stay safe,' I murmur, looking out at the clumps of trees.

When I get to the library, Melody's already in the corner, books open, head down.

She looks up and laughs.

'Come to do some reading practice?' She pauses and takes me in. 'Daniel Margate, what have you been doing? Rolling in straw?'

Looking down in horror, I see bits of straw all over my school jumper. I'll need to be more careful if I'm to keep Jammie Dodger a secret.

'Oh, er, my mum works at the Beckham Animal Rescue Centre. I was helping with the rabbits.' Well, that's only half a lie. I just said rabbit instead of horse.

I go to the computer furthest away from Melody. I don't want her to see what I'm doing. I switch on the computer and type in the school password, which is the Heath Academy motto: Valour is my Bond (all one word).

I type in:

Valerismybond

Your password is incorrect flashes up on the screen.

I never get it right first time.

I try again, typing slowly.

Valarismybonb

Your password is incorrect

I let out a massive, 'Grrrrrrrrrr.'

And I feel as if someone has opened the top of my head and poured glue in my brain and my lightning thoughts stop and my face is pushed flat against a stress wall.

'Let me help you.' It's Melody, standing behind me. She leans over and types in the password and the computer whirs into action – first time round!

'There you go,' she says, turning to go back to her seat.

'Thanks, Melody,' I call after her.

Right. I try to unglue my thoughts. I need to see if there's any reports of stolen horses 'cause maybe Jammie Dodger was stolen and then escaped. I type 'stolin' into Google and a picture of a town near the Ukrainian border pops up.

No, that's not what I am looking for!

I try again. I type

stolan horses   Q

Google says:

Showing results for *stolen* horses

I quickly think to add 'UK', and search again.

The results take me to a long list of links. I scroll through photos of black horses, brown horses, chestnut horses, big horses, little ponies. Every time a white horse appears my heart jolts, just for a second, but it's never Jammie Dodger. They are either smaller than him or dappled grey – not pure white like my boy. I would know my Jammie Dodger anywhere, but my heart aches for the children in the photographs

117

cuddling their horses that are now gone. A little boy in a blue jumper, hugging Freckles, his brown Shetland pony that was stolen from a field. A girl with curly brown hair astride a kingly looking black horse called Midnight, who they believe was snatched in a storm. A storm! Maybe . . . Maybe Jammie Dodger was snatched in the storm but either way, not one of these photographs is of him.

Maybe Jammie Dodger just got lost like me. I can never find my way anywhere.

I type in

List and Fawnd horses	Q

Google says:

Did you mean: *Lost* and *Found* horses

My lightning thoughts start flashing across my brain. It stands to reason that if you had lost a beautiful horse like Jammie Dodger you would tell the world, to get him back. I saw him Sunday night – who knows how long he had been galloping free on the heath before that, and it's now Tuesday. Surely someone would have registered him by now! But none of the horses in the photographs looks anything like Jammie Dodger.

If I am going to be honest, I'm relieved when I can't

find his owner looking for him. 'Cause in my heart and dreams, Jammie Dodger is already mine.

'What's your story, Jammie Dodger?' I whisper. 'Maybe you were abandoned.'

I think of all the abandoned dogs, cats and rabbits at the Beckham Animal Rescue Centre – I know what people are capable of. My conscience pricks me about keeping the horse secret. Jammie Dodger could be at the Pegasus Horse Sanctuary, who would find a new home for him. Beckham Animal Rescue Centre organised a trip there to see the rescue horses last summer. A lady called Joanna showed us around and we had a picnic and then they came to visit us to see what challenges an animal rescue centre in London faces.

They've got so much space at Pegasus, a lot of grass. But then so do we have a lot of grass. The wasteland joins on to the heath, which is enormous, and there are so many clumps of trees for the white horse to hide in. I remember Joanna talking about how some people abandon horses because they can't afford to keep them. So next I type in

| abadand horses | Q |

Google says:

Photos of skinny horses with their ribs showing through their skin, their heads drooping, make my eyes sting with tears. I quickly gulp them back.

The words jump around as I try and make them out and I see horses have been left in woods and tied to fences and one was even left in an ASDA car park. It makes me sad to think that there's a good chance that Jammie Dodger has been abandoned.

'You've got love in your life now, Jammie Dodger,' I whisper as the bell goes for my first class and I turn off my computer, ready to go to history with Mr Samuels.

Chapter 14

I go the wrong way to history, twice! I hear my class before I see them. I turn into yet another corridor and there they are, packed outside the classroom. What's going on?

'Daniel, look,' says Molly-May. Grabbing hold of my jumper, she pulls me through to the front.

A big sign is stuck on the door.

It is October 29th, 1929
You are in America

THE STOCK MARKET HAS CRASHED

You have lost everything!

You are in New York, standing outside the bank trying to get in

The door opens and Mr Samuels steps out wearing a trilby hat and waves his hands in the air, and like magic, our words just stop. Mr Samuels is a magician. Our class never shuts up.

Akin steps out of the classroom to stand on one side of Mr Samuels and Ste is balancing on his crutches on the other.

'You can't come into my bank,' says Akin, ''cause we not got no money.'

'You're angry,' Mr Samuels says to us. 'You're frightened. You want what's yours. I want to hear how angry and frightened you are. Let's hear it!'

I do my best acting ever.

'Give me my money,' I shout. 'I need to go to the shops,' I yell, shaking my fist in the air.

Mr Samuels' hand rises higher and higher in the air and we shout louder and do angry acting. Then Mr Samuels slices his hand through the air and we just stop.

Mr Samuels holds a card in front of Ste, which I can see has big writing on it.

Ste takes a big breath and reads.

'You have lost your homes and your jobs. You

have lost everything. Welcome to H . . . h . . . hoo . . . Hooverville. Come this way.'

We all troop through the door and everyone gasps. There are no desks and chairs; instead there are cardboard huts.

'During the Great Depression, many Americans lost their homes and lived in towns of huts made from bits of metal and wood and cardboard. These shanty towns were known as Hoovervilles,' says Mr Samuels.

'Ours are just cardboard because of health and safety, innit,' says Molly-May.

Mr Samuels laughs. 'Does anyone know why they were called Hoovervilles?'

And I find my hand rising, rising into the air, which it never usually does.

'Yes, Daniel,' says Mr Samuels.

'After President Hoover,' I say.

'Excellent, Daniel,' says Mr Samuels and I feel as tall as a giant. I don't think I've heard the words excellent and Daniel in the same sentence in all my years of going to school.

'A lot of people blamed President Hoover for the bad economy,' says Mr Samuels. 'They believed he was the reason why they lost their homes. Now line up, everyone. You're cold, you're hungry. You haven't eaten for days. This is a soup kitchen – only, today there is no soup on the menu, just bread.'

Mr Samuels lifts a metal urn full of bread rolls and bangs it on to the table.

'I want to be the lady what gives out the bread rolls,' says Molly-May.

'Righto,' says Mr Samuels with a laugh. He brings out a pile of trilby hats and says, 'There's not enough for everyone, so first come, first served!'

We all push and grapple and I manage to reach one.

This is a good day, I think, but then I notice Ste watching everyone scrambling for a hat and he looks really sad. So I put mine on his head. It's not his fault that he couldn't grab one because of his crutches. Ste looks at me, surprised. 'Um, er, thanks, Daniel.'

'You got to have a hat, you're a Biscuit,' I say and I'm sure there's a nearly-smile on his face.

I take my place in the line for the bread and I see Molly-May, quick as lightning, shove a piece of bread roll in her mouth and bury the rest in her pocket.

'Line up properly or you won't get no food,' says

Molly-May and starts plonking bread rolls in our hands.

'When you've got your bread ration, I want you to find yourself a cardboard shack,' says Mr Samuels. 'Four of you in each home. You are now families in the Great Depression.'

Akin is near the front of the queue and when he gets his bread roll, he races to the back in the corner by the window, making all the cardboard huts wobble dangerously on his way.

'DANIEL, STE – OVER HERE,' he shouts at the top of his voice, just as a bread roll gets slammed into my hand by a scowling Molly-May, who's getting well into her part. I feel a warm sparkler in my belly. It's good to be wanted. I don't eat my bread roll. I decide to save it to give it back to Molly-May later.

'MOLLY-MAY, YOU CAN COME IN OURS TOO,' yells Akin. 'You can be our sister.'

'Lucky me,' says Molly-May, rolling her eyes, but then she grins and I know that she likes belonging too.

Mr Samuels brings a chair to put in our hut for Ste. He levers himself into it and we the Biscuits crowd in the hut behind him.

Akin sits with his knees pulled up to his chest with

the biggest smile. I know he thinks this is the best history lesson ever too. I sit with my legs crossed and Molly-May lies on her belly, her chin in her hands, and she's almost laughing but not quite. And as for Ste, his eyes are shining and I think maybe he's forgotten about his leg just for the moment.

'Here,' I say, pulling my bread roll out of my pocket and giving it to Molly-May, who stuffs it into her mouth and gulps it down.

Ste and Akin are just staring at her. Akin pulls the remains of a squashed Twix out of his pocket and shoves it in her hand.

There's a pile of paper and pencils in the middle of our hut home and next to it is a pot and a pan.

'Now,' says Mr Samuels. 'I know this is exciting and different, but I want you to concentrate.'

'Can you be our teacher for all of our subjects, sir?' shouts out Ste.

Mr Samuels laughs. 'I want you to pretend you live here, and what it would be like to have lost everything. Some of you would have been able to grab what possessions you could, which is why I've put some props in each hut. Start writing.'

And I don't have to think twice before I start my story.

My great-great-grandfather Cuthbert H. Brown Junior lived in a car ... And I imagine what it would have been like at night, curled up with his sister Dora and brother Frank on the back seat, under the stars, and I am writing, writing, writing and I don't care about my spelling. It's my story that matters and words are tumbling out of me as my great-great-grandfather climbs a tree to see Red Pollard ride Seabiscuit, the greatest racehorse that ever lived.

After what seems like no time at all, Mr Samuels says, 'Put your pencils down. You're cold and you're hungry, and you need a hero that you can believe in. You need hope. Come out of your huts.'

I do as he says, and my heart stops. Mr Samuels has set up an old-fashioned-looking projector and on the screen is my Seabiscuit.

'I thought you'd be interested in watching this, Daniel,' says Mr Samuels, eyes twinkling at me. 'Class, you are about to witness the greatest horse race ever run. A horse race that brought a nation together. It's November the first, 1938, in Pimlico, Maryland. The great champion War Admiral is about to run against a horse called Seabiscuit – who really isn't built to be a racing horse.

'Seabiscuit was very clever and lost a lot of races in his early years, but a talented trainer, Tom Smith, realised Seabiscuit was fooling around and only ran fast when he felt like it. Tom persuaded Charles Howard and his wife Marcela to buy Seabiscuit so he could bring out his full potential. And Seabiscuit started to win, and became a champion for Americans who had lost everything in the Great Depression. They rooted for Seabiscuit to win because he gave them hope. If this small horse could win, then just maybe they would win too.'

I look around and my classmates are spellbound by his words.

'Red Pollard, his usual jockey, had hurt his leg. So jockey George Woolf rode instead, but Red told him how to get the best out of Seabiscuit.

'Four million people listened to the race on the radio. The president, Franklin D. Roosevelt, stopped a cabinet meeting so that he could listen too. The racetrack was so full that ten thousand people were outside the gate. They climbed trees and stood on cars and rooftops, all to get a view of their hero, Seabiscuit. The voice you are about to hear is the race announcer, and his name is Clem McCarthy,' finishes Mr Samuels just as the race commentary starts playing.

Some of my class stand on chairs. I stand on Mr Samuels' desk so I'm highest of all and even though I know what's going to happen, I'm still yelling with the rest of my class, 'GO ON, SEABISCUIT!' I'm loudest of all. And as he runs over the finishing line I jump up, almost touching the ceiling and Ste is standing holding on to his chair, waving one of his crutches in the air, and the Biscuits are all hugging each other and it's like we are there, back in time, and Seabiscuit has given us hope, 'cause maybe, just maybe the Big Read Off will be OK too.

The bell goes for morning break.

Mr Samuels holds up his hands for us to listen and says, 'As Seabiscuit passed War Admiral, George Woolf turned and shouted back, "So long, Charley" to War Admiral's jockey – a phrase that's still used by jockeys today. So I say, "so long" to you. Go and have a nice break.'

Everyone tumbles out of the classroom except Akin, Ste, Molly-May and me.

'Sir, sir,' I call to Mr Samuels as he walks towards the door. 'Please, I got something to show you.' He follows me as I run to my bag and pull out my scrapbook.

'My great-great-grandad Cuthbert H. Brown Junior. He was there. He saw the race. He used to write letters to Seabiscuit and they are all in here. Look.'

'Oh my goodness,' says Molly-May.

'No way,' says Ste.

'Can I see? Can I see?' says Akin.

Mr Samuels smiles as I place the book in his outstretched hand.

He sits at his desk and Akin, Ste, Molly-May and me crowd round Mr Samuels as he gently turns the pages.

And it's like there is this light, this light shining out of him.

He looks up and says, 'Daniel Margate, you have a piece of living history right here. This is literally one of the most amazing things I've ever seen. Thank you so much for sharing it with me. Your great-great-grandfather Cuthbert H. Brown Junior must have been an extraordinary young man. I see where you get it from.'

Mr Samuels' words – 'I see where you get it from' – do a happy leap into my heart but then wander around in my brain, lost. And before I can stop my own words, they jump out of my mouth and say, 'Me? I'm not extraordinary. I'm dyslexic.'

'Listen to me, Daniel.' Mr Samuels is looking at me with wise eyes. 'Dyslexics have a gift. A different way of doing things and looking at the world. Never forget that you have that gift too. Dyslexics *are* extraordinary people.'

'Sir, I reckon that all the Biscuit Team are extraordinary,' says Molly-May.

'I believe you are,' says Mr Samuels.

'WE ARE EXTRAORDINARY,' shouts Akin, leaping in the air. 'Go on, Ste, say it.'

But Ste just looks out of the window at two Year 9s racing across the playground, biting his lip.

'Can we stay in our hut to do reading practice?' says Molly-May. 'We need all the practice we can get.'

'OK then,' says Mr Samuels, laughing and turning to go.

'Sir,' I say. 'That was the best history lesson ever.'

'Most definitely,' says Molly-May.

'Can we stay with you all day?' says Akin. 'We could be your assistants.'

Mr Samuels laughs. 'It's very gratifying that you enjoyed my history class, but I must go, and you should do your reading practice.'

I wrap my scrapbook in my blue jumper with the hole in the elbow, put it in my school bag and pull out my copy of *Black Beauty*.

When I crawl into the hut, my team are already staring down at their books.

I open mine and try and puzzle out the words.

'Concentrate, Daniel,' I say to myself and open my eyes really wide and stare at the book. But instead I'm wondering if I should tell Akin, Ste and Molly-May about Jammie Dodger and how he could be our reading horse . . .

Then I think, supposing I never see him again? I can't tell anyone about him. Not yet.

As I try and read about Black Beauty, the only horse I can see galloping through my daydreams is Jammie Dodger. I hope he comes back to the Old Shed tonight.

Chapter 15

I'm racing out of school towards the school gate, but this time just as me, Daniel Margate. I trip, stumble flat on my face. Laughter as usual. But then a hand. Someone grabs my arm and pulls me up. It's Michael.

'You all right?'

I nod 'thanks' but my knee stings.

'Where you off to in such a hurry?' he asks.

The truth nearly comes tumbling out of my mouth but I mustn't tell him, 'cause what's the point of a secret if you go telling people?

I feel a shove in my back.

'Oh my days, how you going to do that race on the telly when you can't even run out of school?' Sol, Baz and Nico surround me and Baz is doing his not-so-funny impression of me running, legs and arms everywhere.

'Yeah, you on the TV running and reading – that's jokes,' says Nico.

'We'll be at the finishing line before you even run your first step.' Sol steps into my face.

'If you don't mind, Boyz,' says Michael, squeezing into the middle of them. 'We got places to be.'

'Yo! Prof M,' says Sol. 'Didn't see you there.'

'Prof M, what you doing round these ends?'

Michael's fame has spread.

'I got business with your headteacher,' says Michael.

At the mention of Mr Lawson, the Cinder Street Boyz just melt away into the crowds pushing towards the bus stop.

'I knew that would get rid of them,' says Michael.

'Thanks,' I say, 'you at our school for Science Club thingy?'

Michael nods. 'Yeah, it's good – a proper place to invent things. Usually I plan my inventions in a notebook under the desk instead of doing my lessons.'

I laugh.

'I'd best go,' says Michael.

'See ya,' I say, 'and thanks.'

'Laters,' says Michael as we turn to walk in our separate directions.

'Daniel,' calls Michael.

I turn.

'Come and knock for me sometime if you want. We could get chips from Bernie's.'

I feel like my face is going to crack with my smile and I don't even feel my stinging knee.

Suddenly, I have Molly-May and Akin – and even Ste, even though he pretends he's not one of us. And now Michael wants me to get chips with him. It's good having friends. Things are looking up.

But when I get off the bus ready to head to the Old Shed, things start to look down. Mum is waiting for me outside the Rescue Centre, coat on, pacing backward and forwards. She sees me and comes running towards me.

'There you are, Daniel. Jackson's got a temperature, so we've got to collect him from Lizzie's.'

'But I need to sort out the Old Shed, and I can do my homework there and—'

'No, Daniel. I'll need you to start putting the tea on while I fetch Jackson. Come on.'

And I have no choice but to *come on*, longing with every bit of me to run through Apple Tree Wood to see if Jammie Dodger is waiting for me.

Mum goes to Lizzie's and I let myself into the flat. Dumping my school bag by the front door, I go into the kitchen and open the cupboard to rows and rows of tins of baked beans. They must have been half price or something. So I guess it's beans on toast for dinner.

Nearly cutting myself on the stupid tin opener, I half-open the can of beans when I hear Mum's key in the lock. Thank goodness – I'm not very good at cooking.

'Thanks, Daniel,' she says. Jackson is clinging to her like a sloth clings to a tree. 'Take him, will you?'

Jackson feels hot and so heavy.

'Dan-Dan, Dan-Dan, Dan,' he says over and over as I take him into the bedroom and dump him on his bed.

'Do you want to play racing?' I ask. 'You War Admiral, me Seabiscuit?'

But Jackson just curls up on his bed looking at me. He must be ill, to turn down racing. I pick up a picture book with a bear and a giraffe on the cover from the middle of the floor and plonk myself on the bed next to Jackson and open the book. At least I'll be doing some reading practice. Well, sort of!

I love Jackson's books 'cause the words are big and it doesn't matter if I see the words wrong 'cause the story is told in the pictures as well, so I can guess what the words are saying.

I open the book to a big picture of a bear and a giraffe sitting down to have tea together. It makes me laugh because the giraffe's head is touching the ceiling and the little bear cub is having to stand on the table to pass Giraffe some cake.

'Please can I have some cake, Mr Giraffe asks Mr Baer – no – Mr *Bear*.'

If I find it hard to read a picture book, how am I going to get through the Big Read Off?

'Dinner's on the table,' shouts Mum, but Jackson is curled up in the land of dreams. I take his shoes off and pull the cover over him.

'Jackson's asleep,' I say to Mum as I enter the kitchen.

'Leave him,' she says and we take our plates through to the front room and perch with them on our knees watching the *Seven Show* and I want to tell Mum about the Big Read and Race Off but she is totally engrossed in the telly. I need to get to the Old Shed and see if Jammie Dodger is there. I gobble my beans and toast so quickly it makes me burp.

I take our empty plates through to the kitchen. *Tell her now*, I say to myself, but when I step back into the front room I hear a gentle snore from the sofa.

She's nodded off. I grab my school bag and make my escape, and in no time, I am running over the courtyard and through the wasteland and towards Apple Tree Wood and I'm Red Pollard about to win a race and Seabiscuit is flying towards the finishing line. Day becomes dusk and I slow down to walk so I don't trip, and I weave in and out of the trees . . . and there he is lying under a tree, with his legs folded under him, head up, ears alert, waiting for me.

'You came,' I whisper. I walk towards him slowly, making sure not to startle him. He lets out a small nicker, as if he's saying hello. 'Hello, Jammie Dodger. Hello, boy.'

I put my school bag down and sit next to him. He seems comfortable with me by his side, so I stroke him and bury my face in his mane and smell his beautiful smell. We sit there as the moon comes out and shines on a big red apple hanging from the tree. I want to get it for Jammie Dodger – mad though it seems, mad though the thought is, it will not go away. He just has to have that apple. I stand up and put my foot in a notch in the bark of the tree, reach my arms to the branches and pull myself up, putting my foot in the next notch, and soon I am climbing, climbing. There's a rustling in the branches above. I look up and green cat eyes stare down at me. It's Napoleon. I reach for the apple, and just as I grab it Jammie Dodger stands up. If I climb down to the next branch I can get on his back.

Can I? Dare I? I have never ridden before, apart from on a donkey at the seaside. I know it's dangerous, but I want to ride Jammie Dodger more than anything in the world. I lower myself on to his back as he stands there waiting patiently. I wrap my legs round him and I hold on to his mane and Jammie Dodger starts to walk and I cling on under the moonlight, horse and boy, boy and horse, and I feel complete. Napoleon springs down from the branches and walks ahead of us, tail in the air, leading our parade. A mouse shoots across our path and Napoleon races after it. I think of the Big Race Off, and how I'm going to endure it. I hear Mr Samuels' voice saying, *Dyslexics have a gift. A different way of doing things and looking at the world. Never forget that you have that gift too. Dyslexics are extraordinary people*. And then . . . it comes to me!

Sugden said I had to get from the beginning to the end of the race *somehow* – well, why can't that *somehow* be on Jammie Dodger? I lean forward and pat him.

'Would you like that? Would you? You and me racing on the television?'

I feel strong, I feel powerful on Jammie Dodger's back, but as Jammie Dodger turns towards the shed I see a shadow waiting for me. A glint of silver jacket. It's Michael.

Jammie Dodger stops.

'Your secret's up,' he says.

Chapter 16

I lock eyes with Michael as I look down at him from Jammie Dodger's back, no words coming, till I can't bear it any more. I've got to ask.

'So, are you going to tell?'

Michael shakes his head. 'Who does the horse belong to?'

'No one. I reckon he's been abandoned.'

'A beautiful horse like this?'

'I've searched online to see if he's on the stolen horse register or been reported and he hasn't, so I reckon he must've been abandoned. He runs free over the heath in the day and secretly comes here at night.'

'He's a big secret to keep,' says Michael.

'I know,' I say, 'but now you know, you've got to keep the secret too.'

Jammie Dodger stamps his feet and tosses his head, his mane flying. He's restless.

'Steady, boy,' whispers Michael, walking slowly forwards and stroking the horse's nose. 'I knew you were up to something; I saw you hurrying towards the wasteland early this morning. I've promised not to tell, and I won't, not if you don't want me to, but don't you think we should? We could be in big trouble – now that I know, I'm in it too.'

Panic swims up through my body as I swing my leg over and slide off Jammie Dodger, landing in a heap on the ground. It was further away than I expected.

'Please, you mustn't tell any grown-ups,' I say as I scramble to my feet. 'They'll take him away and he's mine.'

'Have you given him a name?'

'You know Seabiscuit?'

'The racehorse?'

'Well, this is Jammie Dodger, in honour of him.'

Michael bursts out laughing. 'Like the biscuit! That's the best name I ever did hear. Do you like your name? Do you, Jammie Dodger?' he says, kissing my horse on his nose.

'We should get him into the Old Shed. I've made it comfortable for him like a stable.'

I open the door and walk in and Jammie Dodger follows.

'Wowzers,' says Michael as he follows us in. 'I've never had a chance to come in here before. It's enormous!'

Jammie Dodger does a wee then walks into the middle of the straw floor and lies down, just as he did yesterday.

I'm still feeling properly uneasy. I need to make completely sure Michael won't blab to anyone.

'I need to be able to trust you to keep this secret.'

'What do you take me for? I sometimes ride at the weekend with Mr Samuels – you know, he's together with my Aunty Lou. He's taught me to ride. I can help – borrow grooming brushes and horse things and stuff.'

This has worked out better than I thought, I think.

'You know what?' Michael sounds excited. 'We should have a secret society.'

'The Secret Horse Society,' I say.

I run outside and grab my schoolbag and pull out the horseshoe.

'Michael, put your hand on the horseshoe with mine and repeat after me: we, the Secret Horse Society, swear on the Great Seabiscuit's horseshoe to keep Jammie Dodger a secret.'

'We, the Secret Horse Society, swear on the Great Seabiscuit's horseshoe to keep Jammie Dodger a secret,' repeats Michael. He grins and sits in the straw next to Jammie Dodger.

'I got something to show you.' I open my school bag and pull out the jumper and unwrap my scrapbook.

'This belonged to my great-great-grandfather Cuthbert H. Brown Junior. You know Wilbur the reading dog who used to go round all the schools?'

Michael nods.

'Well, I want Jammie Dodger to be a reading horse. So we've got to keep him a secret till I sort it.'

'That's brilliant,' says Michael with a laugh.

I tell him all about the Big Read Off and what the Cinder Street Boyz did with the counters but I don't tell him about my plan to ride Jammie Dodger in the Big Race Off. Not yet.

'Do you want to practise?' says Michael. 'I won't

judge your reading. I'll have a go first – this looks interesting.'

And we open my scrapbook and Michael starts to read to Jammie Dodger.

March 6th 1937

Dear Seabiscuit,

Our automobile is parked on a dusty side-track with a load of other automobiles that families live in and one of them had a radio. We all crowded round to listen to the San Juan Capistrano race.

They said there were forty-five thousand people cheering you on, but I doubt any of them were cheering as loud as all of us crowded round the radio, and as for me, I was cheering loudest of all.

Michael looks up and smiles. 'Your turn.'

I feel my nerves jiggle in front of Michael, but I focus on Jammie Dodger and though the words swim before my eyes and I stumble over letters, I feel that Jammie Dodger is just loving me reading to him. It doesn't

145

matter to him if I say a word wrong, as long as I keep on talking.

The radio announcer said that Special Agent was in the lead with Indian Broom behind, and I could hardly breathe. Then the race caller announced, 'Here comes Seabiscuit,' and you were winning! You won by seven lengths and smashed the track record and people were hugging each other; a man swung a little girl round and he was crying. I was dancing round in circles screaming, 'He's won, Pa, Red Pollard and Seabiscuit have won.' Pa's very words were, 'Well, it makes you believe that dreams can happen.'

Love from,

Cuthbert H. Brown Jr

P.S. Seabiscuit, you brought my pa some luck. His, 'Everyone loves the movies, Cuthbert. People need dreams and movie stars need clothes to act the dreams out' came true. He got hired for two weeks to stitch some

fine costumes on a film called *The Wizard
Of Oz*. Thank you, *Seabiscuit*, from the
bottom of my heart.

Michael's smiling at me.

'I wish I could read as well as you, Prof M,' I say.

'I think you read well, Red D,' he says.

'Red D,' I say, 'Like Red Pollard. I like it.'

'Good, 'cause that's what I am going to call you
from now on.'

It feels good to have my very own nickname.

Napoleon stalks into the Old Shed as if he owns it.
He gives us this look as if to say *what are you even doing
here?* and walks straight up to Jammie Dodger. They
sniff at each other, then Napoleon, purring loudly,
springs on to Jammie Dodger's body, stretches out
and goes to sleep. Jammie Dodger doesn't seem to
mind that he now has a sleeping cat on him, and shuts
his eyes too.

'Napoleon's got big attitude issues,' says Michael
with a laugh.

'It would be good for Jammie Dodger to have an
animal friend,' I say. 'Seabiscuit had a monkey friend

called Jo Jo who slept in the crook of his neck and a little stray dog called Pocatell who slept on his belly and a horse best friend called Pumpkin who shared a stable with him and they went everywhere together.'

'That's so cool,' says Michael. 'You know loads about Seabiscuit!'

I tell Michael about the other Biscuits: Akin, Molly-May and Ste. 'I can't help but think that Jammie Dodger might help them read too,' I tell him.

'Time to swear them into the Secret Horse Society, Red D,' says Michael.

Chapter 17

My fellow Biscuits and I grab bean-bags in the library. I put two bean-bags on top of each other to make it easier for Ste to sit.

'Thanks, Daniel,' he says, letting himself fall backwards on them with his leg sticking straight out in front of him. He seems a bit happier to be with us today.

'Listen up, Biscuits.' I plonk myself down on a bean-bag. 'I got—'

'Up, up, stand on your feet.' Miss Darwin, the drama teacher, appears in front of us with Mrs Johnson. We haul ourselves out of our bean-bags.

'We've been talking, and' – Miss Darwin pauses, looks round at us all dramatically, as Mrs Johnson nods and smiles – 'what we need to do, my little sunflowers, is warm up those voices, get that diction going. If you sound confident, you will feel it.'

She brings a wooden chair into the middle of the library for Ste.

'Sit with your back nice and straight, Ste,' she says. 'You can do this too.'

And she has us massaging our cheeks and pretending to chew toffee and sticking our tongues out as far as they will go and saying tongue twisters like 'Red lorry yellow lorry, red lorry yellow lorry' and 'A creamy cup of coffee in a copper coffee pot', which is a nightmare for dyslexics if you ask me!

'If you sound confident and project loudly you've already won half the battle,' she says.

'No one's ever taught me to be louder before,' says Akin. 'Everyone's usually teaching me to be quiet.'

Mrs Johnson bursts out laughing and even Miss Darwin laughs, though I can tell she's trying not to.

'You can go first, Akin,' she says and he strides up to the front looking cool. He smiles round at us then he opens his book and the smile vanishes. I'm not really listening to the words as they struggle to jump off his tongue, but I watch him twisting and turning his body, shuffling on one foot then the other, screwing his face up. Then he just stops and stares out of the window and I can tell that he wishes he was running over the grass away from here and I just know that Jammie Dodger would make him feel better.

'Thank you, Akin,' says Mrs Johnson gently.

Akin slams the book shut and flings himself back on a blue bean-bag.

'I wish Wilbur was here,' he mutters as his foot starts jiggling up and down.

'Ste, your turn,' says Miss Darwin, dragging a music stand over from behind Mrs Johnson's desk. 'You can rest your book on here.'

Ste hauls himself off the bean-bags and swings himself to stand in front of the music stand. He puts his book on it – it has a boy kicking a football on the cover. He glares at the book like it's his enemy that he's sizing up for battle.

And when the words come, they shoot out of his mouth like bullets one at a time but with big gaps in between so they don't flow into a story.

'The CROWD . . . WENT . . . QUIET . . . AND . . . BOBBY . . .'

'. . . kicked,' I say, guessing, after a long pause.

Ste pushes over the music stand with his crutch and the book goes flying. 'I hate reading. I hate it hate it hate it. I was never any good at it before, but now I can't . . .'

'Ste, you've missed so much school, you've got to be patient with yourself,' says Mrs Johnson.

'I don't want to be patient with words. I want to run. I want to kick a ball. I want . . .'

I quickly look away 'cause Ste must not see my eyes tear up. What have I done, picking him for the Big Read Off and putting him through this?

'Well, Ste,' says Molly-May, 'since you got to do reading 'cause it's the law you might as well do it with us who want to be your friends. If you'll let us.'

'Thank you, Molly-May,' says Mrs Johnson. 'Ste, the Big Read Off will give you something to work towards.'

But it's like all the life from Ste's face has got up and run away. He swings himself over to a chair in the corner, lowers himself down and puts his head in his hands.

Mrs Johnson gets him a glass of water and sits next to him, whispering words of gentleness.

Mr Lawson told us in assembly just before Ste came

back to school that he had been in a coma for a long time and that Ste, one of the most promising athletes at Heath Academy, had to learn how to walk again. Mr Lawson said he thought that Ste was one of the bravest boys he'd ever met and we all had to give him space, time and kindness.

Now that I have picked him I know that Jammie Dodger would help Ste with his reading. I just know he would.

'Daniel,' says Miss Darwin, 'up you come.'

But my heart goes down as I grab my copy of *Black Beauty* and walk with slow steps to the front. I wish with all my heart I was riding away from this moment on Jammie Dodger, but I'm not. I'm here in the library of Heath Academy and I've just got to get on with it.

I breathe. I open my mouth, close it again then open it and begin the first sentence. 'The first place that I can well remember . . .'

I feel as if all the strength has left my body and flown out of the window.

Miss Darwin leans over the book. 'It says, *was a large* . . . Come on, Daniel . . . *pl . . . pl*,' she says, sounding the beginning of the word for me.

I take a breath. 'Was a large pl . . . pl . . . pleasant,' I say and look up and Melody is standing watching me smiling, with a big pile of books in her hand and I just want to die. Melody, the best reader in the school, watching me, the worst reader in the school.

'Can I help you, Melody?' asks Mrs Johnson.

'I've got a study skills period. I thought I'd bring these books back. I've read them all.'

All of them! I think, *How can one person have read so many books?*

Molly-May is staring at my face, which is on fire big time.

'I think it's most probably my go now,' she says, marching up to the front.

'Don't worry about it, Daniel,' she mutters to me. 'We're the Biscuits and don't you forget it.'

That was properly brave and kind of Molly-May saving me like that 'cause she don't like reading in front of people any more than what I do.

Molly-May waits till Melody wanders over to a table far from us and sits down with a book.

Molly-May then opens her book but just stares at it.

She adjusts her wonky glasses, opens her mouth, but no words come. Instead, a big fat tear trickles down her cheek.

'Oh, come now, you can do this,' says Mrs Johnson. 'I believe in you, Molly-May.'

'Me too,' says Akin and bounds up to the front, standing next to Molly-May with his arm round her shoulder.

'I miss Wilbur,' says Molly-May, and now she's shaking. 'Reading was better with Wilbur our reading dog.' And she plonks the book open on her head like a hat and starts to howl. 'We'll never be ready to read on the television. Not ever.'

I know that I've got to introduce the Biscuits to Jammie Dodger tonight.

The bell goes for next lesson which is biology but this kid from Year 7 runs into the library and says Mr Sugden wants to see me and Akin for a meeting on the field for the Big Race Off.

Any hope I had that this day might get better marches out of my body and falls flat on the floor.

As usual, I'm last to struggle into my PE kit, and I can't

do my laces up, so I tuck them into my trainers.

Mr Andrews nods to me to walk behind a tree and bends down and does them for me.

'Tricky things, laces,' he says and smiles, but just as he's doing the second one Baz, Nico and Sol peep through the branches.

'Oh my days, he can't even do his own laces,' says Baz with a snort.

'GET HERE, NOW,' roars Sugden. 'YOU ARE REPRESENTING HEATH ACADEMY BLAH BLAH BLAH . . . YOU WILL NOT LET ME OR YOURSELVES DOWN BLAH . . . YOU WILL TRAIN BLAH BLAH BLAH . . .'

And Sugden has us jogging on the spot and stretching, and then we're at the starting line. 'You will run around the 400 metre track JUST LIKE YOU WILL ON THE DAY.' Sugden's gaze lands on me with an extra sneer before he blows the whistle. Everybody shoots off, leaving me in my usual last place. I'm trying, trying, to catch up with Baz, who's in front of me.

'GO ON, DANIEL!' I turn my head and see Mrs Johnson walking over the field towards us with Molly-May and Ste.

'RUN, DANIEL, RUN,' I hear Molly-May yell.

As I turn to look at them, I somehow manage to fall over my own feet and down in the grass I go, splat. As I peel my face from the mud, Sugden is already standing over me.

'Daniel Margate, somehow you will get from the beginning to the end of this race.'

I will do, I think. *I will get there on Jammie Dodger, though you don't know it yet.*

With this thought comforting me, I start to run again, pretending I am Red Pollard on Seabiscuit even though I'm still last.

By the time I get to the end of the race, the Cinder Street Boyz are already walking back towards the changing rooms and Sugden is talking to Mrs Johnson.

My Biscuits are waiting for me. Akin is bent double, panting, recovering from the race.

'I got something important to show you lot. It's top secret. Can you get away and meet me at the Old Shed on the wasteland at about eight-thirty? Ste?' I say.

He shrugs his shoulders.

'It's a good secret, I promise you. You wouldn't want to miss it,' I say.

I see the tiniest spark of interest run across his face.

'You gotta come,' says Molly-May, 'you're one of us. We've got to get you there somehow.'

'I got a wheelchair from the hospital for when I need it.'

'I'll knock for you,' says Akin.

'Go on, Daniel, tell us what the secret is,' says Molly-May.

'No, you'll have to wait, Molly-May. You'll know tonight and not a moment before.'

Time to swear them into the Secret Horse Society.

Chapter 18

Jammie Dodger is standing in a dark shadow under a tree and nickers when he sees me. He knows he's safe here. My Secret Horse.

'Hello, Jammie Dodger. Have you been waiting for me?' I say, burying my face in his coat as he nuzzles into my hair.

He knows me. He wants to be with me, there's no doubt about that. I also know Jammie Dodger is most probably hungry and thirsty and knows that he'll be fed here in the Old Shed. I get the key from under the stone and undo the door.

I busy myself dragging the water bucket outside, tipping out the old water and filling it up with the hose. Jammie Dodger then follows me into the Old Shed. He's thirsty and drinks and drinks then lies down on his straw bed and goes to sleep. I drag a straw bale

outside to sit on and get the Seabiscuit horseshoe out
ready. I close the shed door behind me so that Jammie
Dodger can sleep, plonk myself on the straw bale and
send a text to my mum.

Got lods of homewurk

I wait. Michael arrives first.

'Everything ready for the swearing-in ceremony?'
I nod. Michael is carrying a big bag which he thuds
down on the ground and perches on the straw bale
next to me.

'Jammie Dodger is inside having some Zs,' I say.

Molly-May comes running up. She's changed into
jeans and a red jumper that's too small for her.

'What's this all about, Daniel?'

'You'll see,' I say.

'Hiya,' she says to Michael, 'you live on our estate
don't ya? You're the one they call Prof M.'

'Yep, that's me,' says Michael.

'I'm Molly-May,' she says.

Then a yell comes from behind the Old Shed.
We run round and see a wheelchair hurtling down
the grass slope towards us with two people squashed
in it. The wheelchair tips backwards. Akin and a pair of

crutches come flying out, landing in a heap on the grass, and all we can see of Ste is his leg cage sticking in the air over the backwards-tipped wheelchair.

'Oh, my goodness. This is meant to be a secret,' says Molly-May. 'Most probably the whole of Camden heard you two.'

Akin scrambles up laughing, and we all run over to the wheelchair and grab a corner.

'Are you OK, Ste?' I ask.

'Have you broken all your bones what aren't already broken?' says Molly-May.

'On the count of three,' says Michael. 'One, two, three.' And we tip the chair the right way up. But Ste's smiling. His cheeks are rosy red, and his eyes are shining.

'This is Michael,' I tell them.

'All right,' say Ste and Akin in unison.

'Follow me,' says Michael. 'We've got important secret business to attend to.'

I run ahead to make sure Jammie Dodger hasn't been frightened by the noise.

He's standing in the shed, his ears pricked. His eyes focus on the others as they catch up with me.

'It's OK, boy. You've got some friends come to see you.' I walk slowly towards him and when I reach him I stroke him calmly. 'There you go, boy. That's it, good boy.'

'What . . . ?'

'How . . . ?'

When I turn around, Akin, Molly-May and Ste are all standing in the doorway of the shed, mouths open, with Michael grinning behind them.

'Meet Jammie Dodger. The Biscuit Team's new reading horse.'

'No way,' says Ste.

'You are full of surprises, Daniel Margate,' says Akin. 'He's amazing!'

'Does Mrs Johnson know we've got this reading horse?' says Molly-May.

'No, no one knows, Molly-May, he's my secret horse. Well, now he's our secret horse.'

'And we got to keep it that way,' says Michael. 'All of us.'

'It's got to be top secret,' I say, 'till the day of the Big Read Off when we reveal our reading horse to the nation.'

Molly-May nods. 'But I'm telling you now, we're going to be in so much trouble.' She walks forward slowly and holds out her hand to Jammie Dodger, who sniffs it. She walks round to his side and strokes him, then she buries her face in his coat. When she looks up at me I see she's got tears shining in her eyes.

'I've never met an 'orse before,' she says. 'Hello, Jammie Dodger. Hello, boy. My name's Molly-May.'

'He's Jammie Dodger in honour of Seabiscuit,' I explain.

'I think it's right and proper that he is named after the greatest 'orse that ever lived,' says Molly-May.

'Hello, Jammie Dodger,' says Akin. 'It is an honour to meet you.'

Ste swings himself forwards on his crutches towards Jammie Dodger, step by step. We're all watching and waiting to see if Ste will be one of us.

Jammie Dodger walks towards Ste and bends his head and sniffs at his cage, then nudges him with his nose.

'He's just checking you out, Ste,' says Akin. 'Just checking you out.'

Ste looks at us and at long last, cracks a grin.

'I think Jammie D's cool,' says Ste.

'Yes, Jammie D! That's gotta be the coolest name ever,' says Akin, 'like he's a rapper or something.'

'Yeah, Red D and Jammie D,' says Michael, flinging his arm round my shoulder, and for the first time in my life I feel cool.

'Red D?' says Molly-May.

'Yeah, it's what I'm known as,' I say, walking a few steps forwards with what I hope is a bit of a swagger and trying to sound like it's been my name for years.

Everybody laughs but I don't mind at all 'cause this is a kind sort of laughter.

'But how come you got the 'orse?' says Molly-May.

'I reckon someone's abandoned him,' I say.

'No way,' says Molly-May. 'Who would do a cruel thing like that?'

'But supposing he's not abandoned,' says Akin. 'Supposing, right, he's been kidnapped and Jammie Dodger ran away from the people what did it and— OH MY DAYS. If I get caught with a secret kidnapped horse I will never get my bicycle back, not ever.'

Michael brings his phone out of his pocket. 'He's not been reported as stolen or missing. Red D's already checked the lost and stolen horse register and I keep checking on my phone. So I reckon Jammie Dodger has been abandoned.'

'But shouldn't we tell someone about him?' says Molly-May. 'I mean, he's a big 'orse wandering round near the Beckham Estate, I mean . . .'

'Why shouldn't us kids on the Beckham Estate, us city kids, have a horse in our lives?' I say. 'We got to keep him secret though, till Read Off day, 'cause otherwise I reckon he'll get taken away to a horse sanctuary in the country,' I say. 'And I want him here with us.'

'But he'll be proper looked after at an 'orse sanctuary in the country.' Molly-May doesn't look convinced.

'I think Jammie D wants to be a London horse,' says Akin.

'A north-west London horse,' says Ste.

'Most definitely. Come on, Molly-May!' I say. My breath stops.

'He does seem to like us . . .' says Molly-May, sitting on a bale of straw, her head in her hands. Then she looks up and grins. 'I'm in,' she says.

'Yes, Molly-May,' I say, giving her a high-five.

'It's time,' says Michael.

I nod and go and get the horseshoe and hold it up in the air.

I say in my deepest, solemnest voice, 'This horseshoe was once worn by the Great Seabiscuit, who is now up in the sky looking down on us all. We have to promise to keep Jammie Dodger, named in honour of Seabiscuit, secret from all grown-ups. Line up, Biscuits.'

I hold the horseshoe out to Akin.

'I swear on the Great Seabiscuit,' says Akin, going to the back of the queue.

'On the Great Seabiscuit,' says Ste, following him.

It's Molly-May's turn. She places her hand on the horseshoe.

'I swear with all of my heart and with all the breaths what's in my body on the Great Seabiscuit to never breathe a single word about Jammie Dodger to no grown-ups.'

'Stand in a circle,' I say, holding the horseshoe out in front of me. 'Everyone place one hand on the horseshoe.'

Everyone does, including Michael, even though he is

already sworn in.

'You are now all members of the Secret Horse Society,' I say.

'The Secret Horse Society,' they repeat.

'We are the Biscuit Team by day, but by night we are the Secret Horse Society who looks after the great Jammie Dodger with all of our hearts.'

Then I lean forward and say in my most dramatic voice, 'Every secret society needs a code word, and ours shall be "biscuit". We will use it to warn each other of danger. You must come immediately when you hear that word.'

And Akin, Molly-May, Michael and me go round and round our circle whispering, 'Biscuit, Biscuit, Biscuit,' getting faster and faster and faster.

Jammie Dodger lets out a breath through his nose and turns himself in a circle, paws his front hooves and settles down, lying in the straw. It's like he knows.

After we toast the Secret Horse Society by eating Jammie Dodger biscuits (and some carrots for Jammie D), it's time for reading practice.

I take the scrapbook out of my bag. 'I think we should all take turns reading this letter to Jammie Dodger – he's learning about Seabiscuit.'

'I want to go first,' says Ste. I catch my breath at his words as I hand him the scrapbook. He's most definitely well and truly in my team now.

Ste rubs his forehead. Jammie Dodger is looking right at him, as if he's waiting.

'Go on, Ste,' says Molly-May. 'You can do this.'

And with stumbles and stops and starts he begins.

April 4th 1937

Dear Seabiscuit,

I want to thank you from the bottom of my heart for making my little sister Dora well again, even though you have not met her. You see, Seabiscuit, she got sick. It was warm outside but she was shivering so.

'Poor little girl,' says Molly-May.

'Don't go interrupting,' says Ste and continues reading.

Ma ordered my brother Frank and me to go and look for old newspapers because Ma said they would keep the heat in if we packed them on top of her blanket. She laid Dora across the two front seats of the automobile and we all crowded in the back seats.

Seabiscuit, so many of those newspapers had your picture on and Dora was so afraid, I placed your photograph where I knew her heart was and started reading bits to her to take her mind off her shivering sickness. You took up the whole page in one paper, and Mr Franklin D. Roosevelt our president had just this tiny little column next to it. That is how mighty you are – more words in the newspaper than the President of the United States of America.

Akin takes my scrapbook from Ste and settles himself down in the straw next to Jammie Dodger. He stops jiggling around. It's like Jammie D has put a calming spell on him as he starts to read to the horse.

One of the articles near Dora's foot said that Tom Smith, your trainer, gives you two quarts of Golden Rod beer before every race and if you don't get it you whinny and stomp.

'Giving a horse beer?' Akin looks up, giggling. 'That's madness.' He then mouths the next few words to himself, before saying, 'It says your great-great-grandfather laughed too,' and he continues to read.

How we laughed at the thought of you drinking beer, Seabiscuit, which I know is not true. I reckon those gentlemen of the press will believe anything they are told. And we laughed even harder when we read from the newspaper that Tom Smith, your trainer, was asked to describe you at length. And he said, 'he's a horse'. A horse! And then just walked away.

'I think I would've liked your great-great-grandfather Cuthbert.' Akin's words make me feel warm and fizzy inside, like Cuthbert H. Junior is right here with us in the Secret Horse Society.

'I wish I could have met him too,' I say, then whisper, 'I really do.'

Akin hands the scrapbook to Molly-May, who settles herself on the other side of Jammie Dodger's head.

'Listen, Jammie D,' she says. 'I'm going to read you a story.'

She starts to read and there are no tears or stresses like there were this morning. The words start to come and when she goes wrong . . . she just carries on.

There was an article by Dora's belly that said there was something up with your leg, but I reckon that's just because you walk a little funny, if you don't mind me saying so, Mr Seabiscuit, sir. Those people just don't know what they are talking about.

We read how they put a muzzle on you to stop you eating all of the time. They say you eat your bedding otherwise.

Well, Seabiscuit, I sure knows what it feels like to be hungry the whole time. I reckon I would eat my bedding if it tasted good.

Molly-May stops reading and bites her lip. I quickly take the scrapbook from her 'cause I know she knows what that feels like too.

It's my turn now, so I plonk myself next to Akin and find my place. And though the words on the page dance around and trick me, they are in my soul and I start to explore them one letter at a time.

But what we liked to read about most was how you were exercised in secret so no one would know how fast you really are.

You take a mighty good photograph, Seabiscuit. There was even a full-page advert for oranges with your picture on it.

The next morning, Dora was not shivering and she even smiled and I know it's 'cause she was wrapped in pictures and words of you, Seabiscuit.

Thank you for saving my sister.

Cuthbert H. Brown Jr

No one speaks, then Michael begins to clap. 'That was properly amazing.'

'It's like Jammie D was helping my words come out better,' says Ste.

'He's really listening,' says Akin. 'It makes you want to read to him.'

'Jammie Dodger won't never laugh at me if I go wrong,' says Molly-May. 'Daniel, could we read your great-great-grandad's letters for the Big Read Off?'

'Go on, Red D, let us,' says Akin.

'I would be honoured,' I say, 'and so would Cuthbert H. Junior.'

I know it's time to tell the Secret Horse Society the rest of my plan.

I stand up, 'cause this needs a proper announcement.

'Fellow Biscuits,' I say. 'I have a plan to win the Big Race Off.'

'No offence, Red D, you are never going to win the Big Race Off,' says Akin.

'Listen up. You know old Sugden said I had to get from the beginning to the end of the race *somehow* and he didn't care how I did it?'

They all nod except Michael 'cause he wasn't there.

'Well, how about if I race on Jammie Dodger?'

They all just stare at me, then Molly-May gasps and

puts her hand in front of her mouth. 'Oh, Daniel Margate, you will be in so much trouble.' Then she starts to giggle.

'This is a genius plan.' Akin jumps up and slaps me on the back.

'You will have to work really hard on your riding,' says Michael. 'I'll teach you, but listen up, Secret Horse Society, only Daniel must ride Jammie D till the Big Race. They got to get used to each other and he will need every moment of practice he can get.'

Ste, Molly-May and Akin nod solemnly.

'I can't wait to see this,' says Ste.

But there's one thing that's been bothering me.

'Akin, I know that you would like to win the race on TV, but—'

'I would gladly lose in the name of the Secret Horse Society,' Akin says before I can finish.

'You know,' says Michael. 'I'm going to be at the festival too. For the science fair on the sports field. The Camden BAM Science Club each have a walk-in booth to present a science project. I've been planning this radio invention for mine – but I can make it a 1930s radio project. I could commentate on the race, like the

Seabiscuit races Cuthbert H. Junior listened to on the radio.'

'Jubilations, that would be amazing!' I say, not quite believing the word popped out of my mouth.

'Jubilations?' says Ste, laughing at me.

'I like it, Red D,' says Akin. 'Jubilations.'

'We're going to be in so much trouble,' says Molly-May again. 'But this is the best secret I have ever, ever kept.'

'Biscuits,' I say. 'Place your hand on the Great Seabiscuit's horseshoe.'

And we all do.

'Secret Horse Society,' I say. 'Till we meet again.'

'Till we meet again,' they all repeat, and the meeting is over.

Life feels different after that very first meeting of the Secret Horse Society. I think we all felt it. We belong together.

Chapter 19

I call into the Old Shed on the way to school, but Jammie Dodger has gone again. Napoleon is curled up in the warm patch where Jammie Dodger had been lying. He must have snuck in after we left. I'm glad my horse has a cat friend.

'Stay safe, Jammie D,' I whisper into the cold morning air, and I set to getting rid of all the poo and wet straw, forking the straw to one side, getting rid of any evidence of our secret horse. I lock the shed door behind me and hide the key under the stone.

I'm already late for school now. But then I miss the bus and it's *years* before the next one comes. I pick all the bits of straw from my trousers and try to brush the horsehair off my jumper on the bus. But by the time I get to Heath Academy I am sooo late.

Miss Raquel's going to get really suspicious if I turn

up late every day, covered in horsehair and straw. I will speak to the Secret Horse Society about this at our meeting today after school. Maybe everyone can help out.

As I try to find my maths class I end up walking past the library. I hear voices and peep through the window to see who's there. The Shakespeares are sitting perfectly in a row, each with a book on their lap, definitely with no horsehair or straw on their jumpers.

Melody is standing in front of them, reading what sounds like Shakespeare. Her voice rings out loud and clear while the rest of them hang on every sound that comes out of her lips.

How are the Biscuits going to look, struggling through our words, next to the perfect Shakespeares?

Alice sees me and waves. I duck down, face on fire, and run down the corridor.

I hear a bang from behind a door followed by, 'Akin, get up off the floor now.'

'It's not my fault, Miss, the chair broke.'

Looks like I've found my maths class.

I walk in to see Akin standing by the broken chair,

the whole class laughing.

'QUIET,' shouts Miss Cranbourne. 'YOU ARE LATE, DANIEL. VERY LATE.' Her tight black curls bounce and her lips screw up as she looks around for a place for us to sit.

'Akin and Daniel, sit over there together where I can keep an eye on you.'

She points to an empty double desk by the window. 'And try not to break any more furniture, Akin.'

'I've just seen the Shakespeares practising. They are—'

'Brilliant,' Akin finishes for me.

'Yep.'

Akin bites his lip and then starts working on the maths problems and I go into battle with a 3 that looks like a 5 and a 4 that becomes a 6 and . . . well, it's just exhausting.

I get through the rest of the day in a daze, counting the seconds till the second meeting of the Secret Horse Society.

When I arrive at the Old Shed after school, the door is already open. Jammie Dodger is nowhere to be seen but there's fresh water and a straw bed set up ready for him.

Michael pokes his head out of the cubbyhole door.

'I thought as I was early, I'd get things ready.'

'It looks good,' I say. 'Thanks.'

Michael disappears back into the cubbyhole and there's the sound of banging. I go and have a peep. There's cogs and tools and bits of metal everywhere.

'I'm going to use this part of the Secret Horse Society HQ as an invention room for my radio project.'

'Good idea. What's that?' I ask, looking at a long wooden object that Michael is hammering a nail into.

'Ah, you'll see,' he says, tapping the side of his nose.

Michael bends down and brings out a riding hat from his school bag, which is under the table.

'It's mine,' he says. 'Try it on.'

It fits! I can't believe I've got an actual riding hat on my head.

'I'll teach you some bareback riding for the Big Race Off, after the meeting,' he says, as Akin pushes Ste through the door.

My tummy flip-flaps at those three words: Big Race Off.

'Where's the horse?' Ste asks, pulling himself out of his wheelchair and grabbing his crutches from Akin.

'He'll come,' I say, as I get a bale of straw for Ste to sit on.

Molly-May comes running in late, but there's still no sign of Jammie D.

I pray to the Great Seabiscuit up in the sky, 'Please let him be all right, Please, please, please.'

'I think we should get on with our meeting,' I say, to distract myself, and everyone is sworn in on Seabiscuit's horseshoe.

'Biscuits,' I say. 'We need to take turns organising the shed in the mornings. Jammie Dodger's poo and wet straw need clearing out.'

'It's called mucking out,' says Michael. 'You do it with a pitchfork.'

'All signs of him need removing, in case anybody from the rescue centre decides to come down here. The straw bed needs forking to one side.'

'What happens if they see the pile of straw on the floor?' says Molly-May.

'If that happens, I'll say that it's my fault and some of the strings on the straw bales came loose.'

I tear out a sheet from the back of my maths
and write down:

> ## The Secret Horse Society's Top Misshon Rota
>
> 1. To Keep Jammie Dodger Secrut from All of our Famleys
> 2. To Keep Jammie Dodger away from Teechurs at school
> 3. To practis reedin a lot
> 4. To make Jammie D happy and to try and keep him safe

'I can't do every morning before school. I keep being late and Miss Raquel's getting suspicious.'

'I can do Tuesdays,' says Michael.

'OK, I'll do Wednesdays,' says Akin.

'I'll do Thursdays,' says Ste.

'I'll come with you,' says Akin, 'and help.'

'That leaves Fridays for me,' says Molly-May.

'Jubilations,' I say, happy that's sorted.

A white horse head pokes round the door and all my anxieties melt away.

Akin jumps up and cheers.

181

'Akin, you're meant to be calm around 'orses,' says Molly-May. 'I watched the Seabiscuit film, I know what I'm talking about.'

We stand back as Jammie D walks into the shed and heads straight for the bucket of water. Droplets go everywhere as he drinks. We watch in silence as he then paces round in a circle and lies down. He's a bit muddy. He most definitely feels safe here with us, you can just tell.

I get my scrapbook out and watch as the others go through it, picking bits from the first two letters to read, but my mind is already under the stars, riding on Jammie D.

Time flies, and before I know it, Molly-May jumps up. 'My dad'll be wondering where I am, and I've not forgotten I'm doing the muck-out tomorrow.'

We all put our hands on the horseshoe.

'Secret Horse Society,' I say. 'Till we meet again.'

'Till we meet again,' they repeat, and the second meeting is over.

'Shall we have our next meeting on Saturday afternoon?'

'Yes.' Everyone nods.

'Weekends are really busy at the rescue centre – with people coming to view the cats and dogs. Remember to watch you don't draw attention to yourselves. Jammie D will be off on his adventures in the woods but we could hang out anyway.'

'Where do you think he goes?' says Akin.

'Well, I reckon that he spends most of the time on the heath,' I say, 'in those thick clumps of trees. But the first time he let me stroke him he was in the trees just behind the school fence.'

'Oh my goodness,' says Molly. 'That's too close.'

'Far too close,' says Akin. 'A teacher might see him.'

'You've gotta stay deep in the trees,' says Molly-May.

'Yes, Jammie Dodger, please stay hidden,' I say, and with that, the meeting is over. Though I know for me the best part is about to begin.

As the others go off through Apple Tree Woods, Michael disappears into the cubbyhole to grab the riding hat.

'Jammie,' I call into the shed. He's on his feet munching hay. 'Jammie D, come to me.'

Jammie D pricks his ears and he walks out of the

Old Shed, right up to me and nuzzles my chest. I want to shout 'Jubilations' to the moon that is peeping from behind a night cloud but I don't, 'cause you don't shout around horses.

'Hey, Jammie D, would you like to go for a little ride?' says Michael, coming to join us and plonking the hat on my head. 'Mr Samuels is going to take me riding tomorrow morning. They have this tack room with lots of saddles and bridles and stuff, but there's this corner where all the old tack that people don't use any more is dumped. There's even a few saddles. I'm going to calculate how big his saddle needs to be.'

Michael puts his hand on the base of Jammie D's mane. 'I need to see how wide he is. This bit's called the withers,' he says. Then Michael squints with one eye at Jammie D's back. 'I'm calculating the length,' he says. 'I'm good at calculating 'cause of all my inventions.'

'How are you going to sneak the horse stuff out?'

'Everyone at that stables loves Mr Samuels and it takes ages to get out saying his goodbyes to people. He always tells me to wait in the car, so I reckon that's my chance.'

'Right, Red D, let's get you up.' I clutch a handful of Jammie D's mane and bend my left leg up so it's sticking out behind me. Michael cradles it and counts to three, then pushes up as I lift and swing my right leg over and . . . I've done it. I am up and on Jammie Dodger.

'Right,' says Michael. 'We're going to do a bit of bareback riding, which is what we call horse riding with no saddle. So hold on to the clump of his mane.'

When I do, Jammie D starts to walk forwards, and my insides are flip-flapping 'cause it's the best feeling in the world.

'Let your legs drop low towards the floor,' says Michael. 'Don't grip too hard. That's good, Red D. Don't slouch – chest open and shoulders back like a soldier. Think like the middle of your body is strong as a steel drum, but feel like you're moving with the horse and Jammie D is moving with you.'

I do as Michael says, and it's magical. I can feel Jammie D's muscles rippling below my bum bones. I feel like I'm going to explode with happiness. I'm actually riding a horse!

A bird flies out of the bushes. Jammie D darts sideways. I feel myself toppling and the ground is coming closer, closer and – thud – I hit the grass.

My legs are shaky as I stand up.

'You gotta get back on. You ain't a rider till you've fallen off a few times – believe me, I know. Look, see, Jammie D could've run off but he's not, he's waiting for you,' says Michael.

Michael grabs the bottom part of my left leg. I clutch a handful of mane and on the count of three I'm back on. I drop my legs towards the floor, imagine my tummy is a steel drum, put my shoulders back, my chest open, wanting to hug the whole world with me and my secret horse in it.

I am Jammie D and Jammie D is me and we are one, like Red Pollard must have felt riding Seabiscuit.

'That's enough for tonight,' says Michael. 'You done well.'

As we settle Jammie D for the night I can't stop smiling. I keep saying in my head over and over, *You done well, Daniel*. I smile all the way home and into bed and am still smiling into my dreams.

Chapter 20

The next morning I try to tell Mum about the Big Read Off and the Big Race Off but Jackson is running around causing chaos (he is definitely feeling better!) and when I enter the kitchen, the first thing I see is half a chocolate cake sitting on the counter. Mum is going through a pile of brown envelopes and letters with red writing on them. She is chewing her lip and punching numbers into a calculator.

'Everything's so expensive,' she mutters.

Maybe today is not the best day to tell her.

Getting to school is painful – my bum is bruised and my legs ache from riding the night before. As I hobble into school, I wonder if Red Pollard felt like this all the time.

I look round for Molly-May. My heart won't rest till I know that she has carried out her Jammie D duties and that all is still secret.

But in registration there is no Molly-May and no Akin.

'Where are they?' I mouth across the room to Ste. He shrugs his shoulders, looking worried.

Still no sign of Akin and Molly-May by the time assembly starts. Mr Lawson starts waffling on about the BAM festival, but I'm not hearing his words. Then the door swings open and in comes Molly-May looking a right mess. There's bits of straw hanging from her hair, and all over her uniform. My heart stops. Kids are sniggering. I can see Ste madly waving to try and get her attention.

Miss Raquel whispers something to Molly-May and they both disappear out of the assembly hall.

I just want Mr Lawson to finish his words 'cause I got to find out if Molly-May let slip to Miss Raquel about Jammie D. I know she wouldn't mean to, but supposing it just blurts out?

At long last, the bell goes and everyone starts crowding out of the hall. Ste beckons me over.

'Come with me to Miss Raquel's office. I'm allowed to go and sit there when things get too much. We can see what's happening with Molly-May.'

'Sit down, Ste,' Miss Raquel says when we get to her office. She brings out the comfortable blue chair that sick kids sit in.

Molly-May is sitting in the corner in clean uniform from Miss Raquel's stash of spares. She's eating toast – which Miss Raquel must have made for her. She's kind like that. I can see Molly-May's uniform going round and round in the washing machine in the corner.

'I was just telling Miss,' she says, 'about them Beckham Street Boyz throwing straw over the balcony this morning. One of them's got a pet rabbit and they thought it was funny throwing straw everywhere. All over me it went.'

'What about the white hair all over you?' says Miss Raquel. 'Come to think of it, you were also covered in white hair the other day, Daniel.'

I think with lightning speed. 'It's that big white dog that belongs to someone in Cinder Street, Miss.'

'Yes, Miss,' says Molly-May. 'It's properly friendly.'

Miss Raquel looks from me to Molly-May then back to me again.

'Why isn't Akin at school, Miss?' says Ste, changing the subject.

'Oh, he just has to be somewhere this morning,' says Miss Raquel. 'Remember you've got your extra reading in the library this period. Mrs Johnson will be waiting for you.'

'Result! Missing English,' I say.

'Daniel, that's not the attitude,' says Miss Raquel, trying not to laugh.

'Oh, Miss, I don't know what's worse: battling numbers or punctuation. It's both equally exhausting, if you ask me.'

Molly-May hands her empty toast plate back to Miss Raquel and picks up her school bag. 'Thanks, Miss Raquel. You coming, Ste?'

'No,' he says. It looks like everything that makes him Ste has marched off and left him. He must really need some quiet time. He wasn't just saying it before.

'Hope you feel better soon,' I say.

As soon as we're out of earshot I turn to Molly-May.

'Is everything OK with Jammie D? Had he left the shed? Did you lock the door?'

She straightens her wonky glasses and glares at me.

'Of course everything's OK. What do you take me for? Jammie D had gone off wherever he goes. He'd made a lot of mess. I cleared it up and locked the door. End of story.' She rubs her arms. 'It's heavy work is cleaning up after a 'orse. I am a proper member of the Secret 'Orse Society, I'll have you know.'

'Sorry, Molly-May, I didn't mean . . . It's just it's a big secret we're keeping.'

'The biggest secret ever,' whispers Molly-May, as we hurry off to the library.

Mrs Johnson is waiting for us in our corner.

'Akin's not here, Mrs Johnson. And Ste's with Miss Raquel.' Molly-May plonks herself down on a yellow bean-bag. 'It's just us.'

I make a pile out of some of the bean-bags and plop myself next to Molly-May.

'Pretend the bean-bag mountain is Jammie D,' I whisper as I get out my scrapbook.

'Don't look much like him,' Molly-May whispers back.

She starts to read, and though she is stumbling and stopping and sighing and taking her glasses off and putting them back on again, the words start to come.

Dear Seabiscuit,

I hope you are healthy and happy and looking forward to your next race. Even though it is nearly dark, I am lying on the grass trying to write this to you whilst I can still see just a little bit.

Every time Ma looks over at me, I quickly pretend I am sleeping, but, Seabiscuit, I just got to tell you what happened today.

Today was my birthday. I'm thirteen years old. Ma, Pa, Dora and Frank made a circle and danced round me, singing 'Happy Birthday'. Some of the other people in the automobiles and shacks nearby joined in and, well, it was joyful to hear all those voices, raised just for me.

I know lots of people send you gifts, it says so in the newspaper, and I could tell that Pa and Ma were sad that they didn't have a gift to give me, but I gave them a hug and thanked them for their singing.

Ma marched us down to the mission relief kitchen, but Pa was dragging his feet behind *us, hands in his pockets, looking sad as sad can be.*

Seabiscuit, I got a secret to tell you — I heard Pa crying last night. The sound of his sobs woke me from my dreams of riding you. I could see, under the moonlight, Ma had her arm around him like he was a little child and it broke me in pieces to see it.

Molly May just stops.

'My dad cries sometimes,' she whispers. 'I hear him in the night.' I put my arm around her.

'Oh, child, everyone has to cry sometimes,' says Mrs Johnson. 'It's so you can pick yourself up and start again. You read that so beautifully. Do you want to read some more?'

She shakes her head and hands me my scrapbook and I take a big breath and start to read. I stop and start but the words start to come out of my mouth one by one.

It seems like we were in that line for ever, waiting for soup.

Pa said we should all stick together but Ma said, 'Let them be, Joseph, let them be.'

I found us a place at the kids' table and told Frank to stay and guard my soup and bread whilst I went back for Dora, 'cause there sure were some hungry-looking boys who wouldn't think nothing of eating my food as well as theirs. Dora was slopping her soup over the sides as she carried it and lost half of it to the floor, so I grabbed her bowl in one hand and her hand in the other and marched her to the table and poured some of my soup into her bowl.

I took a big bite of bread and started spooning soup into my mouth, fast. It was very watery but it felt good in my belly and the bread — well, I chewed and chewed to make it last longer, and all around me the air was filled with talking so I started to listen.

These boys along our bit of table were all train-track kids — this means they had travelled from all over the United States of

America by clinging to the box cars on trains. Their chitter chatter filled the air around me. William, well, his pa and ma couldn't feed him and asked him to make his own way in the world. Same with Henry, who was on the other side of me. But Norman, well, he just wanted an adventure. Imagine that, Seabiscuit.

'You can come along with me if you want,' he said, and my heart skipped a beat for a second at the thought of clinging to a box car and travelling far, far away from our automobile home. Dora and Frank both put down their spoons and clung to me, then I looked over at Ma on the other side of the hall and she gave me a little wave, and I knew I was going nowhere.

'Thank you, Norman,' I said, 'but I am just fine where I am.'

'Couldn't you do with a friend to tell your troubles to?' said Norman.

'Oh, I got a friend,' I said. 'I tell all my troubles to Seabiscuit.' And I told him about climbing high, high in the tree to see you.

'You actually caught a sight of Seabiscuit?' says Norman, his mouth open so I could see all the chewed-up bread and, Seabiscuit, I wish you'd been there 'cause all the train-track kids put down their spoons and the hall was just full of talk of you — how they'd heard a race on the radio, or read this and that in the newspaper. It seemed like you give everyone a little piece of hope.

'So long,' said Norman, and I locked eyes with my friend of the moment that I knew I'd never see again.

When we got outside to walk back to our automobile, Pa had a skip in his step and clapped his hands. 'This man, Jake, who was sitting right next to me, says he knows where there is some work going clearing rubble. I'm meeting him tomorrow.'

Ma looks at Pa's slender hands and sighs.

'I think it's Seabiscuit's doing,' I say.

'So do I, son, so do I. He gives us all hope.'

Mr Seabiscuit, sir, thank you for giving me

the best birthday present ever: a skip in my pa's step.

Yours respectfully,
Cuthbert H. Brown Jr

'Mr Samuels told me about this wonderful scrapbook of yours, Daniel,' says Mrs Johnson. 'Something's changed with you both, and I can't quite put my finger on it.' And then she smiles and keeps on smiling.

'C'mon, Big Racers,' shouts Mr Sugden. 'To the starting line.'

Any happy bubble I had after the morning's reading session burst as soon as I struggled into my PE kit.

As I stand on the starting line shivering, I see kids swarming towards the track. It looks like the whole of Heath Academy is coming to watch!

I feel my face – even my legs and arms – start to burn red, and I am no longer shivering but on fire. I can feel the laces that I couldn't even tie, tucked inside my trainers, rubbing against the top of my foot.

Mr Andrews walks past us. I pray he doesn't look down and see them. So I distract him so he looks at my face, not my feet.

'Sir, what are they all doing here?' I ask.

'Mr Sugden wants you to get used to running in front of a crowd,' he says.

The whole of Heath Academy slowly spreads out, surrounding the track, and I am trapped.

I wish Akin was here, I think, 'cause he would glory in running in front of the whole school like this.

But it's my biggest shameful nightmare: just me and the Cinder Street Boyz racing in front of the whole school.

The whistle blows and we are off.

Nico shoots to the front and without Akin, he is the fastest today. Most probably all that practice running away from teachers and the police.

Behind him is Sol, and Baz is just in front of me. It goes without saying that I'm last. I am hating it, hating it, hating it. Everyone can see my legs and arms flying everywhere *but* in the direction they are meant to be going.

'You can do this, Daniel. You are tremendous,' shouts this girl in my year called Delilah. I like Delilah, she's kind. Even though I'm a bit scared of her best friend, Marcus Sparrow. But that's another story.

'Yes, Daniel, you are tremendous,' I say to myself. 'You are Red Pollard on Seabiscuit.' But all the pretending in the world can't make my feet fast enough and I'm trying, trying, trying to catch up with Baz but I just can't. I'm well and truly last, as always.

Then – shame of all shames – my trainer flies off! I hear laughing, but I carry on running, one sock, one trainer.

One by one, the others pass the finishing line, till it's just me running and all the school's eyes are watching my funny run.

I focus on the finishing line, now just a few strides away. I see Sol standing there snarling, but I refuse to look at him as I get closer . . . I'm almost there . . . and then my leg hits something. I stumble and then I'm tumbling flat on my face, centimetres from the finishing line.

'Loser,' Sol hisses. And I realise that the thing I stumbled over was his foot. 'It's great having you in the race 'cause you make us look good.'

As I get up, Nico walks straight through me, knocking me sideways like I don't even exist.

'Daniel!' It's Mr Samuels, calling me over – he has my trainer in his hand.

'Thanks, sir.'

He waits for me as I squash my foot back into it.

'Come for a little walk with me.'

We walk away from the Cinder Street Boyz and before I can stop them, big hiccupping sobs are breaking out of me.

'I run funny,' I say. 'And everyone saw.' I wipe my face on my PE top.

'So did Seabiscuit,' said Mr Samuels.

'Yes, sir,' I say. 'He used to swing his foreleg out and he had really short legs for a racehorse.'

'Exactly,' says Mr Samuels. 'And he was a champion. Daniel, you are one of the bravest boys I know. It's easy to keep doing things you are good at. It takes courage to do the things that you find hard. Remember that.'

'I will. Thank you, Mr Samuels.' And I think about how it's going to take the most courage of all to ride Jammie Dodger in the race. But I'm ready to face that challenge.

Chapter 21

Mum is called in to work at the rescue centre on Saturday morning, which gives me the perfect excuse to go with her and spend the afternoon in the Old Shed. I'll be able to hang out with the Secret Horse Society right under Mum's nose and she won't even know it.

By the time we've dropped Jackson off at Lizzie's and walked to the Beckham Animal Rescue Centre huddled under Mum's umbrella, there are lots of cars parked outside and people milling around. The weekend is really busy with people coming in to adopt cats, dogs and rabbits.

A small boy in a blue coat and dungarees comes out with a grey rabbit in a carrier. He's laughing as he splashes through the puddles, holding the hand of what must be his mum. 'Come along, Hector,' she says.

As we open the door to the Beckham Animal Rescue Centre, Silver the greyhound streaks past us, heading towards Apple Tree Wood, followed by Buster the Staffie. Jessica grabs a lead and has one foot out of the door to go after Silver.

'Hi, Amy-Beth. Hi, Daniel. Buster's so naughty! I actually caught him using his nose to shove the catch up on Silver's kennel to let her out, but I was too late to stop him.'

I turn to see more people surge through the rain towards the rescue centre.

'I'll look for her,' I offer and take the dog lead from Jessica. 'I'm going down to the Old Shed, and they ran in that direction. Let me help. Silver likes me.'

'OK then, Daniel. Text me if you find her. Fingers crossed she won't have gone too far – she hates the rain. Please be careful, Daniel.'

'Thanks, Daniel,' says Mum, and I hurry off towards Apple Tree Wood, the rainwater trickling down the back of my jacket and my jeans getting splattered with mud.

I find Silver standing shivering under an apple tree, with Buster bounding round her wanting to play.

I walk up to her slowly, slowly and hold out my hand for her to sniff.

'Good girl, Silver, good girl.'

I take the lead out of my pocket and clip it to her collar and walk through the apple tree branches towards the Old Shed chatting to Silver, calming her all the way. Buster follows.

Jamie Dodger isn't there. I let Silver off the lead, and she runs round and round the Old Shed, followed by Buster, and then they both settle on the straw, snuggling up together and go to sleep.

I text Jessica.

> **I got dog. I will keep her with me as she is sleepin & Carm. Will brung bak later when peoples gone & I tidid shed.**

Jessica texts back.

> **Thanks Daniel. Still busy here & Silver would be fretful with all these people. Text me straight away if u need help.**
> **J x**

I set to mucking out and decide to leave the straw bed down as no one from the Beckham Animal Rescue Centre will come to the Old Shed today. They are all too busy, besides I don't want to disturb Silver and Buster.

Thunder rumbles in the sky but in between the rumbles I hear a bang, bang, bang against the back wall of the shed. I run outside and round the back. It's Jammie Dodger, kicking his hoof against the wooden wall.

'Clever boy. You came for shelter and you knew to come in the back way in case anyone saw you. Come on, Jammie D.'

And do you know what? He follows me round to the front and in through the door, but he stops when he sees Silver and Buster. My breath catches; I plead to the Great Seabiscuit in the sky that Jammie Dodger likes dogs.

Silver opens one eye, then the other. She rolls on to her feet, stretches and walks up to Jammie D. They stand nose to nose for the longest time, then they start walking round the shed together like the oldest of friends and I breathe again. Buster does one last snore, wakes up, rolls over and joins them, wagging his tail like he doesn't want to be left out.

Molly-May appears with her coat over her head. Buster runs up to her, wagging his tail.

'Buster, what are you doing here?' she says, stroking him. 'And who's this?

'This is Silver, she's stressed with all the people up at the rescue centre.'

'I know – there's loads of people. Will she let me stroke her?'

'Walk up to her . . . that's it, careful.'

Molly-May puts her hand out to the dog and Silver immediately presses her whole body against Molly-May and hides her face in her red jumper. Jammie D nudges Molly-May with his nose.

'Do you want some attention too, Jammie, do you? There you go.' And she gives him lots of pats.

Akin wheels in Ste, who breaks into a massive smile when he sees the dogs.

'This is Silver,' says Molly-May as Akin helps Ste out of the wheelchair. 'You gotta introduce yourselves so's she knows you're her friends. And this is Buster. Everyone on our estate knows him.'

Ste makes a fuss of Silver and Jammie D and Buster while Akin just sits on a bale of straw and watches. I don't think I've ever seen him so still and silent.

'You all right, Akin?' I ask.

He just nods his head.

'Oi! You lot, help me.'

I run to the door and see Michael staggering towards the shed with a massive laundry bag. Akin and I run out to help, Buster bounding in front of us.

Buster jumps up at Michael, nearly knocking him over.

'Buster, get down, boy. I got loads of stuff,' says Michael. 'I told Jemima who runs the stables that it was for a demonstration on animal care that we are doing for enrichment at school.' He looks at us and grins. 'It's not really a proper lie 'cause the Secret Horse Society is the best enrichment I could ever have.'

'And me,' says Akin, a smile flickering across his face at last.

It's good having friends to share secrets with. He dumps the bag on the shed floor and we all crowd round. Buster and Silver sniff it then wander off to play their own game at the other side of the shed. Napoleon struts in, sees Silver and Buster and changes his mind and walks back out again.

We swear ourselves in and the Secret Horse Society meeting begins as thunder crashes outside.

Michael starts teaching us how to look after a horse and it's the best lesson ever – right up there with Mr Samuels' lesson on the Great Depression, and we're all listening spellbound until there's the loudest thunder crash and Jammie Dodger rears and we all stumble backwards. Buster and Silver start barking but I've got to calm my horse. As his hooves hit the floor again, I walk slowly forwards, gently placing my hand on his nose.

'Everything's all right, Jammie Dodger,' I whisper. 'You're safe, we've got you, boy.' And my horse actually pushes the side of his face hard against my chest and closes his eyes. My world fills with happiness.

I look across to the stack of hay bales where Buster and Silver are still barking. Akin is with them and takes a tennis ball out of his pocket and gives it to Silver, who butts it with her nose. Buster tries to snatch the ball, so Akin takes his sock off and gives it to Buster to chew. It's in shreds in seconds but it has done the trick; the barking stops. Silver is calm again, which I am very glad about as she is my responsibility.

'You're going to be in so much trouble with your mum about your sock,' says Molly-May.

Akin shrugs and grins. 'I'll say the rain washed it away, if she notices.'

'Gather round, ladies and gentlemen,' Michael says, like the greatest showman.

'White horses are called greys by horse people,' says Michael.

'That don't make no sense,' says Molly-May.

Michael parts a bit of Jammie Dodger's horsehair. 'Look, see? His skin is grey. White horses usually have grey or black skin. It's very rare for their skin to be white.'

He brings out a tangle of straps and buckles with a lead rope dangling from it. 'This is a head collar.' He untangles it and slips it on Jammie D. He must have worn one before because he don't object.

'Hold him, Daniel,' Michael says, handing the lead rope to me. Then he cuts twine that's tied round one of the bales of straw and attaches it to a small metal hoop sticking out of the wall. I walk Jammie Dodger over to Michael and he shows us how to do a quick release knot as he ties the end of Jammie D's lead rope to the twine.

'This is for safety. If Jammie D panics, he can

208

break free,' says Michael.

I'm not good at knots so I'll have to practise.

'Molly-May, move from behind Jammie D. He can't see you there and he could kick out. Always put your hand on the rear of a horse if you are near his back legs and talk to him so he knows you are there,' says Michael.

'Sorry. I'm here, Jammie D,' says Molly-May and puts her hand on Jammie's bum, then comes round to stand next to me.

'Grey horses are the hardest to get looking clean, as you can well imagine,' says Michael as he gets an armful of hay for Jammie D to munch on.

He picks up a funny-looking round rubber brush and lets Jammie D sniff it. 'This is a curry comb,' he says, and starts moving it, doing small circular movements down Jammie D's neck and along his body. 'This will loosen dirt and bring up all the loose hair out of his thick winter coat.'

Jammie D leans into Michael.

'Ah, you like this, don't you, boy. It's like a massage,' he says.

Then we all have a go while Jammie D munches his hay and it's the best thing ever.

'This is the dandy brush.' Michael shows us a wooden brush with bristles. 'We use this with short flicking strokes, following the direction of Jammie D's coat, to brush off all the dirt and hair we brought up with the curry comb. We can use it on his legs too.'

Michael hands the dandy brush to Molly-May, who begins to brush Jammie Dodger.

'Harder than that, Molly-May, otherwise Jammie D will think you're tickling him.'

Molly-May giggles, does a few more strokes, then hands the brush to Ste, who leans on my shoulder so that he can have a turn. Once we've all had a go, Michael runs his hand down the inside of Jammie Dodger's leg, which tells Jammie D to pick his foot up. Michael then gets the dirt out with a hoof pick and continues with each leg in turn.

I look round at the Secret Horse Society: Michael has happiness jumping out of him (maybe right now he's not missing his best friend Nell quite so much), Ste looks like just for the moment, he isn't hurting because he cannot run free and win races, Akin seems to have forgotten whatever it was bothering him just for now, and Molly-May – well, she looks like her dad-worries have packed their case and gone and her whole wide world is Jammie Dodger. I don't know what I look like 'cause there ain't a mirror, but I reckon if I was to look in one I would just be zinging.

There's a lull in the storm.

'You lot should go before it starts again,' says Michael.

'I could stay here for ever,' says Molly-May.

We all put our hands on the horseshoe. 'Till we meet again.'

Jammie D is still munching hay while Silver is wandering round sniffing in every corner of the shed.

When they have gone, Michael pulls out a bridle from the bag and hangs it on a hook. He then hauls out a saddle.

'Wow! I don't know what to say.'

'It's an old one, was in the corner, cobwebs all over it, but I've cleaned it. Get the numnah out. It's a saddle cloth that goes underneath.' I dip into the bag and pull out a faded blue saddle pad.

'We are not going to ride in this storm, but I want to check the fit and see if he's OK with it. Can you put the numnah on him?'

I pat Jammie D. 'There you go, boy.' As I put it on his back, he pauses and raises his head as if he's thinking about it, then goes back to munching hay again.

Michael puts the brown leather saddle on top of the numnah on Jammie D's back and does up the girth. 'Yes, it fits! Told you I was good at assessing measurements. It's so important it's right for Jammie Dodger, otherwise it would feel like when you have shoes on that pinch.'

Silver growls, her hackles up.

Voices.

I freeze.

Buster runs to the door, sniffing. Jammie D immediately side steps, pulling against his head collar, and the twine snaps. I grab the end of the lead rope, whispering, 'Shh, Jammie D. It's OK, I'm with you.'

Michael quickly lifts the saddle off and runs over to Buster, kneeling next to him, whispering, 'Shhh, boy, shhhhh,' over and over, so that he doesn't bark.

The voices get closer.

'When we're on TV, we'll be famous innit.'

It's the Cinder Street Boyz!

'Yeah, we'll all look fast next to Daniel.'

'He'll most probably still be running when everyone's gone home,' I hear Baz say, then they all laugh so he's obviously doing his impression of me again.

'He can't even read,' says Nico.

I feel sick with shame, but this time it turns to anger. *I'll show them*, I think through gritted teeth as I stroke Silver, who has come to stand next to me and Jammie D, praying they don't hear her low growling.

The rain starts again, hammering against the roof. Michael and I obviously have the same thought at the same time, as Michael flattens himself against the door and I drop the lead rope and run across the straw to join him. We lean our weight against the door, so they can't open it.

'We should break in here to shelter,' says Sol. And sure enough, the door latch flicks down as they try it.

'It's locked.'

Then one of their mobiles rings and Nico starts shouting down the phone, 'Yeah, we're coming all right. See you in ten.' And I hear their squelchy footsteps as they run off through the trees.

'That was close,' I say.

'Don't let their words get to you, Daniel. Don't let their words count,' says Michael.

'I won't,' I say, but I'm lying 'cause it hurts. It really hurts.

My phone buzzes. It's a text from Mum.

> **Leaving in 10 mins**
> **Bring 20 tins of cat food**
> **up with U we r running low.**

'I've got to go,' I say, stuffing tins of cat food in each pocket and the rest in my bag. I clip on Silver's lead.

'I'll settle Jammie D for the night and then take Buster home. I want to do some work on my radio project anyhow,' says Michael.

'Goodbye, Jammie D,' I say, giving him a kiss on the nose. 'I am glad you've got animal friends like Seabiscuit had. Buster, Napoleon, Silver and Jammie D.'

'Sounds cool, like members of a rock band,' says Michael.

'Yeah, the coolest friends ever,' I say, as me and Silver head off in the rain.

Chapter 22

I've got such a long way to go, but I LOVE RIDING, especially now I get to ride Jammie D with an actual saddle on. I'm learning how to use the reins properly and also gradually learning how to be at one with Jammie D.

Aunty Lou and Mum think that I'm assisting Michael with his science project and that, in return, he's helping me with my maths homework. They both said that as long as we didn't get in anyone's way, didn't stay out too late and made sure we walked home to the Beckham Estate together, then it was fine. Not only that, our Secret Horse rota worked like a dream. I wanted to shout 'jubilations' to the stars and back.

There was only one thing stopping me.

Akin was still not himself. All through lunch break, he sat by himself on what we call the thinking bench, near the school gate. We call it that 'cause it has a gold plaque that says *A place for quiet thinking*. No matter how much we tried to talk to him, he stayed locked in his own world. Even Ste had no luck. Akin was so quiet that he didn't get into trouble once in class, whereas I did lots of times for not concentrating 'cause I was worrying about Jammie Dodger. Where was he? Was he safe?

Then, on the Friday, Ste was having a rest in Miss Raquel's office and Akin and I were in our maths lesson when we heard Molly-May's voice extra loud and clear from outside in the corridor.

'Mrs Ojo and Daniel's mum, yes, if you would like to come this way to our most lovely library what I have been given special duty to show you.'

Akin and I shoot upright in our chairs in horror. Then Molly-May's face appears flat against the window and she's mouthing, 'Biscuit, Biscuit, Biscuit,' to us with her face flat against the glass. And then we see our mums walk past. Mrs Ojo looks really smart in a blue dress and matching jacket and my mum still has her parka on and her hair pulled back in a scrunchie. They are chatting and haven't seen us. Why are our mums here?

'Do you think the school has found out about Jammie Dodger?' I hiss in Akin's ear. But Akin keeps his head in his hands and ignores me. Mrs Ojo is one of the school governors. This looks serious.

Miss Cranbourne is glaring at me. I try and get on with my work, but I can't. Akin still won't look at me, even when I nudge him.

There's a knock on our classroom door and Miss Raquel enters. 'If Daniel and Akin can come with me to the library,' she says.

And as we do our walk of dread with Miss Raquel, Akin doesn't even look at me, not even once.

Mum and Mrs Ojo are sitting round a table with Mrs Johnson and Mr Samuels.

'Welcome, Daniel and Akin, please take a seat.' Mrs Ojo takes the lead. 'Would you like a puff-puff?' She offers us the yummy sweet fried dough-balls and I think, we can't be in trouble if there's puff-puff!

But Mum is looking really upset. My heart stops. They must know about Jammie D. I feel sick as I sink down in the chair.

Akin remains standing, looking down, scuffing his foot on the carpet.

'Akin, if you want to get your bicycle back from you father, I suggest you sit.'

He sits.

Unlike our mums, Mrs Johnson and Mr Samuels are smiling at us. So I guess we definitely aren't in trouble. I try and focus on the words as they come out of Mr Samuels' mouth. 'Heath Academy, together with Mrs Ojo and the school governors are setting up a peer-to-peer support scheme, where students with something in common are paired up to support each other.'

My thoughts race. Peer support? What does he mean, something in common? Have they found out about me and Akin both being in the Secret Horse Society?

'I don't understand,' I say with my best I-have-done-nothing-wrong face.

'Daniel, Akin has something that I feel would be good if he shared with you, his friend,' says Mrs Ojo. What is going on?

'Go on, Akin,' says Mrs Ojo. There is a silence as everyone looks at Akin, who won't look at any of us.

'I got that dyslexia,' he mutters.

A laugh of relief comes up all the way from my toes.

'There you go,' says Mrs Ojo, smiling. 'It was not hard to say, was it?'

'Is that it?' I say. 'Is that why you've been quiet?'

'Stop laughing,' says Akin. ''Cause I don't want it, OK? I don't want it.'

'What's wrong with being dyslexic?' I say, annoyed now. 'I'm dyslexic.'

'Well, maybe I don't want to be like you.'

We stare eye-daggers at each other.

'Akin, that is not kind and you are a kind person,' says Mrs Ojo. 'I know you have both become good friends and you should share that your brains have this neurodiverse wiring. Being neurodiverse is a gift. That is a good thing.'

Akin puts his head in his hands.

'Daniel,' says Mum. 'I am so glad that you boys are friends. You need friends. But why didn't you tell me about this Big Read?'

Mum looks uncomfortable with every bone in her body. I feel sick.

'I'm sorry, Mum. I tried to tell you. But it's just you are always so busy and I didn't want you to worry . . .'

Mum looks like she wants to cry. I want to cry.

'Amy-Beth, life is full of challenges,' says Mrs Ojo, reaching out and putting her hand on Mum's arm. 'Do not be hard on yourself. It seems as if there are a lot of words that need to be said today.'

'Gentlemen,' says Mr Samuels. 'I brought you in today to talk about your strengths, not because of the things that you find challenging. When a baby is born it does not move, it wriggles, then eventually crawls, toddles, walks and one day that baby will run across the room. Those are logical steps and some people spend their whole life in that straight line and they have no concept that your brains are . . .'

'Flying round the room,' finishes Akin a tiny twitch of a smile. 'I can't settle. I don't mean to be in trouble, but I just can't settle my thoughts.'

'And me. I am always dreaming,' I say. 'I try to make the teacher's words go in my brain, I really do – honest, Mum – but one minute I'm in class and the next I'm on Seabiscuit winning a race with the crowds cheering.' Mum gives me a small smile. 'To be honest, though, without my dreams I don't think I could cope with going to school at all. I don't dream in your lesson, Mr Samuels, or yours, Mrs Johnson. My brain dreams when it needs to escape from sounds, words and letters attacking me and confusing my brain.'

'Dyslexics are good problem-solvers,' says Mrs Johnson. 'Daniel, when you had to pick your team members for the Big Read Off, I was watching you and could see you working it out. You picked such a good group of people, who can all support each other and bring something to the group.'

'I think we all need each other,' I say.

'Akin,' says Mr Samuels. 'You say your brain flies all over the room – but don't you see? It means you have the gift to see things from every angle. You are such a gifted footballer because you can see where the ball needs to be before anyone else, and you are an extremely intelligent young man.'

'When my son does focus, he is amazing,' says Mrs Ojo. 'He showed such kindness and patience in helping his friend Ste step back into school life after he had left the hospital.'

Mrs Johnson brings out a pack of plastic see-through sheets in different colours. There are blues and yellows and greens and pinks – all sorts of colours.

'These have just arrived. They are called overlays,'

she says. 'For some dyslexics, the contrast of the white page and black letters is too much. These can help.'

'My eyes and my head hurt when I do my schoolwork, Miss,' I say. 'I feel all crumpled.'

'You do always look so tired, Daniel,' says Mum.

'I'm always losing my place,' says Akin.

'I am really hoping this will help,' says Mrs Johnson. 'If you put them over the page you are reading, they can help the letters look clearer and stay in place. Everyone's brains work differently, so different people need different shades of colour. I suggest we enjoy this lovely food and experiment with different colours.'

And we do. I open one of the books and try all the different overlays. When we get to the lime green overlay it's as if the words jump off the page to greet me. 'This one's for me,' I say.

'The bluey colour's best for me,' says Akin, a proper smile on his face, picking up a teaspoon and balancing it on the end of his nose.

'Bicycle, Akin,' says Mrs Ojo.

He quickly puts the spoon down. I bite my lip so I don't laugh.

'Ah, that's aqua blue you've got there, Akin,' says Mrs Johnson, making a note in her book of both of our colours.

Nudging Akin with my foot under the table, I say, 'I promise to support Akin with his dyslexia in this peer-to-peer thingy and I know that you will help me, won't you, Akin?'

All the grown-ups have smiles on their faces. Little do they know that I mean we'll support each other in the Secret Horse Society.

Akin mutters, 'The Biscuit,' so low that only I hear it, but I know that is his way of saying sorry. 'The Biscuit,' I whisper back, to show we are friends again.

I travel home from school with Molly-May, and we are just stepping on to the Beckham Estate when we hear a scream coming from the courtyard. We round the corner and see Mrs Patel with her hands on her head, looking as if she's had a fright. The basket arrangement outside her shop is strewn everywhere. I see Mum and Molly-May's dad, Joe, darting across the courtyard from where the lift is.

'It was a horse, I tell you, a great big white horse, eating all my carrots.'

My heart forgets to beat and I run towards her, for once not needing to pretend I am on Seabiscuit. Mum and Joe get to her at the same time.

Molly-May and me stare at each other, fear between us.

Mum goes into the shop and brings out a chair and makes Mrs Patel sit down.

'I'll make you a nice cup of tea,' she says, before disappearing back into the shop again. I help Molly-May and her dad pick up all the baskets and bits of carrots that are left.

'A big horse, I tell you,' she keeps saying, over and over.

The sound of cheers comes from our estate and I hear football blaring from TVs.

'I reckon more people would have seen Jammie D if it weren't for the football on the telly tonight,' Molly-May whispers.

'Mrs Patel,' I try. 'Maybe it was a big dog.'

'It was a horse, I tell you.'

'Well,' says Molly-May. 'It must have belonged to a

policeman and ran away from him and maybe the policeman has caught him again now.'

'I'll need to let the rescue centre know,' says Mum, bringing out the cup of tea. 'We'll need to keep an eye out if there's a horse on the loose. Joe, can you mend those baskets?' she asks Molly-May's dad.

'Already on it!' says Joe as he starts fixing the wooden display for Mrs Patel.

I need to go to the Old Shed to see if Jammie D is there.

'Molly-May and I will have a quick scout around, Mum,' I say. 'See if anybody's caught sight of a horse.'

'Don't be long, or late,' says Mum, 'and please be careful if you see this horse, I don't want you to be bitten or kicked.'

We run off before she can change her mind. We run all the way across the wasteland and don't stop till we reach Apple Tree Wood and there he is, Jammie Dodger, standing by the Old Shed door with a carrot top dangling from his mouth, looking like butter wouldn't melt.

'Jammie D,' I say, giving him a hug. 'You can't go eating Mrs Patel's carrots.'

'Or go wandering round on the Beckham Estate,' says Molly-May. 'They'll take you away from us,' she whispers, and that thought is so dreadful we can't even look at each other.

Chapter 23

It was as if all the Secret Horse Society's hearts were beating as one, faster, quicker, now that Jammie Dodger had actually wandered on to the Beckham Estate to sample Mrs Patel's carrots. Our secret had nearly escaped. We were on high alert, ears listening, eyes watching, hearts thudding.

'Fellow Secret Horse Society members, I have an announcement to make,' Michael declared one day. We had gathered in the shed and had just sworn ourselves in on the horseshoe, when he made us follow him outside into the warm October sun.

At the back of the shed were two wooden oblongs nailed into the wall, like a giant number eleven. On one was a picture of a carrot, on the other, an apple.

From the top of each of them was a tube of rubber piping leading to a wooden box.

'Lady and gentlemen, gather round, gather round. I give you the one, the only – designed by Prof M himself – the amazing Jammie Dodger Carrot and Apple Dispensing Machine!' As if on cue, the sound of horse hooves trots up behind us.

Jammie D sniffs the two wooden oblongs; he nudges the bottom of the left-hand one with his nose and out of the bottom shoots a carrot. Jammie D grabs it with his teeth and munches. We all applaud.

'As my assistant has demonstrated, he may now eat a carrot whenever he wishes.'

'Jammie D's got his very own snack shop,' says Molly-May in awe.

'Come on, boy,' says Michael, tapping the other oblong, 'come on.'

Jammie D looks at him, then swings his nose and nudges the bottom of the other oblong and out shoots an apple. Jammie D crunches it up. He nudges again and again and apples are pinging out here, there and everywhere. We try to catch and grab them, rolling on the grass laughing, and Jammie D is walking among us now, nudging us with his nose, which makes us laugh harder. Ste is leaning against the shed watching the scene, tears of laughter rolling down his face. I've never seen him look happy like this, not since the accident.

'I haven't never seen anything so funny, not in all the years I've been born,' says Molly-May, wiping tears from her eyes.

'Prof M, this is the best invention ever,' says Akin, trying to stand up but laughing so much he can't. Michael is rolling on the grass, belly-laughing, trying to grab hold of the apples. And as for me – well, I'm lying on my back looking up as the dusk creeps across the sky, trying to stop my hiccupping giggles. Jammie D bends over me and touches his nose to mine and when I feel his sweet horse breath and hear the laughter of my friends, my life is complete.

Michael is a genius. Now Jammie D has no reason to hunt around the estate for food. I hope with every bone in my body that now, he'll be safe.

'We got two weeks till the Big Read Off,' says Michael.

I go cold and our laughter vanishes.

We gather all the apples and carrots and put them in the right sections of the wooden box.

'Time to work,' says Michael.

'Secret Horse Society,' I say. 'It's time to choose which one of the letters you want to read in the Big Read Off.'

'I bag the one where your great-great-grandfather climbs high up in that tree to cheer for Seabiscuit,' says Akin, ''cause that would have been me all right. I'd have been cheering the loudest.'

'I want to read the one where they go to the relief kitchen on Cuthbert's birthday.' And I know why Molly-May has picked that letter. I think all of us do.

'I can't decide. I gotta think about it,' says Ste and his face has gone really, really white and he leans on Michael, who puts his arm round him to steady him, and do you know what? Jammie D walks right over to Ste and nuzzles his head in Ste's chest. I reckon he just knows that Ste's not feeling good. Akin fetches his wheelchair and Ste doesn't even complain as he sinks right down into it. I think I know which one Ste should read, 'cause Ste needs some hope.

I flick through the pages of my scrapbook till I find the Dear Seabiscuit letter I am looking for and I lay it on Ste's lap. As he reads it to himself, the colour ever so slowly starts to trickle back into his face and his eyes shine and he just looks at me and nods.

And as for me – well, it's a no-brainer which letter I'm going to read. A letter I haven't shared with the others yet. I haven't shared it with nobody.

We get comfortable and practise our reading until it's time to do our 'Till we meet again' on the horseshoe.

'Aunty Lou wants me home to tidy my bedroom,' huffs Michael, 'so no riding today I'm afraid.'

As Michael, Molly-May and me head back towards the Beckham Estate, Obo drives up in his white van and toots his horn. He winds down his window and shouts, 'Michael, I got something you might be interested in.'

We wander over as Obo hops out of his van and opens up the back.

'I've just done a house clearance. The old man was a collector and you were telling me about your radio project, and I thought . . .' He trails off as he swings the door open and inside is an older than old brown mahogany 1930s radio like I've seen in films.

'Wow!' says Molly-May. 'It's beautiful.'

'It's perfect,' says Michael, letting out a big breath.

And there are boxes and boxes of metal bits and valves and . . . well, I don't know what they are, but Michael obviously does as he is dancing around, clapping his hands. There is also a crate full of old transistor radios and some microphones.

'Thank you, Obo, oh, thank you. This is all so perfect,' he says.

Mr Samuels emerges from Aunty Lou's and comes and joins us. When he sees what we are crowding around, he lets out a low whistle.

'Oh, this is a find.' He grabs one side of the radio and helps Obo lift it out of the van and carry it into Aunty Lou's flat.

Molly-May and I help Michael carry boxes of metal bits and bobs and microphones into his bedroom – which, I gotta say, is even messier than mine and Jackson's, which is saying something – while Aunty Lou is shouting, 'MICHAEL, TAKE IT OUT. TAKE IT OUT! YOU'RE MEANT TO BE TAKING ALL OF YOUR RUBBISH OUT, NOT BRINGING MORE BACK IN! Oh, Michael, no please.'

'But it's for my project, Aunty Lou,' Michael keeps saying, over and over and over, and Mr Samuels is trying to distract Aunty Lou with a cup of tea and I'm chewing my lip so I don't laugh. Molly-May – well, I can just tell she's trying to choke back snorty giggles.

When the van is empty, I walk Molly-May back to her flat on the second floor and then head up in the lift and past the no entry sign to the roof. I look up at the night sky and as I watch the stars come out, I say a silent thank you to Seabiscuit.

'And please keep Jammie Dodger safe,' I say. 'Don't let anyone find him.'

Chapter 24

The countdown to the Big Read Off begins. We work on our reading every second we can grab at school.

And then half term comes round and our Secret Horse Society meetings last all day long. We read to Jammie Dodger with the sound of thuds and scrapes and bangs coming from the cubbyhole as Michael works towards his radio project. We try to have a sneaky peek at what he's doing, but he always catches us.

'You'll know, when it's time,' he says.

When the rest of the Secret Horse Society go home, it's time for my riding lesson with Michael. Through the apple trees we go as day becomes dusk, and I think I am improving every day, but I know that I need to get stronger, so I feel at one with Jammie D.

Half term rushes by and before we know it, we are back at school and the days are racing towards the Big Read Off and Big Race Off.

And every time I think about it, I can't actually breathe.

I look at my fellow Secret Horse Society members and they look as if they can't breathe either – even Michael looks scared.

'Remember what Miss Raquel always says,' I say to the Secret Horse Society.

'Akin, what have you done now?' Akin says, grinning.

'Not that,' squeaks Molly-May. 'She says do things in manageable chunks.'

'That's right,' I say.

I look round at the Secret Horse Society gathered around me, eating up my words, and I realise with a jolt that I don't have to pretend to be Red Pollard – I am just me, Daniel Margate, and I am leading the Secret Horse Society.

'Manageable chunk one,' I say. 'Let's begin.' And I open the scrapbook to a page where there's a headline stuck in.

SEABISCUIT RIDES TODAY

As Jammie D turned in a circle and settled down in the straw for us to read and Michael disappeared into the cubbyhole and started banging around, so started another meeting of the Secret Horse Society.

Manageable chunk 2 – getting to the Old Shed

There will be no meeting of the Secret Horse Society tonight! My Biscuit Team are all in detention apart from me, who escaped. Raindrops trickle down the back of my neck as I climb on the bus.

The rain started with Miss Darwin's smile as she walked into the gym for our drama class. But she stopped smiling when I shouted 'YES!' before I could stop myself, because of course the rain meant *no big-race practice*.

'Daniel, be quiet,' she said, and then everything went wrong from that moment.

'Choose an animal that inhabits our planet,' she said. 'Feel how they move. Be free.'

I, of course, was a horse – Seabiscuit to be exact – and started galloping round the gym. But the trouble started when Akin decided he was a T-rex having a pretend fight with Ste, who was waving his crutches in the air being a Giganotosaurus, and then they both decided to eat Molly-May, who was a sleeping kitten, but she started letting out big snorty giggles, saying that they were tickling her.

Miss Darwin said that dinosaurs had no place in her drama class and put them in detention along with Molly-May, even though it wasn't her fault.

It has stopped raining by the time I get off the bus and I arrive at the Old Shed at exactly the same time as Michael and tell him about the dinosaur antics.

We hear thuds from behind the Old Shed. Jammie Dodger is playing with his apple dispenser. 'Good, it's working,' says Michael as we bring him in. 'Keeping him occupied and out of harm's way.'

Michael disappears into the cubbyhole to work on his project and I look after Jammie Dodger, getting him water and drying him off.

When it's dark outside, Michael appears from the cubbyhole.

'I am not sure you should ride tonight,' says Michael, standing outside and squelching the mud with his trainer.

Disappointment and panic all mixed together flood

me from top to toe.

'But I've got to ride,' I say, 'or I will never be good enough.'

Michael screws up his face for a second, bites his lip, then disappears back into the cubbyhole and brings out the saddle.

We tack Jammie D up and lead him out into the night air with the moon shining her light down on us. Michael gives me a leg up and it's like I feel right all of a sudden – my weight is equal on my bum bones, my heels are down, my back is straight, I feel the gentle connection from the bit in Jammie D's mouth to my reins. I am at one with Jammie D.

'Let's have some rising trot,' says Michael.

'One, two. One, two. One, two.' I count my rhythm, still at one with Jammie D.

Then the moon disappears behind the cloud and I hear barking. Buster is running towards us, and without warning, a fox runs out of a bush across my path. Buster starts chasing the fox. Jammie D side steps, stumbles, I smack my head on the branch of an apple tree and Jammie D breaks into a canter. *But I cannot canter. We have not cantered yet. I DO NOT KNOW*

HOW TO CANTER. I try and wrap my legs round Jammie D but I am slipping sideways . . . and then I am off and hit the ground.

Jammie D carries on cantering. I know that I have lost him – but then . . . he stops.

He actually stops and walks all the way back to me.

Michael is behind me, his hand under my armpits, pulling me to my feet. My legs are shaking.

I touch where I hit my head. There is bit of blood on my finger. I hate blood.

'It's just a graze,' says Michael. 'You're lucky, you could have cut your head open.'

It's like all my bravery has got up and walked away and all that is left is fear.

I know I have to get back on again so I put my hands on Jammie D's saddle.

'No, not tonight, no more,' says Michael. 'I shouldn't have let you. It's dangerous.'

'No, I got to get back on. Otherwise I might . . .'

I see something change in Michael's face.

'No,' he says. 'No. No. No. No. No.' He leads Jammie Dodger back into the Old Shed.

'There's more to life than the Big Race and the Big Read. You could have hurt yourself and it would have been all my fault.'

'No, it wouldn't,' I say as my panic rises. I can't have Michael quit on me now. 'Look – I'm fine, no bones broken.'

'Don't you get what just nearly happened? You could have been seriously hurt and so could Jammie D, stumbling like that. We can't afford a vet and that would have been it, the end of the Secret Horse Society.'

I nod my head with misery. I know I've been selfish. Jammie D's welfare matters more to me than the whole world.

Buster returns to us with his tail between his legs.

'You may well look ashamed, Buster,' says Michael, grabbing his collar.

But it's me who feels ashamed.

'I need to think,' I say to Michael. 'Would you mind leaving me so that I can be alone with Jammie Dodger? I need to show him I'm sorry.'

'But Aunty Lou said we got to walk home together.'

'Please, Michael,' I say.

Michael nods, turns on his heels and disappears

into the night.

I take off Jammie D's tack, talking all the while I am doing it.

'Sorry, Jammie D, I wouldn't hurt you for the world.' And his ears are cocked and he's listening to me. 'I can't believe you came back to me, even though that old fox had startled you. You and me are proper friends. We get each other, don't we, Jammie D?'

I get the old towel and start to rub the mud off Jammie D, drying him all the while, and as I do, I see Red Pollard talking to Seabiscuit, rubbing him down. It's as if they are right there with me. Both of us caring for and loving our horses.

Jammie D settles down in the straw like Seabiscuit all those years before him. I check his water, turn off the light and after I've closed the door I pull out my phone and text Michael.

Sorry You R Rite. Forgive me.

Manageable chunk 3 – getting past Mum

'What have you done to your forehead?'

I'm barely awake. Jackson is bouncing on my bed

and Mum is standing over me, pointing at my head.

Think quickly, Daniel!

'I, er, slipped off a straw bale and hit my head on the shovel handle. You know how clumsy I am.'

'I'm not sure I like you spending all that time down there.'

'I'm fine, Mum, I just wasn't thinking and from now on I *will* think, I promise.'

And I jump out of bed to show her just how fine I am, and even though every one of my bones is aching, I get to school in what I reckon is record speed but I still somehow manage to be late.

Miss Raquel tuts and marks me in the late book again as I hand over my mobile to her. 'The late book should just be called The Timekeeping of Daniel Margate,' she says.

The school day drags and in the afternoon I am made to run round the playing field track in practice for the Big Race Off *again*. It hurts 'cause all my bones feel achy after my fall off Jammie Dodger and I am *last again*. I give up halfway round as I just can't run any more.

'Somehow, somehow you will get to the end of the race,' growls Sugden and I just smile as I think of me on Jammie Dodger.

Akin and me got kept behind after school to help tidy the classroom and are the last to leave, even though that is totally unfair 'cause we didn't make the mess in the first place.

'See you at the Old Shed tonight,' I call and it sounds all echoey in the empty corridor, except, as I turn the corner my bones jump 'cause Baz is sitting on top of the caretaker's cupboard, swinging his legs.

'He must have heard,' I whisper to Akin.

'I don't know. Let's get out of here,' whispers Akin, grabbing my arm and pulling me past him as we run all the way to the school gate.

Manageable chunk 4 – getting to the Secret Horse Society meeting

Jammie Dodger arrives late at the Secret Horse Society that evening, panting like he's been galloping to get here. He goes straight to the water bucket and drinks lots of water, sloshing it everywhere.

'Hey, boy, hey, Jammie D,' I say. 'Where have you been, then?'

He paces round the Old Shed sniffing at things, inquisitive, restless.

After we are all sworn in on the Great Seabiscuit's horseshoe, Jammie lies down in the straw – he knows it's reading practice time. Ste is sitting on a hay bale with his leg stretched out on another hay bale. He reaches out and takes the scrapbook from me. He reads, hesitant at first, but then his words start racing along with Seabiscuit.

Dear Seabiscuit,

There I, Cuthbert H. Brown Jr, was, squashed in a crowd on the sidewalk, listening to the radio, waiting for you to run the Brooklyn Handicap. People were pushing so I got separated from Pa. Folks were talking about how you travelled back east on a train specially converted for your every comfort, with oats, hay and straw and your good horse-friend Pumpkin.

Seabiscuit, as you know, the east is where I've come from, and it feels good that you are going there to meet your mighty opponents because, let's face it, you have beaten every horse in California.

Pa told me there are some mighty horses in the east for you to conquer. Aneroid, Rosemont and the mighty War Admiral himself.

The radio announcer said there were twenty thousand people to cheer you on and that Pumpkin was there to keep you company and they put him in between you and your many fans so that you could have your saddle put on in peace.

And then the race started and you were off, shooting to the front. You should have heard how quiet the crowd went so that we could listen to the radio. And then Rosemont began to catch you up and I swear I stopped breathing and for a moment you and Rosemont were neck and neck.

Rosemont hesitated and you shot ahead. And I was sure you had this race in the bag but then Aneroid was upon you and you were running together, both in the lead, and I couldn't breathe and Aneroid's nose moved in front.

No, I said, run, Seabiscuit, run! Then, at the very last second, your nose was in front and you won again. I was crying and Pa found me and pulled me into a hug and strangers were hugging and kissing each other.

The radio announcer said that you and Mr Pollard cantered back to the winning stand and that you loved posing for the photographers. How I laughed.

The next day, Pa found a newspaper that says you had hundreds of telegrams congratulating you from stars like Bing Crosby and Fred Astaire.

Well, I hope this letter from me is just as special to you, Seabiscuit.

You are my hero.

Love from,

Cuthbert H. Brown Jr

Ste looks up, his eyes shining. 'What a horse,' he says.

'You read that beautiful, Ste,' says Molly-May. 'You would never think you was in the Silver Reading Group.'

'You're getting way too good,' says Michael. 'I couldn't have read it like that.'

'Don't laugh or nothing,' says Ste, glaring round at us, 'but when my leg throbs in the mornings, well, I just say to myself, "Seabiscuit, Seabiscuit, Seabiscuit" over and over and it gives me the strength to carry on, and I think of us lot right here at the Secret Horse Society and well, I just feel—'

'None of us are laughing, Ste. It's the same for all of us,' says Akin.

'I don't know what I'd do without you lot,' says Molly-May.

We fall into a group hug. Jammie D nudges us with his nose.

'He wants a group hug too,' says Molly-May with a giggle and we all put our arms round Jammie D, our most precious Secret Horse of the Secret Horse Society.

I take my scrapbook from Ste as Jammie lies back down in his usual place, and then—

Thud.

Something is smashed against the back wall. We freeze.

'Oh my days, Nico. What do ya think this mental thing is what's stuck to the wall?'

Then the sound of scraping wood and laughter and the thud of apples and carrots.

It's the Cinder Street Boyz!

Michael turns on his heel so he is facing us, horror splashed across his face.

'Hide,' he hisses as he tiptoes over to the light switch and switches it off.

I run to where we have dumped our jackets and throw them over Ste.

Molly-May and Akin bury themselves in the straw but I know I can't hide – I've got to stay strong defending my Jammie D.

I kneel next to his head, praying that I don't kneel on any part of Akin or Molly-May. I feel a hand snatched away from under me.

'Sorry,' I whisper. Jammie D is listening.

'It's all right, boy,' I whisper in his ear. 'Nothing will hurt you.'

Michael kneels next to me. 'I'm staying with you,' murmurs my friend as the sound of kicking and whoops get louder.

We hear a car drive over the wasteland.

'POLICE! RUN!' screams Sol. And then thudding feet disappear into the distance.

The car engine stops, slamming doors, sticks breaking underfoot as booted feet get nearer and nearer, then walk round the shed and back to the front again.

I know that as Biscuit Team leader it's up to me to head them off before they find us.

I get to the door just in time, as the latch starts rattling.

I open it a crack and pop my head round. Two police officers stand in front of me, a man and a woman. The man is holding in his hand the bent and splintered Amazing Apple and Carrot Dispensing Machine. I swallow hard and take it from him.

'It was a school project,' I say, which is not really a lie.

'What are you doing here in the dark?' asks the policeman.

'My mum works for the Beckham Animal Rescue Centre and Matt the Vet's put me in charge of the shed while they are in India.' I lean forward and whisper, 'It's my den. I like doing my homework by torchlight here, to get some peace from my little brother. I'm going home soon.'

The policeman chuckles. 'I had a den when I was your age. If those boys that ran off come round here again bothering you, call us.'

'I will, thank you,' I say.

'Does your mum know you are here?' says the policewoman.

'Yes, I've texted her. I'm nearly finished up here then I'm going home. I live on the Beckham Estate.'

The police officers turn to go then the man says over his shoulder, 'This may seem like an odd question, but you haven't seen a white horse galloping around these parts have you?'

I hear Molly-May gasp and quickly cough to cover it up.

'No,' I say, cold trickling through me. 'I haven't seen a horse galloping.' Which isn't technically a lie because I haven't seen him galloping around 'cause he's in here with the Secret Horse Society, safe, where he should be.

'There's been reports of a white horse around here. He stole an apple off an old man sitting on a bench reading the paper and then was spotted galloping over the heath by the bird-watching society. Let us know if you do see him,' says the policeman. 'We can't have a horse galloping around creating mayhem.'

'I will do,' I say, crossing my fingers.

I wait for them to get in their car and drive off.

I switch the light on. Ste's face appears from beneath the coats as Molly- May and Akin pop up from the straw. Jammie D is watching me as Michael takes the broken dispenser from my hand.

'Oh, well,' he says, shrugging, but he looks so sad. 'It'll mend. At least none of us got hurt.'

'Oh, no, they'll catch Jammie D, I know they will,' says Molly-May, 'and take him away and we won't be able to read and . . .'

'I can't read in front of people without Jammie D helping me,' says Ste.

'And I won't be able to win the Big Race Off without Jammie D,' I cry out. 'I can't imagine not ever seeing Jammie D again. What'll we do without the Secret Horse Society?'

'We all know that day will come, though,' says Michael. 'After the Big Race and Read Off, Jammie Dodger won't be a secret – they will come for him and we will be in trouble.'

Molly-May nods, lets out a strange hiccupped sob from the back of her throat. She slams her hand in front of her mouth and I know that she don't trust herself to speak.

Ste hides his face in a coat and Akin looks down at the ground, scuffing his foot in the straw. And as for me, I know that Michael's words are true, of course I do, and that truth visits me in my night-dreams, prickles my thoughts, spoils my daydreams – but I stamp it down, 'cause it's a truth I don't want to think about.

It's not a manageable chunk.

It hurts too much.

Today is the manageable chunk that matters right now and I've got to get my friends believing again.

'Listen up, Secret Horse Society,' I say, holding my scrapbook in the air. 'We ain't beaten yet. You got away from people, didn't you, boy?' I say, patting Jammie D. 'And he'll do it again. The only people I reckon he trusts is us. Did Seabiscuit and Red Pollard give up? No, they didn't, and neither will we.'

Akin bumps his fist to mine, knuckle to knuckle in strength.

'It will be worth it,' he says, 'even if it means I never get my bicycle back, 'cause these Secret Horse Society days are the best of my life.' Ste nods at me and slowly grins and Molly-May flings her arms around me in a hug.

I breathe; my words have worked. I am leading the Biscuit Team again.

'That's right,' says Michael. 'Nothing can stop us.' He gets the Great Seabiscuit's horseshoe and puts it on a bale of straw and we all stand in a circle around it.

Akin turns to the middle of the scrapbook, where my great-great-grandfather Cuthbert H. Jr had written a list of races Seabiscuit had won, and starts to read, pretending he's a racing commentator.

'Seabiscuit's conquering track record, by Cuthbert H. Brown Jr . . . Seabiscuit goes back to Empire City and wins the Butler Handicap. Two weeks later, Seabiscuit wins the Yonkers Handicap, breaking the mile-and-sixteenth record that had been held for twenty-three years.'

Molly-May takes the scrapbook and reads,

'Seabiscuit goes to Suffolk Downs, runs head to

head with Fair Knightess in the Massachusetts Handicap, but Seabiscuit wins again.'

She holds the scrapbook in front of Ste to read. Faster and faster come our words, our hope rising, racing to fill us with Seabiscuit's victories.

'Seabiscuit comes third at Narragansett. It's not your fault, Seabiscuit, it was wet and muddy. I know you don't like mud in your face and ears.'

I feel the Secret Horse Society's hope falter with Seabiscuit's loss.

I grab the scrapbook, my words fast, beating with the rhythm of Seabiscuit's hooves.

'Seabiscuit wins Continental Handicap at New York's Jamaica Race Track. Seabiscuit ties for first with Heelfly, ridden by George Woolf. Seabiscuit wins the Riggs Handicap, breaking the track record.'

I hand my scrapbook to Michael.

'Bowie Handicap, everyone hoped War Admiral would come – he didn't, Seabiscuit had a hard race and lost by just a nose to Esposa.'

The Secret Horse Society groan.

'No,' I cry. 'Seabiscuit shall not be defeated. He has only one horse left to beat and that is . . .' And we all place our right hands on the Great Seabiscuit's horseshoe and chant, 'War Admiral, War Admiral, War Admiral.'

We tack up Jammie Dodger and I know that I, Daniel Margate, must get on Jammie Dodger, even though I fell off yesterday. As I start my moonlight riding lesson, the Secret Horse Society stay and watch, cheering me on. Michael shortens my stirrups so that I am sitting more like a jockey and I do my first canter – and I actually stay on, at one with Jammie Dodger, and it's the best feeling of my life.

But on the way home to the Beckham Estate that best feeling vanishes. On the tree is a poster:

POLICE NOTICE

WHITE HORSE LOOSE ON HEATH
CONTACT CAMDEN POLICE IF YOU SEE HIM

I rip the poster down, even though I know that most probably makes me a criminal, but then we see another one and another one and it feels as if everything is closing in on Jammie Dodger and us, the Secret Horse Society.

Chapter 25

It's the last lesson on Friday afternoon. I'm exhausted as the sixes became fours and the threes became fives and I think, *What is the point of maths when all I can think about is Jammie Dodger?*

Please stay hidden, I will him in my head. *Please don't get caught.*

The blinds are down because the sun is shining freakishly brightly today, and we are still squinting to see the whiteboard. It's then that I hear it. An unmistakable neigh, coming from outside.

I go cold. Akin digs me in the ribs as I peep through the slats of the blind and there is Jammie Dodger rolling in the long-jump sandpit. He scrambles up and starts cantering around the track, jumping over some hurdles that have been left out. I've got to catch him, now!

I nod at Akin. 'Cover for me,' I whisper.

'Miss, I'm going to be sick.' I jump up from my chair and run out of the classroom with my hand over my mouth, making dramatic retching noises.

I run down the corridor praying that no other bored kid peeps through the blind slats and sees him. I round the corner, expecting the exit to the playground to be there, but it's just another long corridor of classrooms. Where's the door to the playground? Where is it? When will I ever find my way round this school?

At last, I find the right door. I burst through it and run through the playground and on to the playing field. Jammie D is rolling in the sandpit again.

'Jammie, Jammie, no!' And he actually nickers to me and gets to his feet and trots over. I pull off my school tie and loop it round his neck, and hold the ends as he nudges me in the chest with his nose.

'We've got to get out of here,' I whisper. 'Now!' I lead him to a patch of grass at the side of the school where the old caretaker's hut is situated. Thankfully the roof leaks, so Burt the caretaker now has a new shed near the school gate. But I know for a fact he sneaks back here with his assistant Will for a cigarette. I've seen them.

No sign of anybody now, though. I look through the dirty window to check that it's empty.

'Come on, Jammie D,' I say, leading him round the side of the hut nearest the fence, where no one will see us.

'We are lucky that Year 9 have swimming over at Camden Leisure Centre, or Sugden would have caught you for sure. Game over!'

But Jammie D does not seem to understand the importance of the situation and is munching grass.

Now what? I'm going to have to wait. I'm not sure what time it is, or how long until the school bell. I wish I had my school bag with me. I don't like to ever leave my scrapbook unattended.

An alarm pierces the air. Jammie D rears up; I step back as the ends of the tie are pulled out of my hand.

As his front hooves hit the ground I grab the ends of the tie. 'Whoa, whoa, easy, boy.'

At first I think it's the school bell, but it doesn't stop, and soon there's the sound of hundreds of trampling feet.

It's the fire alarm.

Something's happened.

The gathering place for the fire alarm is at the front of the school in Cinder Street so they'll be heading in the other direction. Relief makes me relax a bit – but then Jammie D rears up again. The alarm must be loud to him. Horses' hearing is a million times better than ours.

'It's OK, boy, it's OK, Jammie D,' I say as his hooves hit the grass again. 'I'll take care of you.'

Molly-May is running across the grass towards me, carrying both my school bag and hers.

'You lifesaver, Molly-May,' I say, grabbing my bag.

'I told the boys you'd be here!' she says and flops over to get her breath back. 'It's the only place I could think of where you could hide an 'orse.'

'Good detective work, Molly-May,' I say.

'I escaped from Miss as she was marching us out on to Cinder Street,' she puffs. 'The Cinder Street Boyz have flooded the boys' toilets by the cloakroom, water all down the corridor, there is. And then they set the fire alarm off for a joke. Loads of people saw them. Everyone's gathering in Cinder Street. It's chaos! They are sending us home 'cause it's so near the end of the day. Ste and Akin will join us when they get their phones back off Miss Raquel. She's standing in the street with her big box, dishing them out. Good thing I haven't got one, eh.'

Molly-May starts stroking Jammie D. I look up and see Akin sprinting across the grass towards us, followed by Ste swinging himself along on his crutches faster than I've ever seen him.

'Year 9 are getting straight off the minibus and they are sending them home, so the school is empty which is good,' puffs Akin. 'I managed to grab your phone,' he says, handing it back to me.

'I heard Mr Lawson say today's science club is still going ahead – but in the art room, away from all the water,' says Ste.

'Michael!' I say.

'Exactly.' Ste nods at me. 'We need to get Michael out of science club. He'll know what to do.'

'Akin, Ste, give us your ties,' says Molly-May, taking hers off. She ties them all together and loops it around Jammie Dodger's neck then hands the end to me. She then takes my tie from round Jammie D's neck and adds it to the end of the new school-tie lead rope.

'There, that's better,' she says.

'I'm starving,' says Ste.

I pull a squashed packet of Jammie Dodgers out of my school bag and pass them round and hold one in the palm of my hand for Jammie D, who munches it up in no time.

A genius plan jumps into my brain.

'Ste and Akin, you look after Jammie D. Molly-May, come with me, we are going to get Michael.'

Truth is, I need Molly-May in case I get lost going to the art room and besides, she's a good blagger.

We creep past Mr Lawson's office and hear him shouting at Baz, Nico and Sol. 'I AM PHONING YOUR PARENTS . . .'

I see a plate someone has left lying on Miss Raquel's desk; she has long gone home. I nip in and grab it and tip some Jammie Dodger biscuits on to it as we walk along.

'We got to use code so Michael knows we need him,' I whisper.

Our steps sound really echoey in the empty school. Along a corridor, up some steps, along another corridor, up some more steps and at last we reach the art room. I knock on the door.

'Come in,' says a voice.

A teacher I've never seen before with long curly hair and glasses is standing by the whiteboard wearing a white lab coat.

Michael is in the front row next to Max from the Shakespeares, scribbling in a notebook. He jolts his head up, startled, when he sees us.

'Excuse me, Miss,' I say. 'We thought you and your science club would be hungry, so . . .'

'We brought you some Jammie Dodgers,' says Molly-May, and she winks at Michael. 'To make you most welcome to Heath Academy. Here you go, Miss,' she says, taking the plate from me and shoving it in the surprised teacher's hands.

'The biscuit is what you all need, I think,' I say, staring at Michael.

'Yes, the biscuit,' says Molly-May, glaring at him. 'Yeah, you lot must be hungry doing all this clever science work.'

'Yes,' I say. 'We got these Jammie Dodgers from the old caretaker's hut.'

'That's so kind of you,' says the curly-haired teacher. I am staring at Michael and he gives the tiniest of nods. Barely noticeable, but I've seen it.

Molly-May and I dash out of the art room and out of the school and back to the old caretaker's hut.

Napoleon is sitting on the fence, watching us all.

'Napoleon, you get everywhere,' says Molly-May, stroking the ginger cat.

'Look – he showed us how Jammie D got into the school grounds,' says Ste as he pushes at the fence with a stick next to where Napoleon is perched and a part of it swings back.

'It's brilliant, isn't it? We need to keep it hidden so the caretaker don't see it and mend it, so we can sneak Jammie D in for the Big Race Off on Monday,' says Akin.

'Good idea,' I say, pure fear filling me at the thought of the day of the Big Race and Read Off. As I help Akin get piles of twigs to put in front of the broken bit of the fence, Michael runs towards us.

'Excellent code work, Secret Horse Society,' he says. 'You wanted to be with your friends, didn't you, boy.' He strokes Jammie D.

'Oh, Michael, what are we going to do?' says Molly-May.

'You're the best horseman among us,' I say.

'We can't lose Jammie D, we just can't,' says Molly-May.

We've got to find a way to get Jammie D out of here.

'I'll never get my bicycle back if we get caught,' says Akin.

'Is that all you can think about?' says Molly-May. 'Your stupid bicycle? There's an 'orse at stake here.'

'Just saying,' says Akin.

'Give us a moment to think,' says Michael.

We all watch Michael as he paces up and down then jumps in the air.

'I think I've got it,' he says. 'What we've got here is a chance to display confidence in the Secret Horse Society and an opportunity to build confidence in Jammie D.'

'What do you mean?' I ask.

'Well, think about it – if I nip back to the Old Shed and get his tack and then come back here, I can ride him back to the Old Shed with confidence. No one will think he's the abandoned white horse everyone's looking for. That is, providing we don't bump into no one from the Beckham Estate who knows us.'

'People will think he's your 'orse,' says Molly-May, clapping her hands.

'Genius,' I say.

'And while I'm gone . . .'

'We should show Jammie D the track he'll be running on and take him into the school hall,' I say. 'So he's ready for Monday.'

'Yes, it's the only chance we will have to get him used to our school,' says Akin.

'So he don't freak out at the Big Race and the Big Read,' says Ste.

'Exactly,' says Michael. 'Meet me back by the hole in the fence.' He steps over the piles of sticks, flips it open and disappears.

'Secret Horse Society – to work,' I say. 'Akin, can you go and see where Mr Lawson is?'

He nods and speeds off.

'I've got a big apple in my bag somewhere,' says Ste, peering inside. 'Got it.' Before giving it to Jammie D he takes a small bite out of the apple so that it's easier for him to get hold of with his teeth.

While Jammie D chomps away, we fuss over him to keep him occupied.

Ten minutes later my phone bleeps.

> **Spy report......**
>
> **Lawson in big chat with Burt & Will Other End**
> **Of School NOWS YOUR CHANCE BISCUITS**

'Come on,' I whisper to Jammie D and, grabbing hold of the ends of the school-tie rope, I start to lead him towards the running track.

'People will be cheering and making a proper racket, Jammie D,' says Molly-May.

'Yes, and you mustn't be frightened,' says Ste.

As we lead Jammie D round the running track, Molly-May runs around cheering and clapping her hands to get him used to it. Ste joins in with the cheering. My heart flip-flops at the thought of what it's going to be like on the actual day of the Big Race Off.

Jammie D bends his head and starts eating the grass.

'Come on, Jammie D,' I say when we reach the end of the track, 'let's go to the school hall so that you can see where you are going to be our reading horse.'

'Do you think he'll even step inside?' says Ste.

'Let's hope so,' I say, keeping everything crossed and texting Akin.

But Jammie D shies away from the open door. Handing the tie rope to Molly-May, I delve into my bag for the Jammie Dodgers and hold one out to the horse in the palm of my hand.

He munches it up. I walk backwards through the door, making a biscuit trail. Jammie Dodger steps in through the door, eating the biscuit trail as he goes.

Jammie Dodger looks up from following his biscuit trail, curious at the corridor he is now standing in. He seems particularly interested in a wall display the Year 7s have done about 'Our city'. He grabs the corner off a picture of the London Eye and munches it.

'Oh, no, Jammie, no.' But it's too late, the picture is destroyed. Ste pulls the rest of it off the wall with one hand and stuffs it behind the radiator.

'So it looks as if it fell,' he says.

We lead him to the hall. I stand inside the entrance and hold a biscuit out and Jammie D steps right in, walking towards me to get the biscuit.

'This is where we are going to read to you,' I say.

Jammie D blows through his nose and promptly does a massive poo.

'Oh, no,' says Molly-May. 'I'm going to get some paper towels.' And she sprints off.

Jammie D walks around, sniffing at everything.

'I think he likes it,' I say.

Molly-May runs back in, scoops up the poo and chucks it out of the window into a flower bed just as my phone bleeps.

GET OUT NOW LAWSON
WALKING TOWARDS HALL

Footsteps coming this way.

Quickly, I lead Jammie D behind the blue velvet curtain that's pulled across to hide bits of scenery from last year's Christmas play, *The Wizard of Oz*. There's a space for us to stand in between a wall of Aunty Em's cottage and a giant wooden sunflower from Munchkinland. I peep through a moth hole and see Molly-May run towards the other curtain, ducking behind it with Ste swinging himself across the hall behind her, getting there just as Mr Lawson walks into the hall talking on his phone.

Jammie D presses his head into my chest. I am

mouthing, 'Stay still, please, please be still.' And he is.

I swear he is the cleverest horse on the whole of Planet Earth.

I reckon he understands that I, Daniel Margate, who loves him SO MUCH, is in danger.

Mr Lawson sniffs the air. He must be able to smell the horse poo. He walks across and opens a window as he is chatting.

Then his words sail across the room and into my ears where they burn and will never be forgotten.

'Yes . . . Yes, I am really worried that they'll go to pieces in front of the cameras. Our librarian says they are working really hard and she thinks I'll be pleasantly surprised but still, they are not good enough . . .' And then his voice trails off and I can't quite hear the next bit because Jammie D swings his head and sends the wooden sunflower flying. My breathing stops. I hear the sound of Ste's crutches banging on the floor.

'Sorry, sir, I knocked a pile of chairs over.'

Peeping through the moth hole I see Ste swinging himself across the room towards Mr Lawson.

'Ste . . . I was just . . .'

'I heard you saying that we are not good enough, sir.'

Mr Lawson tries to change the subject. 'Ste, what are you doing here?'

'Miss Raquel put my bag behind the curtain in assembly this morning 'cause people kept tripping over it as they was coming in. My pencil case fell out, so I just came back to find it,' he says, waving his yellow pencil case in the air.

'Let's see about getting you home. Come with me.'

And Ste swings himself after Mr Lawson as they leave the hall.

Ste has sacrificed himself for the Secret Horse Society.

Molly-May dashes across and holds the curtain aside so that I can lead Jammie D out.

'Did you hear . . . did you hear him, saying we are not good enough? We'll show him.' Her fists are screwed into tight little balls, her glasses crooked. I reach out and straighten them.

'I heard him, but we've got to get out now.'

In no time at all, Jammie D is in a fast trot towards the broken bit of the fence – we run by his side, just about keeping up. Akin and Michael are waiting for us, holding Jammie D's tack.

'I got some funny looks on the bus back with this saddle, let me tell you,' says Michael. 'Quick, get him through the hole in the fence in case anyone sees us.'

I lead Jammie D to a clearing in the woods.

'Silver's run away,' says Michael. 'I bumped into some volunteers from the rescue centre, setting out to look for her on the heath, when I was on the way back to the Old Shed. They say she got away on her walk, shot off over the wasteland and towards the woods beyond our school.'

'Oh, no,' I say, feeling like a million ants are jumping in my tummy. 'I hope they find her.'

'I hope Silver keeps safe,' says Molly-May.

'Greyhounds are so fast,' says Ste, looking suddenly sad. 'They can out-run anyone.'

'Listen up,' says Akin. 'I got something that will make you lot smile. When I was spying, I overheard Lawson say that Cinder Street Boyz are being suspended *after* the Big Race Off. He says they got to do that so they don't let even more people down than they have already.'

'Result,' I say, giving him a high-five.

'Good they are still doing the race,' says Ste. 'Or you

two would have no one to beat.'

'We need to get going,' says Michael.

Akin hands Molly-May the body brush and she starts to brush off all the leaves and bits caught in his coat so they don't irritate Jammie D under the saddle.

Akin and I untangle the reins as I tell them of Ste's sacrifice.

Jammie D is now ready.

'I'll give you a leg up, Michael,' I say.

'No,' he says. 'I will give you one. 'You should ride home with us, the Secret Horse Society minus one by your side.'

My heart soars to the sky as Michael gives me a leg up. I take the reins and smile at the clouds in the distance as we start our parade back to the Old Shed, making sure to go the long way round so there's less chance of anyone we know seeing and we won't bump into the search party for Silver. I hold my head high just as Red Pollard did as he paraded Seabiscuit before the men, women and children of the Great Depression that loved him and the horse who put hope in their hearts.

Chapter 26

> **Secret Horse Society B at Mine 4 10**
>
> **Do not B late fellow Biscuits. Red D tell M-M**
>
> **Luv Prof M**

It's Saturday! *The Big Read Off and the Big Race Off are tomorrow.* I shout 'goodbye' to Mum and Jackson and as I rush down to Molly-May's, I notice one of Michael's old transistor radios on the balcony with a Post-it note that says:

> ## DO NOT TOUCH
> ## School Work

What's Michael up to now?

Molly-May and I take the lift down to Aunty Lou's and see that there is another transistor radio with another Post-it note leaning against the wall. I'm just about to knock, when Akin's mum drives into the courtyard in a steel-blue car.

'Remember, Akin, bicycle,' says Mrs Ojo as she walks Ste and Akin to Aunty Lou's front door – which we all know is code for he'd better behave.

Michael appears at the door and grins and beckons us all into a very smart front room. Figurines of angels and Jesus stare down at us from display shelves.

Molly-May stares up at the angels as if she is in wonderland. I hear Aunty Lou and Akin's mum introduce themselves to each other and then start droning on about schools the way that grown-ups like to do.

'What's happening?' says Ste as we take off our jackets, draping them over a chair.

'Yes, why are we here?' asks Molly-May.

'Because, Secret Horse Society,' says Michael. 'I have a surprise. I need you all to dress up in 1930s costumes for my walk-in booth.'

'Costumes!' says Molly-May, clapping her hands.

'Do we have to?' says Ste. 'Last time I dressed up I was a sheep in juniors and it itched.'

'Well, at least you never had to be the donkey, like me,' says Akin.

'No, these are good costumes, I got it all planned,' says Michael. 'We're all gonna be different people in Seabiscuit's world. Akin will be Mr Howard, Seabiscuit's owner. Molly-May, you are Marcela Howard, his wife, and Ste – you are going to be Tom Smith, Seabiscuit's trainer. And you, Daniel, are . . .'

'Red Pollard,' I finish, feeling as if my smile will crack my face open.

'Who are you going to be, Michael?' Molly-May asks.

'Clem McCarthy – he was a 1930s radio broadcaster. He did the commentary for the Seabiscuit versus War Admiral race.'

Michael runs to the door and peeps through a crack. 'They are still going on,' he says as Aunty Lou and Akin's mum's voices trickle through the doorway. 'We are safe for the moment – look,' he says, and he brings out from behind the sofa two pairs of horse stirrups fastened together with a leather strap.

He drapes one pair over the big arm of the sofa and the other pair over the other arm. 'I found out that some young jockeys use sofa arms to practise on,' he says.

'Daniel, you are on Seabiscuit and I am on War

Admiral,' says Michael.

We climb on to the sofa arms, putting our feet in the stirrups.

Ste starts commentating as Michael and I pretend to race.

'And they are off and Seabiscuit takes the lead but War Admiral is catching up and overtakes Seabiscuit but no, Seabiscuit is in the lead again.'

Akin and Molly-May jump up and down cheering and clapping and—

'GET OFF MY SOFA!'

Aunty Lou stands in the doorway, lip quivering, arms folded.

Michael jumps off his arm as I scramble down and get my feet caught in the stirrups. I end up a heap on the floor.

'I am so sorry, Aunty Lou,' I say, my face burning. 'I didn't mean to disrespect your furniture.'

'You are Michael's guest and he should have known better. Michael, I will be having words with you later. Put your coats on and follow me.'

We are soon all squashed in the lift, going up to the eighteenth floor.

'We are going to my friend Gracie's,' says Aunty Lou. 'She is an absolute wonder with a needle and thread.'

As we walk along the balcony I trip over another transistor radio with the same Post-it note:

DO NOT TOUCH
School Work

I try to catch Michael's eye to see what's going on but he won't look at me.

'Come along,' says Aunty Lou, who is bustling along and doesn't appear to have spotted the radio. She rings on the doorbell.

An old woman I recognise from round our estate opens the door. She has twinkly eyes and determination literally sparking off her.

'Good, you are here. Come on in. Nothing I like better than a costume challenge. Ever since Michael came to see me three weeks ago I've been on a mission. Car-boot sales, vintage shops and rooting around to find things that I knew I had somewhere. I've finally got everything I need.'

'Three weeks ago?' I say, looking at Michael.

'I've been planning this for ages,' says Michael, tapping the side of his nose. 'I want my walk-in science booth to be the best.'

There's a sewing machine set up on the kitchen table, a box of different-colour threads, a bowl full of pins and a big pair of scissors.

'Give me your coats,' says Aunty Lou. 'Shall I pop them out of the way in Willem's room?'

'Yes please,' says Gracie. 'Willem's my grandson and he is away studying aerodynamics.'

'He must be very clever,' says Molly-May.

Gracie smiles. 'Now come with me.' We follow her into another bedroom which must be hers, only you can't see an actual bed 'cause it's covered in clothes. There are lots of different-coloured dresses laid out and slowly, slowly Molly-May walks to the bed, perches on a corner and starts stroking a coral silk dress. Aunty Lou brings a chair by the dressing table for Ste to sit on and Akin plonks a pile of hats with brims on to Ste's lap.

'They are called fedoras,' says Aunty Lou. 'Very smart. Gentlemen knew how to dress back then.'

Ste and Akin are trying the hats on and laughing at

themselves in the mirror. It's then that I see them hanging on a hook, and I let out a gasp. The red-and-white racing silks of Red Pollard and Seabiscuit.

'Would you like to try them on?' Gracie says.

All I can do is nod.

Aunty Lou hands the racing silks to me and shows me to the bathroom.

My hands are shaking as I try and detangle myself from my jeans and jumper and wriggle into the white jodhpurs and sturdy leather riding boots that are nice and roomy. Then I put on the red silk top with white arms and red cuffs. On the front and back in white is an upside-down triangle with an H for Howard in the middle to show who Seabiscuit's owner was. They are a perfect fit. There is a knock on the door. It's Michael – he hands me a riding hat with red and white silk panels on it and a tiny white bow on the front.

'I gave Gracie my old riding hat to make this for you,' he says. 'She told me their jockey caps weren't even proper hard hats to protect them back in Seabiscuit's time. Imagine that! It's a good thing our heads are the same size 'cause you gotta wear this to be safe for the Big Race Off.'

I don't trust myself to speak. I put it on my head and 'cause my hands are trembling too much, Michael does the strap up under my chin and I look in the mirror and Red Pollard stares back at me. Michael squeezes my arm.

'Come on,' he says. As I follow him back into Gracie's bedroom everyone claps. Ste and Akin look smart in their suits, complete with ties and waistcoats, shirts and jackets.

'These are yours, Michael,' says Gracie. In her hands are a shirt and bow-tie, a tartan sleeveless jumper and trousers with braces.

A loud hiccupped sob explodes from Molly-May. A silence, as we all just stop and gape at her.

'I ain't never seen such lovely things,' she hiccups. 'Not ever.'

Aunty Lou sits on the bed next to her and Gracie shoos us all out of the room and into the kitchen.

'I got to be first for my alterations,' says Michael. 'I've got places to be.'

'You, young man, will do exactly what Gracie tells you to do,' calls out Aunty Lou, 'after the disgraceful way you treated my sofa.'

Michael stands on a chair like a statue, with a fixed smile on his face. Me, Ste and Akin all look at each other and laugh. He knows he is in big trouble with Aunty Lou.

Gracie pins up our hems and takes in our waists, one by one. While she is cutting Ste's trouser leg to make room for his cage, Molly-May comes into the kitchen wearing the coral dress with puffy sleeves and a pleated skirt.

She has a brown felt hat on her head and brown shoes with a strap on her feet and she is smiling her biggest smile and she looks . . .

'Pretty, you look really pretty,' says Akin.

Ste nods. 'You look brilliant, Molly-May.'

'I'm going to make this child some dinner to eat,' says Aunty Lou.

'There's a chop in the fridge,' says Gracie.

Aunty Lou opens the fridge and brings out a plate of ready-made sandwiches for us all to eat, and starts to make Molly-May a proper dinner.

'Your turn, Akin,' Gracie says, but he is as usual so hoppity-hoppity that he nearly falls off the chair while Gracie is pinning his trousers.

'Your dad won't give you your bicycle back,' says Molly-May, wagging her finger. This starts a game and every time Akin moves, one of us shouts 'bicycle'.

'Bicycle, bicycle, bicycle,' I shout and we are laughing so hard that none of us notice that Michael had gone until we hear his voice loud and clear from the radio outside.

'This is your Beckham Estate radio station with Prof M in the house . . .'

We rush out of Gracie's front door.

'. . . I hope that you all come on down to Heath Academy tomorrow to meet Red D & Jammie D for the Big Read Off.'

So that's what Michael has been building in the cubbyhole! A radio station.

He is so clever. No one will have a clue what he is talking about, except for us, the Secret Horse Society.

'This is one for all the stressed ladies on the Beckham Estate and especially for you, Aunty Lou, and sorry about your sofa. Here is Bob Marley and his famous song about not worrying.'

Aunty Lou starts dancing with a smile on her face, muttering to herself, 'That boy,' and then Mr Samuels joins us and does teacher dancing outside Gracie's front door. I look down which makes me feel dizzy but I can see people coming out on the balconies listening to the radios and Michael plays something for everyone, from Beyoncé to hymns. I see a diddy Mr and Mrs Patel and Bernie coming out of their shops to listen. And when he plays that song about price tags by Jessie J I see a tiny Mum, dancing with Jackson way below in the estate courtyard.

Everything is so happy, but I know I got to get the Secret Horse Society properly focused on tomorrow.

When Molly-May has finished her chop and mash, and we have demolished the sandwiches and given our costumes to Gracie for last-minute alterations and safekeeping, it is time for the Secret Horse Society to make our way over to the Old Shed to bed down Jammie D.

Through the setting sun we walk, whispering our plans for tomorrow. The Secret Horse Society and me.

Secrut Plan

1. All Sucrut horse Society to set alarm for 4 o'clock (Daniel DOUBLE CHECK that you put 4 NOT 6. This wood bee a dizasta!)

2. Daniel must kreep out of flat without waking Jackson

3. Akin to go to Ste's and help him eskape from his house with weel chair

4. All meat at HQ befor Jammie D wakes up

5. Groom Jammie D to look smart and redi for Big Race and Read off

6. Michel go bak to Beekam Estate and sneek bak into bed so Aunty Lou will think he has been zzzz all night

7. Michel get taxi to skool in morning with Aunty Lou and Gracie wit all props and costums 4 Walk-in science booth

8. We the Sucrut horse socity promise to do Jammie Dodger, Red Pollard and Seabiscuit prawd

Good luck, Biskits
From your leeder

Chapter 27

I sleep with my headphones on so that no one hears the alarm when it vibrates at four. Jackson wakes up for a second as I'm struggling into my clothes. He murmurs 'Dan-Dan' but then falls back to sleep.

I scribble a note for Mum so she doesn't worry, and then I creep out.

C U & Jackson at
scool laiter

'Psst. Red D – we're over here.'

A pinprick of torchlight blinds me from across the forecourt. Shielding my eyes, I see Molly-May and Michael, huddled outside Bernie's Burger Bar, waiting.

I hurry over to join them.

'It's freezing,' whispers Molly-May. 'I hope there

ain't going to be no storm, it will ruin everything.'

My heart hits my boots as I look up at the thunder-clouds. *Please no, no, no – no storm*, I pray silently to the Great Seabiscuit in the sky.

We hear the clattering of claws on concrete and panting. It's Buster, tearing over the courtyard towards us.

'Oh, Buster, you are naughty. You got out again,' says Molly-May.

'We'd best take him with us,' says Michael. 'We'll get caught if we take him back to Finn's now.'

'Yeah, we should get going,' I say. 'We got so much to do.'

Our breath steams as we hurry over the courtyard with Buster at our heels. Once we get to the wasteland, Michael turns the torch full on and we make our way over the lumpy bumpy grass, me stumbling on to my knees again and again.

'BISCUIT, BISCUIT, BISCUIT!'

It's Akin, shouting as he runs at top speed towards us.

'Jammie D's gone,' he says. 'It's the Cinder Street Boyz – they've smashed up our headquarters.'

'Noooooooo,' I hear echoing through the dark and I realise it's coming from me as I run with the others through Apple Tree Wood.

The shed door is swinging off its hinges and on it is sprayed:

CINDER STREET BOYZ

Inside, Jammie Dodger's bed lies empty. Bales of straw have been pushed from the top of the mountain. Hay is strewn everywhere. Cans of dog and cat food have been thrown across the floor, squashed carrots and cabbage trodden into the straw. Ste is trying to balance on his crutches and pick up a can of cat food.

There is deathly silence apart from Buster's whining as we take in the scene.

Our Secret Horse Society headquarters are wrecked.

'We've got to find Jammie D,' I say, filling head to toe with the panics. 'I hope they haven't hurt him.'

'There's not much poo,' says Michael. 'So it looks

like Jammie D got out of here a good few hours ago.'

'I reckon he'd have got away from them quick, no problem,' says Molly-May, squeezing my arm.

'But the heath is huge. How will we know which way to go?' says Ste.

'Manageable chunk, by manageable chunk,' I say.

'Buster,' says Michael. 'He'll be our sniffer dog. He found my friend Nell once when she was missing.'

'I'll hold you up, so I'll stay and tidy up as best I can,' says Ste.

'You're coming with us,' says Akin.

'Yeah, all the Secret Horse Society together,' I say, helping him into his wheelchair.

'We'll look and look till we find our 'orse,' says Molly-May.

I spy a clump of white horsehair lying on the straw. I scoop it up and hold it in front of Buster's nose. 'Find Jammie Dodger,' I say, 'find your friend.' And off we go into the night.

Michael shines his torch ahead as we make our way through the trees, twigs and apples crunching under our feet and Ste's wheels as Akin pushes him. Buster keeps bounding ahead then runs back to us, tail wagging. When we reach the edge of the wasteland we all stop and stare at the dark heath that goes on and on and on.

'It looks even bigger in the dark,' says Molly-May.

Buster jumps up and licks her. Dogs just know when people are sad and frightened.

'How are we going to find him in time for the Big Read Off?' says Ste. 'It's impossible.'

'All our plans'll be ruined,' says Molly-May.

'We'll find him,' says Akin, putting his arm round Molly-May's shoulder. But I can tell he don't believe the words that are coming out of his own mouth.

Michael is shining the torch around him, biting his lip. 'Give Buster another sniff of the horsehair,' he says.

I fish it out of my pocket and hold it in front of the dog's nose again.

'Buster, find,' I say. 'Find Jammie Dodger, find him, boy.'

Buster wags his tail, barks, and shoots off straight ahead and out of sight.

I know as head of the Secret Horse Society it's up to me to keep everyone believing that we will find our horse.

'Seabiscuit won when everyone said he couldn't and so will we. Come on, Biscuits.' I take the torch from Michael. 'Follow Buster.'

We walk and we walk and we walk through a clump of trees and out the other side towards a big oak tree standing alone in the dark night, and as I take each step, a list of jittery fears jump through me.

We might never find Jammie Dodger.

Supposing he's hurt.

Supposing someone has caught him and we never see our horse again.

Supposing . . .

'Going somewhere, bone boy?' Nico swings himself down from the branch of the huge oak tree ahead of us. Sol drops down next to him and Baz jumps from another branch, landing behind Nico.

I gulp a breath. 'Let us through, please,' I say, but my voice sounds shaky, not like the leader of the Secret Horse Society should sound.

'Nah, this is our tree,' says Sol, prodding me in the shoulder.

'No, it ain't,' shouts Molly-May. 'It belongs to everyone.'

'What you lot doing out this time? Come to practise your running with your little friends, have you?' says Baz, and he does his impression of me running round in a circle, legs and arms everywhere.

'Nah, maybe they are practising their reading in the dark, so no one can hear how rubbish they are,' says Sol.

A rumble of thunder.

'Prof M?' says Nico to Michael. 'What ya doing out on the heath with these losers?'

'The only losers I see are standing right in front of me,' says Michael.

'You'll be sorry you said that,' says Sol. 'Very sorry indeed.'

Another rumble of thunder.

Akin helps Ste out of his wheelchair so he is standing supported between Michael and Akin and we are all in a row facing our enemy.

'We ain't scared of you,' says Ste.

'If you ask me,' says Molly-May. 'Anyone who's stupid enough to vandalise a building then spray-paint their name to show the world it's them what done it, ain't got no brains at all. I'm just saying. You're going to be in so much trouble.'

'Who are you calling stupid, Molly-May?' says Nico. 'You haven't even got clothes what fit you properly.'

'Leave her alone,' says Akin.

'We rule these ends and don't you forget it and nothing'll stop our night-time tagging,' says Baz. 'Nearly got trampled on by a white 'orse but that didn't stop us.'

Nico slaps him round the head and hisses, 'Shut up, Baz.'

I breathe out. Jammie Dodger got away, but supposing . . .

'You better not have hurt the horse!' explodes out of me.

A flash of lightning.

'Look!' shouts Michael, and under the electric sky, galloping towards us is Jammie Dodger, side by side with Silver the greyhound! Gleaming in the lightning, under the thunder-clouds, they speed straight at us, and behind them is Buster, barking, running, and they are not going to stop.

'Run!' shouts Nico and the Cinder Street Boyz disappear, sprinting into the trees. A burst of rain falls down on us. I step into the path of the galloping horse, holding my arms outstretched.

'Daniel! Get out the way, what are you doing?' Molly-May cries.

But my beautiful boy stops, his head bowed, panting.

'You came back to me. You came back to me, Jammie D,' I say, burying my face in his mane.

'He loves you, that's why, and he found Silver,' says Molly-May, grabbing hold of her collar so she doesn't escape again.

And the rain stops, as if by magic.

'You know what I think – that horse was protecting us,' says Michael.

Buster stands on his hind legs, his front paws on my tummy.

'Clever boy, Buster. Clever boy,' I say.

'Buster, you found them. You are the Secret Horse Society's hero,' says Molly-May, making a huge fuss of Buster and Silver.

Ste is sitting back in his chair and Molly-May takes Silver over to him and he starts talking to her gently.

'We are all back together again,' says Akin, grinning round at us all.

'We should get going,' says Michael. 'We've got a lot to do. It will be light soon and we don't want to be caught.'

And, as a happy parade of the Secret Horse Society, two dogs and a horse, we make our way back over the heath, the wasteland and through Apple Tree Wood. We step into our headquarters as night becomes dawn, but a dark shadow falls over me. What will happen after today, when Jammie Dodger is no longer a secret?

Chapter 28

I stand outside the Old Shed feeding Jammie Dodger apples with Ste, who has hold of Buster and Silver's collars, while the rest of the Secret Horse Society are inside, clearing up the mess the Cinder Street Boyz made and making it safe for the animals.

Then we set to work grooming Jammie D. Molly-May, Akin, Michael and me make our secret horse – who will no longer be secret after today – as smart as he can be.

They've got to let us keep our reading horse, they just have to. I swallow back my fear as I brush and brush and doubt slices through me. Michael picks the dirt out of Jammie D's feet and Molly-May combs his mane and tail till our beautiful boy is ready. Michael brings out a red numnah from his bag.

'I saved up and ordered this. It will look really

smart with your red jockey silks.'

'Thanks so much, Michael,' I say, and we tack Jammie D up.

'He looks so handsome,' says Molly-May, and he does.

'Slight change of plan,' says Michael. 'I've got to take the dogs back. I'm going to tell Aunty Lou I couldn't sleep and went for an early morning walk.'

'Me and Ste will go the road route and get the bus,' says Akin.

'Yeah, we'll attract less attention that way,' says Ste.

Molly-May and me start our long walk through the cold night air, leading Jammie D across the heath. We don't talk; no words are needed. We both know what we are about to do.

After what seems like for ever and a day we reach the woods that backs on to our school. A rat scurries past; Jammie D startles and steps backwards.

'Whoa, boy,' I say, and we carry on our journey till we reach the patch of wood by the broken bit of the fence.

I take out my scrapbook and we practise our reading

to Jammie D as the sun comes out. And then it's time to wait.

The sound of a crutch on broken sticks.

'Biscuits, Biscuits – where are you?'

'We are over here,' I hiss through the trees.

It's Ste, dressed in his costume. Fedora hat tilted forwards.

'You look so cool,' says Molly-May.

'It worked. I told Aunty Lou and Gracie I felt a bit funny, so they told me to go and sit down. They think I'm with Miss Raquel. You two go!'

'Ste will look after you now, boy,' I tell Jammie D before squeezing through the broken bit of the fence after Molly-May, and hurrying across the field to where the walk-in science booths are being set up.

We hurry past a Spitfire booth, a History of Television booth and a Space Travel booth that looks amazing. Michael's booth is right at the end. Aunty Lou and Gracie have already helped him set it up to look like a 1930s radio station. There's a mic and a table with props for radio sound effects.

'Try them out, go on,' says Akin. 'They're good.'

He is already in his costume.

'Looking smart, Akin,' says Molly-May.

'Thanks.' Akin grins, tilting his hat to a jaunty angle. He holds a picture of President Franklin D. Roosevelt straight while Aunty Lou fixes it to the wall with a staple gun.

So I do as Akin suggests and have a little play around with the sound effect props. It's brilliant! There is a sheet of metal that I shake to make thunder. A small tin bath with a full watering can. When I pour it into the tin bath it sounds like rain. A wooden creaking door with a key to fit into a lock. There is a crate of gravel with a pair of shoes in it for the sound effect of walking up a path.

Gracie walks towards us with an armful of costumes. She hands Molly-May hers and she rushes off to change. She drapes my racing silks over a chair.

'For when you're ready,' she says.

'Thanks,' I say as I have another go of walking the shoes with my hands on the gravel.

Mr Samuels and Michael are fixing up the big old radio on a table with a label that says *1934 Atwater Table model*. Michael has hidden a laptop in the hollow of its back so that a recording of Seabiscuit's race against War Admiral is coming from the radio.

'This is magical,' I say.

Gracie and Aunty Lou are putting what I assume are 1930s style chairs around the radio.

'In your characters, you are going to be listening to the radio,' says Michael, 'as if this is your front room.'

I plonk myself on the brown leather chair with my racing silks draped over the curved arm. It's really comfy. I gaze up at the other pictures on the wall. I'm guessing it's posters from famous children's radio programmes of the day: *Flash Gordon*, *Dick Tracy* and *Little Orphan Annie*, all with big colourful lettering that's easy to read. I wish all writing was like that.

The excited buzz of chat around us rises. I turn to see the *Seven Show* camera crew have arrived with Carrie Crawford. People are surging forwards to meet them.

I watch Melody and Polly take a selfie with her.

'I'm gonna get changed,' I say, grabbing my costume.

I head across the playing field towards the broken fence and climb through, making my way in the trees to where Jammie D and Ste stand hidden.

Jammie D gives a little nicker when he sees me.

'He's a bit restless,' says Ste, who is perched on a log holding Jammie D's reins.

'I'll take him for a little walk,' I say.

With my silks over one arm and the reins in the other I start walking Jammie D up and down, whispering to him over and over.

'You are the very best, Jammie D, do you know that?' Over and over.

I lead Jammie D back to the log so that Ste can sit down and hold him, and nip behind the tree to get into my silks.

I'm telling you, it's hard enough for me to get dressed in the bathroom, let alone behind a tree, but eventually I do it.

'I'll stay with Jammie D,' says Ste, ''cause you and Akin got to have that meeting about the Big Race Off with Sugden.'

I nod and, stuffing my school uniform in my school bag, I give Jammie D a pat and head back through the trees.

The general public have started to arrive so I rush back to Michael's booth and sit down in one of the 1930s chairs and get into character. I am Red Pollard through and through. Molly-May and Akin are wandering around arm-in-arm being Charles and Marcela Howard and then they sit down and listen to the radio broadcast. I can tell Michael is loving showing people round his radio booth and it's like we, the Secret Horse Society, are a piece of living history. Then Sugden goes and spoils it all by marching up to me and Akin, having no respect that we are in character, and says, 'Meeting about the Big Race Off, now.'

He shoos Akin and I to the boys' changing room. The Cinder Street Boyz are already there in their PE kits, hair all combed and warming up like they are Usain Bolt or something.

'You will not disgrace the school BLAH,' Sugden starts.

'You will behave BLAH.

'You are representing the school to the nation BLAH.

'AND DANIEL MARGATE, YOU WILL GET FROM THE BEGINNING OF THE RACE TO THE END, SOMEHOW.'

I look him straight in the eyes and say, 'Somehow, I will.'

Akin quickly turns away and I know it's 'cause he's laughing.

'Get changed out of those ridiculous clothes and into your PE kit.'

'Rude,' says Akin under his breath.

Luckily, Delilah comes with a message for Sugden, which gives me the opportunity to nip out of the door and I run across the playing field to the broken bit of the fence.

Michael has taken over from Ste as planned and is walking up and down with Jammie D. He gives me a leg up and adjusts my stirrups high like a jockey.

I am obviously not going to ride as fast as a jockey, but I still want to look the part. I slide my feet into them, first one, then the other.

'Michael, I am sure Clem McCarthy is looking down on you proud. You look every bit like a 1930s gentleman who would announce a race.'

Michael grins and adjusts his spotty green bow-tie and smooths down his sleeveless tartan jumper. He has what looks like an old mic but he's attached it to a modern-day microphone lead draped round his shoulders.

'I am going to pop this into your headteacher's tannoy when he's not looking. You are safe. Your Mr

Sugden is at the end of the race with some of the camera crew and that girl Melody – she's going to do the "on your marks, get set, go" bit.' He fiddles with his fedora hat. 'Are you all right from here? I need to get into position.'

I nod and as Michael disappears through the trees, I take my reins, my tummy somersaulting at what I'm about to do.

'It's just you and me now, Jammie D,' I say, and he starts to walk towards the hole in the fence.

Chapter 29

The Cinder Street Boyz are posing in front of the TV cameras in their new trainers. They strut up and down, looking like idiots, and when the crowd start cheering they think it's for them. The fools. They have no idea that they are being photobombed by a horse. Jammie D has stuck his head in the background of every one of the Cinder Street Boyz' camera shots.

He is loving the cameras – just like Seabiscuit! People are clapping and cheering. Akin comes running out in his PE kit and is cheered by our school. 'Akin, Akin, Akin.'

He flings his arms around Jammie D and kisses him on the nose.

Baz, Nico and Sol turn round and literally jump six foot in the air.

'It's that horse!' squeals Baz.

'Yes, it is. Go to the top of the class, Baz,' I say.

Jammie D snorts and steps backwards. I know he remembers the Cinder Street Boyz from last night.

I lean forwards and whisper in my horse's ear. 'It's all right, Jammie D, you are safe.'

I see Mr Lawson and Sugden marching towards us but with lightning quickness, Michael appears next to me and announces over the mic, 'This is Clem McCarthy, speaking from Heath Academy. So, tell me, Daniel. Why are you riding on a horse today?'

'Well, Clem,' I say, 'you see, I am not good at running. I trip over my own legs a lot and Mr Sugden – that's my PE teacher here at Heath Academy – said I was to get to the end of the race *somehow*, so I thought I'd get to the end of the race somehow on a horse.'

'That's a very clever interpretation of Mr Sugden's words.'

'Well, you see, Clem, I'm dyslexic and us dyslexics are good at thinking in a different way and finding creative solutions to problems. It's our gift.'

Carrie Crawford is laughing and clapping her hands and the camera crew are surrounding me and Jammie D and I can see Mr Lawson and Mr Sugden have stopped in their tracks and can't get through the crowd.

'OH MY DAYS, THAT'S NOT FAIR,' Nico is shouting. 'That horse has four legs, I've only got two. That's taking liberties.'

Sol is stomping up and down, saying to anyone who will listen, 'I've got my new trainers though. I've got my new trainers though.'

Then Melody walks over and, as if she's a celebrity, gives Jammie D a kiss on the nose and winks at me.

'Gentlemen, if you would like to take your places.'

'Walk on, Jammie D,' I say, and we take our places at the beginning of the race. Akin is in the lane to the right of me and Baz is three lanes over to the left, trying to be as far away from me and Jammie D as he can. Somewhere in the gathering crowds will be Mum and Jackson but I can't think about them now. I look straight forwards, focused, ready.

'On your marks,' says Melody in her best dramatic voice, 'get set, GO.'

And we are off, and there is nothing anybody can do about it.

Jammie D and I start off at a trot. I hear Michael

commentating on the race in the background. Baz and I are neck and neck with Nico, Sol and Akin ahead of us. But then Baz trips over his trainer laces and falls, with a splat, flat on his face.

'Who's running funny now?' I say as we pass him.

I can hear Michael laughing over the mic.

Jammie D picks up his speed and passes Sol, no trouble, and then Nico, and then he is eyeball to eyeball with Akin, just like Seabiscuit was with War Admiral on this exact date in 1938. Jammie Dodger now has the urge to win and he breaks into a canter and we streak ahead.

I look behind me. 'So long, Akin,' I shout to my friend.

And me and Jammie Dodger are one, like Red Pollard and Seabiscuit were one . . . Together the years merge and we win the race for Seabiscuit and my great-great-grandfather Cuthbert H. Brown Junior, and the crowd go wild.

Chapter 30

'Jammie D, we won! We actually won,' I say, leaning forwards and patting him on the head.

I am surrounded by the television crew and Carrie Crawford is standing in front of me, taking her position in front of the cameras, as Akin, Molly-May, Ste and Michael push through the crowds, cheering, smiling, laughing, till they are standing next to Jammie D, in their rightful place as members of the Secret Horse Society.

'You did it, Daniel, you did it,' says Molly-May.

Michael reaches out and grabs the halter, ready to lead us to the school hall.

From my position high up on Jammie D's back I see Mr Sugden and Mr Lawson just staring, mouths open, at the back of the crowd and there is nothing they can do even if they could reach us. They are not going to tell me off in front of the TV crew.

'Well, Daniel,' says Carrie Crawford, holding the mic up to me, 'you certainly found an ingenious way to do what your teacher Mr Sugden said and get to the finishing line *somehow.*'

'Thank you,' I say, looking straight at the camera, blinking. 'It seemed the best way to solve the problem.'

'Would you all like to introduce yourselves to the viewers of the *Seven Show* and tell them who you are dressed as?' She is holding the mic up to me again and I feel my mouth go dry and I swallow and swallow.

'I am dressed as Red Pollard, the hero jockey who rode Seabiscuit, the greatest racehorse there ever was.' The words tumble out of my mouth on top of each other as my face reds up. 'And this is Jammie Dodger, named in honour of Seabiscuit.' Carrie Crawford then holds the mic in front of Ste, who just stares at the camera. Akin nudges him.

'Oh, I'm Ste and I am dressed as Tom Smith, Seabiscuit's trainer, who could work miracles with horses.'

'I am Charles Howard,' Akin says, waving at the camera. 'I own Seabiscuit.'

'His real name's Akin and I am Molly-May, and I am Marcela, who is married to Charles Howard and who loved Seabiscuit very much.'

'And you are?' says Carrie Crawford, holding the mic out to Michael.

'I am Clem McCarthy, who did the commentary for the famous race between Seabiscuit and War Admiral.'

My heart is hammering so hard it feels like it's going to smash my ribs up and jump out of my body but I know what I've got to say it and say it *now*, or I will miss my moment. I lean forward and say into the microphone, 'Excuse me, but I've got something to tell the *Seven Show* viewers.'

Carrie Crawford smiles and hold the mic up to me.

I stare into the camera and take a deep breath. 'Akin, Ste, Molly-May and me are in the Biscuit Team for the Big Read Off. We don't find reading easy but now we've got Jammie Dodger. He's our reading horse. We can read to him, 'cause he don't judge us. I would like the viewers to see how he helps us. Please follow us as we go into the Big Read Off.'

I hear one of the crew say, 'This is television gold, the producers will be happy.'

As if by magic, Mr Samuels appears in front of us, his eyes twinkling.

'Daniel Margate, there are obviously questions to be answered after today as to where this horse has come from, but for now, go and take your places for the Big Read Off,' says Mr Samuels.

I take my feet out of the stirrups and swing my leg over and dismount. My legs wobble as they hit the ground.

'I'll see to Jammie D,' says Michael. 'Good luck, Biscuits.'

Akin, Molly-May, Ste and me walk into the school hall. Everyone's eyes are on us.

A semicircle of chairs is set out on the stage and the Shakespeares already occupy one side of the semicircle.

Mrs Johnson's jaw drops when she sees us. I guess she was too busy preparing for the Big Read Off to watch the Big Race Off.

Mum and Jackson wave from their seats next to Aunty Lou and Gracie, as I make my way on the stage with my Biscuit Team.

On each of our chairs is an enlarged photocopy of one of my great-great-grandfather's letters. Mrs Johnson has put my lime green layover on top of my letter and an aqua blue one over Akin's,

Miss Darwin, who is judging, claps her hands. 'Costumes! How lovely,' she says.

The camera crew take their positions and the audience quieten. One by one, the Shakespeares stand up and read Shakespearean sonnets. Red Pollard would have enjoyed hearing them, I think.

And then it's Melody's turn and she becomes Shakespeare's Juliet in front of our very eyes.

'O Romeo, Romeo! Wherefore art thou Romeo?

Deny thy father and refuse thy name . . .'

I look around and everyone is hanging on her every word. It's like she's hypnotising us all.

The hall erupts with cheers and whistles and now it's the Biscuit Team's turn.

I spy Michael bringing in Jammie Dodger at the back of the hall.

I nod and he leads him down the central aisle. Everyone turns and stares and Mrs Johnson gasps but Jammie D is holding his head up and, I swear, he is enjoying the attention as much as Seabiscuit did posing for his fans back on this very day in 1938. Michael stops at the top of the aisle so that Jammie Dodger is facing us, and we can read to our reading horse.

We, the Secret Horse Society, walk to the front of the stage. Akin, Ste, Molly-May and me. I see the Cinder Street Boyz sitting in the back row, nudging each other and smirking. But I don't care about them any more.

I hold up Seabiscuit's horseshoe to the audience and announce, 'Ladies and gentlemen, let me introduce you to the Biscuits and our reading horse, Jammie Dodger. We are going to read you letters that my great-great-grandfather Cuthbert H. Brown Junior wrote to Seabiscuit, this little brown horse with too-short legs and a funny run, who was a hero to all the people who had lost everything in the Great Depression, and to bring us luck I present to you a horseshoe worn by the Great Seabiscuit himself.'

Molly-May, Akin and Ste all place one hand on the horseshoe. Molly-May waves at her dad, Joe, in the front row.

It's time to start.

'My great-great-grandad, Cuthbert H. Brown Junior, lived in a car in the Great Depression in America during the 1930s,' I say. I look round at all the eyes staring at me and falter. *Do it for Cuthbert. Do it for Red Pollard. Do it for Seabiscuit.* I continue. 'He wrote letters to Seabiscuit, the racehorse, that we, the Biscuits, would like to read to you.'

Molly-May steps forward.

'This letter was written by Cuthbert H. Brown Junior on his birthday when they had to visit a relief kitchen, which is what they called food banks.'

I see her fix her eyes firmly on Jammie D before she begins to read.

'Dear Seabiscuit, I hope you are healthy and happy and looking forward to your next race . . .'

I look round at the audience, listening as her words swirl around them, and as Molly-May reaches the part where Cuthbert had written, 'Ma marched us down to the mission relief kitchen, but Pa was dragging his feet behind us, hands in his pockets, looking sad as sad can be . . .' I see Molly-May turn her head and look straight at her dad.

'Seabiscuit, I got a secret to tell you – I heard Pa

crying last night. The sound of his sobs woke me from my dreams of riding you. I could see, under the moonlight, Ma had her arm around him like he was a little child and it broke me in pieces to see it.'

We have all heard Molly-May read the letter a million times but it has never sounded like this before. Though she stumbles on some of the words, it doesn't matter 'cause her voice is strong and every word she reads is from her heart.

As she reaches the end, I look at her dad and there is a single tear trickling down his cheek.

'Mr Seabiscuit, sir, thank you for giving me the best birthday present ever: a skip in my pa's step. Yours respectfully, Cuthbert H. Brown Jr.'

The audience applaud; she bows her head. Jammie D is stomping his feet, like he is clapping too. He's restless, impatient. *Stay calm, my beautiful boy*, I pray but as soon as Akin starts to speak, he is calm, listening to his every word.

'Daniel's great-great-grandfather, Cuthbert H. Brown Junior, watched Seabiscuit run the Santa Anita Handicap in 1937, February 27th, 1937. Dear Seabiscuit . . .'

I look round at the audience, eating up Akin's every word, then a glint of blue catches my eye. Mrs Ojo is standing at the back of the hall with Mr Ojo, and he is holding the handlebars of a blue bicycle. I look at Akin standing tall and proud, reading to Jammie D, and although at times hesitant I just know the words come to greet his eyes through his aqua blue overlay. His foot is jigging but apart from that he is more focused than I've ever seen him. His mum and dad look so proud.

Akin reaches the part in Cuthbert's letter where they are waiting for the judge's decision. The audience are eating up his words.

When he reaches the part: 'Guess what? I have one of your actual horseshoes. A reporter who was walking away from the racetrack told us that Mr Howard, Seabiscuit's owner, gave it to him,' Akin suddenly looks up and sees the bicycle and his face cracks into what I am guessing is the biggest smile of his life as he finishes reading.

Akin says to the audience, 'As you heard, Seabiscuit didn't win that race, a horse called Rosemont won. But I want to say to Seabiscuit, don't feel downhearted that you didn't win because the way I see it, all those people wanting you to win makes you a winner in my eye.'

The audience cheer and Akin does the most dramatic bow you have ever seen. He puts his arms round Ste so that his friend can lean on him as he reads. Molly-May takes Ste's crutches and I put his letter in his hand. Ste looks at Jammie D, who is calm, waiting for his words.

Ste clears his throat and announces to the audience, 'On June 23rd, 1938, in Boston, Red Pollard had a horrific accident. He shattered his leg completely, doing a favour for a man called Bert Blume, galloping a horse called Modern Youth. The horse spooked and he ended up in hospital. Seabiscuit also got injured. He ruptured a part of his leg. Red Pollard was told he would never ride again.'

Then Ste focuses his eyes on Jammie Dodger and starts to read.

February 9th 1940

Dear Mr Red Pollard,

My heart broke when I heard that both you and Seabiscuit were injured.

I read how you were staying at Mr

Howard's ranch to get better, and you would go for walks on your crutches, Seabiscuit hobbling beside you step by step. I reckon you poured strength into each other.

I want you to know that my family and I prayed for you every night. We followed how, bit by bit, you got better until the rumour was Tom Smith lifted you into the saddle and you were able to go for gentle canters on Seabiscuit.

I heard that Mr Howard was worried about letting you ride ever again, but that David Alexander the newspaper columnist said, It's better to break a man's leg than his heart.

He was right. Today, I listened to you win the Santa Anita Handicap on Seabiscuit.

I know that is the last race you will ever run on Seabiscuit, as he is to retire. I would like to thank you both for being the heroes of my childhood and for teaching me that anything is possible.

To Seabiscuit I would like to say, have a

well-deserved rest. You will always race on in my heart.

Your friend,
Cuthbert H. Brown Jr

Ste looks up at the audience and says, 'I know just how Red Pollard felt lying in that hospital bed after his accident and not being able to ride Seabiscuit and thinking everything was over. That's how I felt after my accident. The Secret Horse Society, that is no longer secret, and Jammie Dodger here, helped rebuild me and I know I will walk again and I will run again. Red Pollard proved the doctors wrong and so will I.'

The whole audience in the school hall rise and they cheer and cheer and clap till I guess their hands are raw and I look at my friend Ste and I know his heart is complete. Jammie D shoots his head up and looks around. I swear he thinks the applause is all for him. The noise does not seem to be bothering him but still Michael is stroking and talking to him to keep him happy.

'Seabiscuit wold be proud of you,' I whisper, and no word of a life, Jammie D looks straight at me.

Now it is my turn.

I take a deep breath and say to the audience, trying not to look at Mum and Jackson, who is waving at me, 'On this date back in 1938, the 1st of November, was the most famous race in history. Seabiscuit versus War Admiral. I am now going to read to you the letter Cuthbert H. Brown Jr wrote on that day.'

I look down through my lime green layover and the words become clearer, sharper and jump up at me. I turn to Jammie Dodger and I start to read and though I stumble, and not every word is perfect, I read with my soul. I feel Cuthbert H. Junior there beside me as I share his letter.

> November 1st 1938
>
> Dear Seabiscuit,
>
> Today, the United States of America stood still in your honour. Stores were closed and workmen were sent home early so they could listen to the greatest race ever run: Seabiscuit versus War Admiral.
>
> They say even President Mr Franklin D. Roosevelt halted a meeting so he could listen

on his radio in the White House.

But here's a special surprise for you, Seabiscuit. I was actually there. Yes, some folks were gunning for War Admiral, but it seemed that the folks around us who, like me, had holes in their boots and too-thin winter coats, all wanted you to win. We got there six-and-a-half whole hours before the race. Pa lifted me high up on his shoulders so's I wouldn't get squashed against the fence, and people kept on coming. When they let us in we swarmed to the infield. Pa had a bread crust stuffed in his coat pocket and broke some off to give to me but, though my tummy was rumbling, I didn't feel hunger at all as all I could think about was you, Seabiscuit. I could see the folks who hadn't got in climbing on rooftops and up trees, all to try and get a glimpse of you.

And then I saw you with my very own eyes as you were led out with your horse friend, Pumpkin.

Then you swung your head up and even

though to you I was a little dot in the distance, I swore you looked straight up at me, Cuthbert H. Brown Junior.

'Seabiscuit, win, please, please win,' I whispered into the air, praying it would reach you on the breeze.

And then you walked to the start and I stopped breathing. Seabiscuit, I saw you behind War Admiral, head down, then you looked up at all the people. 'I'm here, Seabiscuit. I'm here,' I called, waving.

I could see a man, who Pa said was Mr Clem McCarthy the race caller, struggling to get through all the people that love you to his calling post. In the end he had to call the race from the rail.

The bell rang and off you went, neck and neck, and then you shot ahead, but then it was like your jockey, Mr Woolf, slowed you down so that you could see your opponents, because they say that once you look your opponent in the eye, there is no way that you will lose. And then you were running neck and neck again, and War Admiral bobbed his head in front, then you bobbed your head in front, and then you went into the far turn still head-to-head and either of you could've won.

'Go Seabiscuit, GO!' I screamed. 'You can do it!' And then you broke away and were in front by a bit, then a bit more, then you shot far ahead and over the finishing line, and the crowd went wild. People were crying and laughing and thumping each other on the back because you, Seabiscuit, the greatest horse that ever lived, had given us hope. You belonged to us who have lost everything.

There were tears splashing down my cheeks and I swear I could feel my pa's shoulders below me get wider and stronger and I know that you — the horse that no one thought could win — winning against War Admiral has given my pa his pride back. Because if you can win, Seabiscuit, then so can we.

I look into Jammie Dodger's eyes and whisper, 'Thank you,' and to the sound of applause, I take my bow.

Miss Darwin walks on to the stage waving her hands to quieten the audience. Both teams go back to our seats.

Carrie Crawford steps up behind her, carrying the silver star trophy.

'It is time,' says Miss Darwin, 'to award the Body and Mind festival trophy to the best reading based on diction, fluency and general performance. The judges and I have decided to award it to . . . the Shakespeares, for their superb reading, with special commendation to Melody for her stunning reading of Juliet.'

Everyone cheers as Melody steps forwards to receive the cup from Carrie Crawford. I am clapping really loudly, because she was the best reader.

Melody stands in the middle of the stage but she doesn't say anything.

Everybody waits for her to speak and there is an awkward coughing and shuffling.

Eventually, she says, 'I can't accept this trophy. I really can't. Shouldn't the journey that has been taken to achieve something be taken into account? Reading comes naturally to me and the other Shakespeares, but the journey that the Biscuits have gone on is incredible. I mean, they even found their very own reading horse!'

The audience laughs.

'You heard what Akin wanted to say to Seabiscuit: don't feel downhearted that you didn't win, because all those people wanting you to win makes you a winner. I think in my eyes and everybody's in the room, the Biscuit Team are the winners.'

She turns to Carrie Crawford.

'Please, Carrie, will you award this to Daniel Margate and the Biscuits.'

Carrie nods and I step forward and take the trophy, just like Mr Howard would have taken it every time Seabiscuit won a race. I bet he would then have handed it to Red Pollard on Seabiscuit's back, who would have held it high, high up in the sky for the crowds to see.

And that is exactly what I do. I hold it above my head and the audience stand up and cheer. I spy Nico, Baz and Sol looking properly shocked.

As one, the Secret Horse Society walk down the steps to stand with Michael and our horse, Jammie Dodger.

People surge forwards to meet us; Mr Samuels and Miss Raquel jump in and ask people to step back so that Jammie D does not get frightened.

Mr Samuels lets Mrs Ojo through, though. Mr Ojo is behind her wheeling the blue bicycle towards us.

'You must give it to your son,' she says, 'as you promised. He has earned it.'

Mr Ojo hands the bicycle to Akin, who is hopping on one foot he is so excited.

And Mr Ojo strokes Jammie D and says, 'You are a fine beast, helping my son concentrate on his books.' Jammie Dodger rubs his head against Mr Ojo's jacket.

Mr Ojo then shakes my hand and says, 'You have done your ancestor Mr Cuthbert H. Brown Junior proud, today. Daniel, you are a fine friend to my son and I congratulate you.'

Mrs Ojo nudges her husband and points over to

Molly-May's dad and he hurries over to talk to him. Before I have time to wonder what they are talking about, Molly-May's dad is swinging her in the air and she is crying out, 'Dad, you've got a job!'

Mr Samuels, a big smile on his face, is making sure that none of the crowds get too close to our reading horse. I calm Jammie D, stroking his neck, but he seems as if he is really enjoying himself, lifting his head and looking at everything going on around him.

Carrie Crawford is talking to Melody in the corner and I see her hand Melody a business card. Mrs Johnson is pushing her way towards us, her face beaming. Ste leans on one of his crutches with one arm round Jammie D, and I can tell today is the best day he has had since the crash and that now he has hope. Jammie D does a big wee and everyone jumps out of the way laughing as the puddle on the floor spreads.

I look for Mum and my heart stops. There she is, in the corner with Mr Lawson, Mr Sugden and Aunty Lou. They look up in my direction and my heart does an extra stop as I see Matt the Vet join them. He is back from India. Someone must have called him about

Jammie D. They start walking towards us.

'Biscuit, Biscuit, Biscuit!' I call out to Akin as he rides past on his bicycle.

'BISCUIT,' I shout over to Molly-May, who is still chatting to her dad.

Akin leans his bike against a chair and runs towards us, and Molly-May turns and dodges through the crowds, till we are standing together, the Secret Horse Society who are secret no more, as we are surrounded by the grown-ups. There is no escape.

Chapter 31

It's one thirty on a Saturday afternoon and we, the Secret Horse Society, have met as we were instructed to, outside the Old Shed. There is frost on the ground and an exciting nearly Christmas tingle in the air . . . but not for us. *Our hearts are broken*. We have to say goodbye to Jammie Dodger, and this is going to be the worst Christmas ever. Joanna from the Pegasus Horse Sanctuary is coming to pick him up and take him away.

Jammie Dodger is having a snooze on the straw inside the Old Shed, totally oblivious to the fact that he is to leave us for ever.

'It's time,' says Michael, and I open the door and go inside. I kneel in the straw and bury my head in his coat.

'I love you, Jammie D,' I whisper.

Michael gets the head collar and a carrot. Jammie

D opens one eye and I get out of the way, so he can stand up and start to munch his carrot. I put on his head collar and lead him out so we can say our goodbyes.

Akin is chewing his lip and has his arm round Molly-May, who is sobbing, 'I can't bear it, I can't bear that I'm not going to see Jammie D no more.'

Ste is sitting on a log and Jammie D nudges him with his nose. Ste is stroking and stroking him, avoiding looking at any of us. I think it's 'cause he's scared he might cry too.

I fetch Jammie D's body brush so that I can brush him one more time.

As I brush and brush and brush I think over the happenings of the last few weeks: we have been praised for our reading and scolded for keeping Jammie D secret. Shouted at by Mr Lawson, who said that he has never been so proud and so angry at the same time, ever. The Secret Horse Society have been whispered about and pointed at by kids in our school.

The good thing is, the Cinder Street Boyz are still suspended and are in even deeper trouble after their vandalisation of the Old Shed was reported. Whenever any of us bump into them in the street, they turn and walk in the other direction, 'cause we have made fools of them when it was them who tried to make fools of us. Ha!

The worst telling-off was from Matt, who said he had left me in charge of the Old Shed and trusted me. I've never felt so shamed.

I got to say, it was all worth it, though. We looked brilliant on TV. The Secret Horse Society came round to mine and watched it. We ate chocolate cake and crisps. The Big Race Off was well funny at the beginning when Jammie D photobombed the Cinder Street Boyz. There he is in every shot as Baz, Sol and Nico strut around like idiots. It was just so exciting watching us win the race, and the crowds cheering, and as for the Big Read Off, well, Mum watched it with Jackson with tears of happiness in her eyes. Happy memories to hang on to and keep, because it's all we will have once Jammie D has gone.

I will have to make my own scrapbook so that my great-great-grandson can know about the Secret Horse Society.

I will stick the newspaper articles in it, so that he can read about us bringing a horse into Heath Academy.

The headlines said:

LONDON KIDS WANT HORSE
Beckham Estate goes to the races

And my favourites were:

RED POLLARD & RED MARGATE

JAMMIE DODGER and SEABISCUIT:
The Greatest Horses There Ever Were

But the one that I shall remember with pride every day till I am an old, old man is:

BOY FLUMMOXES PE TEACHER WITH ALTERNATIVE DYSLEXIC THINKING

And guess what? The *Seven Show* are going to do a feature on the gift of dyslexia and they are going to interview me and Akin.

'Daniel, Daniel.' It's Molly-May, tapping me on the shoulder. She takes the brush out of my hand.

'You've made our Jammie D look properly handsome,

333

but it's time to say goodbye.'

She takes my other hand tight in hers and I turn and see a horse-box backing carefully through the trees with Matt the Vet directing it. My heart is literally in my throat, choking me. I can't imagine my life without Jammie D.

The horse-box stops, the engine is turned off and Joanna from Pegasus jumps out and walks towards us. She opens the back of the horse-box and brings a ramp down, ready for Jammie D to walk up and leave us for ever.

But wait . . . the horse-box is not empty! We watch as a beautiful little oatmeal-coloured horse with a white mane and tail is led down the ramp towards us, and Joanna is laughing and so is Matt. What's going on?

'Meet Hob,' Joanna says. 'Jammie Dodger's new friend.'

Jammie D nickers and the little horse nickers back, and the two horses touch noses and nuzzle into each other, neck against neck, giving each other a horse hug.

'I don't understand,' I say, walking over to stroke the beautiful little horse.

Then all of the Secret Horse Society speak at once and my head's just spinning.

'What's happening? Whose horse is that? What's going on?'

'He's cute,' says Molly-May, after the word cloud has stopped.

'Yes, he is,' says Joanna, 'and he's all yours.'

'What?' I say, walking over to stroke the horse.

Then, from behind the trees, Mum and Jackson appear with Molly-May's dad and ... *What's Mrs Johnson doing here?*

Matt holds his hands up so he can speak.

'Daniel, I want to apologise, I was really harsh on you and the rest of the Secret Horse Society, but you have changed everything for us at the Beckham Animal Rescue Centre. After you appeared on the *Seven Show*, the donations started flooding in and after the "London Kids Want A Horse" headline, an anonymous donor contacted us and gave a very generation donation – enough for us to keep Jammie Dodger. We felt that he should have a friend and little Hob here was in need of a companion. We've been given permission to build an extension to the Old Shed and make it into a proper stables and paddock. Mrs Johnson, do you want to tell them the school's news?'

'Absolutely!' Mrs Johnson steps up next to Matt. 'The generous donor gave the donation on condition that we start an education programme at Heath Academy in conjunction with the Beckham Animal Rescue Centre. So, Silver Reading Group, Jammie Dodger is now officially Heath Academy's reading horse.'

I can't believe this is happening. We, the Secret Horse Society, all cheer and laugh and hug each other.

'In the summer, we shall have sessions on the sports field with Jammie Dodger and in winter, you can come down to the rescue centre,' Mrs Johnson continues, 'because the centre's expansion will include a new space to educate and spread awareness about rescue animals.'

'Hob is the colour of an oatmeal biscuit,' I say.

'He's a strawberry roan,' says Michael.

'We should call him Hobnob,' says Molly-May. 'So he's a Biscuit too.'

'That is genius,' says Michael with a laugh.

'Hobnob it is,' I say.

'Hello, Hobnob,' says Akin, and Ste heaves himself over on his crutch to greet his new horse friend.

So, just like Seabiscuit had Pumpkin all those years ago, Jammie Dodger has Hobnob.

As if things couldn't get any better, Jessica walks past with Silver pulling on her lead, trying to play with Jammie Dodger. 'I've adopted her,' says Jessica. 'I fell in love, couldn't let her go.' Then there is a barking, as Buster comes tearing up in hot pursuit. I spy Napoleon, judging us all from a branch of the apple tree. I love it that Jammie Dodger has his animal family to keep him happy, just like Seabiscuit did.

Matt invites Mum, Mrs Johnson and Molly-May's dad back to the rescue centre for coffee. I hear Jackson screaming all the way through the trees that he wants to play with the horsey.

Joanna stays to settle in Hobnob; together we are mucking out and watering and feeding.

'You all look like you know what you're doing,' Joanna says to us, impressed. 'But you must call me any time you want advice about the horses.'

She is a very kind lady, I think.

When it's time to go say goodbye, we wave Joanna

off in the horse-box and say good night to the horses now lying in the straw together, and it looks just like a Christmas card and I know with all my heart this is going to be the best one ever. 'Happy Christmas,' I whisper.

We walk back through the trees. Mum's in front, carrying Jackson, who is now asleep. Molly-May's dad is talking to Mrs Johnson and we, the Secret Horse Society, walk behind them slowly so that Ste can keep up. Akin is wheeling his bike, making a cracking sound as he runs over all the twigs that have fallen from the trees.

'Hold the bike,' Akin tells me when we reach the wasteland.

So I do, and Ste sits on the handlebars with his leg stuck out in front and his crutch balanced over his lap and Akin hops on the bike and away they go.

'Happy Christmas, Secret Horse Society,' yells Akin, pedalling furiously away.

'Happy Christmas,' yells Ste.

The grown-ups all turn around at the commotion.

'AKIN, AKIN, GET OFF, GET OFF NOW,' shouts Mrs Johnson. 'That boy.'

My mum looks completely horrified but the rest of us are laughing.

'I would have done the same when I was a boy,' says Molly-May's dad.

We watch the blue bicycle disappear into the distance and then walk Mrs Johnson back to her car before heading back to the Beckham Estate. Molly-May, Michael and me run ahead and I don't care how I look running.

Molly-May stops and gives me a hug.

'Thank you for changing my life, Daniel,' she says.

'Mine too,' says Michael.

'Thank you, Seabiscuit,' says Molly-May and as we all stand together looking up at the sky I realise that I no longer wish I was Red Pollard. I am glad to be me, Daniel Margate.

THE END

(Well, nearly! There is one more manageable chunk to go.)

I take the sleeping Jackson from Mum, so that she can find her front door key in her bag, which as usual, involves her tipping her bag upside down on the outside doormat and rooting through all the screwed-up bits of paper, lipsticks, and general clutter that she seems to carry around with her. A group of Beckham Street Boyz are trying to get past.

'Alright, Red D. Saw you on the telly,' one of them calls out.

I smile. I guess I'm not invisible anymore. It's nice to have a nickname.

Scooping up the key from between her hairbrush and an old receipt, Mum throws everything back in her bag and lets us all in.

I take Jackson into my bedroom – no, *our* bedroom – and as I put him on his bed he wakes.

'Play horsey,' he says.

'OK,' I say, cracking a smile, not quite believing that now instead of two paper horses, I actually have two real horse friends: Jammie Dodger and Hobnob.

And I am such a good older brother that I say, 'You can be Seabiscuit.' I thump the bit of wallpaper that is now hanging down, with my fist, so that the paper horses can ride over it.

I put one string in Jackson's sticky hand and we

begin to jiggle them and the paper horses begin to move. I am deliberately losing because I am now a brilliant older brother, but also if I am properly truthful with myself, it's 'cause Seabiscuit has to win. 'Go on, Seabiscuit,' I shout. 'Go on!'

Mum comes in and watches the end of the race. Jackson has such a proud gleam in his eye as he wins, I want to kick myself for not letting him win other times too.

'And Jackson is the winner,' Mum says, trying to scoop him up but he is too fast. He runs to my bed and reaches under it and grabs my jumper bundle.

'NO,' I cry.

'Me make it crackle,' says Jackson and starts waggling my precious scrapbook. I run to grab it but there's a noise like something snapping.

'Jackson, you've *broken* it!'

Mum scoops Jackson into her arms and watches while I hold my breath and turn the pages, trying to find the damage.

I find a split along the top of the last page.

But – hang on – it's like two pages have been stuck together and – wait – there's something inside it.

'Mum, look,' I say, carefully parting the hole. 'I think there's something hidden here.'

'Hang on, I know what you need to get it out,' she says, and disappears for a few moments. She returns and hands me a pair of tweezers.

I slowly put them in the tear and clasp them shut on the bulge I can feel inside. I pull oh so gently and with it comes . . .

Another letter!

'I'll give you some time on your own.' Mum takes Jackson and closes the door.

I grab my jacket and run through the dusk all the way back to the Old Shed.

Jammie D and Hobnob are still snuggled in the straw.

I bring the letter up to my nose and smell the scent of old paper and far-away dreams.

With shaking hands, I start to read.

To whoever in the future has found this letter, my dearest wish is that you love horses like me.

Dear Keeper of the Scrapbook,

I wanted to say hello to you across all the years that have gone past. By the time you get this, I will no longer be on this earth. I send you love and hope that you have Seabiscuit's horseshoe and my scrapbook safe in your possession and that you love horses as much as I do. More than anything, I hope you have somewhere to live and enough food to eat.

You probably wonder why the letters are in a scrapbook, not with the Great Seabiscuit himself. Well, Ma didn't have the money for the stamps and she kept them all and put them in the scrapbook because she thought they were a record of my childhood, something to keep and pass on, which I have now done to you.

You probably feel sad that Seabiscuit did not get these letters, but I have a story for you. We moved back to New York when times got a bit better and Russo and Sons welcomed my pa back with open arms, as they said he was one of the finest tailors they had ever had.

Sadly though, my beautiful pa, Cuthbert H. Brown Sr, passed away of T.B. The years on the road had taken their toll. I knew that I had to stand on my own two feet and not be a burden to Ma, so I ran away. I remembered Norman from the relief kitchen and the stories about boys clinging on to trains to take them some place. So, early one morning I went down to the rail track and when the train came, I jumped and clung on for dear life. It was time for my adventure.

Well, I made my way to the Santa Anita Racetrack. First, I ran around doing odd jobs. I would walk the horses, muck out, clean boots. I wanted to learn to ride like a jockey. One of the trainers, Albert, eventually took pity on me and said that if I helped him with his letter-writing he would teach me to ride, and that's what happened till I was good enough to become a bug boy — an apprentice jockey. Life was hard, but I was determined. Then one day, when we were galloping the horses early in the morning, I saw a man standing watching, leaning on a cane. After we had taken the horses back to the stables, Albert told me to go on up to his house as he had a letter he wanted me to write for him. As I passed the track, I saw the man still standing there, staring at where we had galloped past him moments before. 'Excuse me, sir,' I said. 'Is there anything that I can do for you?' The man turned and I realised that it was Red Pollard.

'Oh, sir,' I said, shaking his hand. 'It is an honour to meet you.'

Red Pollard said, 'I was just reliving—'

'The 1940 Santa Anita Handicap, when you won on Seabiscuit,' I finished for him. He smiled at me and I could see dancing in his eyes, the cheering crowds the minute he went over the finishing line, riding the greatest horse there ever was.

'Sir,' I said, 'I have something to show you. Would you do me the honour of meeting with me later today? I could be back in two hours. I have a letter to write for Albert, but I'll be back.'

He nodded to a tree. 'I will wait for you there,' he said.

I hurried my letter-writing, then dressed in my one suit that my father had made me, with its fine stitches. I grabbed my scrapbook and Seabiscuit's horseshoe and ran, and there was Red Pollard, waiting for me under the tree. It wasn't until I looked up at the tree and saw the horse's head carved in the bark that I realised it was the very tree that Pa and I climbed to watch him race all those years ago.

I told him of that day as we sat on the grass; the greatest jockey and the bug boy, side by side under the tree. He kissed the horseshoe and read every word of my letters, tears shining in his eyes as he talked of Seabiscuit and the happy times they had spent together. It started to grow dark but I did not want to say goodbye, I wanted to talk to him for ever, but I had to get back to the horses. I walked backwards as I went, watching Red Pollard as he dreamed of Seabiscuit beneath the tree.

I think that was the greatest afternoon of my life. Please keep this story and pass it on to your children and their children and tell them to tell all the children they know, so that the story of Red Pollard and Seabiscuit, the little horse that gave hope to a nation, is kept alive.

I wish you a happy life.

Cuthbert H. Brown Jr

Hobnob and Jammie Dodger have their ears pricked, listening to every word. I fold the letter carefully and put it back in the envelope.

I lie back and rest my head on Jammie Dodger's belly, breathing in his lovely horsey smell and I think about how I am glad to be dyslexic, 'cause otherwise none of this would have happened.

When it's time to go, I walk back to the Beckham Estate, looking up. I can almost see Red Pollard and Seabiscuit riding across the night sky above me. I imagine Cuthbert H. Junior looking down on me and smiling.

'Thank you for the letters,' I call up to him. 'I will always treasure them. Good night, Cuthbert.'

THE VERY END

Aknolagements
Acnolidgmants
Acknolegdgmants
GIVE UP

Seriously, though, every time I have come to write the acknowledgements for my books, it takes me about three attempts to spell it!

So in this book, I shall call them this:

TO ALL THOSE THAT HELPED SEABISCUIT, JAMMIE DODGER AND ME RACE TO THE FINISHING LINE

It's taken a team of people cheering me on to help me win this race!

Thank you to all my team at Hachette for celebrating my neurodiversity and for working with me in a visionary way.

Naomi Greenwood, thank you for your exquisite editing and, most of all, for your kindness, patience, sense of fun and for your belief in the Secret Horse Society.

Jodie Hodges, my agent – from the moment your peal

of infectious laughter hit the air (when I told you I was calling the horse in my book Jammie Dodger in honour of Seabiscuit) I knew I was on to something. Thanks for your wisdom and never-ending support.

Emma Roberts, my copyeditor, for your wonderful attention to detail and your expertise in explaining to this very non-sporty author what a 400 metres track would even look like!

Now for the dream-come-true book cover: Michelle Brackenborough, I am truly blessed to have you as my designer, and thank you Keith Robinson for making Jammie Dodger and the Secret Horse Society come alive in your stunning art.

For Daniel and Akin, my neurodiverse members of the Secret Horse Society: dyslexia affects people differently. My brain works in the same chaotic way that Daniel's does. During the writing process I watched Kara Tointon's moving documentary *Don't Call Me Stupid*. I wasn't diagnosed till I was an adult, so I had a tough time at school but, through my challenges, I found that I was able to find my own way to do things and tune in to other neurodiverse young people and mentor them. I would like to pay tribute here to all the pupils of The Moat School in London who I worked with through the years. Thank you for your trust as we found ways together to meet challenges, your mind-blowing creativity and for defying the odds again and again, stunning your parents with your dramatic performances in our productions and our legendary poetry tea parties! You astound me. Also gratitude to Dell Smikle and Kate Zamira Mummery for the many deep conversations we have had about the dyslexic brain. For me it's been – and still is – such a journey: from being written off at school to becoming a published author. I entered Soho Theatre's Westminster Prize just for fun – it hadn't entered my head that I could ever be a writer – and was stunned to reach the shortlist. I told Jonathan Lloyd, the then Artistic Director of Soho Theatre, that I couldn't be a writer because I can't spell and he said to me, *'We don't care. It's the stories that matter.'* Those words were life changing for me. Thank you, Jonathan. It was author Lou Kuenzler's brilliant Writing for Children Workshops at City Lit that set me on my path, and I never dreamed it would lead to me writing my sixth children's book and the honour of making the list of the Top 50 Neurodivergent Women by the movement Women Beyond The Box, founded by Emma Case.

I believe the seed for Akin, the fiercely intelligent boy who can't sit still, was sown in my brain back in 2005 when I was brought in by my dear friend, producer of Collective Artistes, Semsem Kuherhi, to work as a script coach on Chuck Mike's production of Wole Soyinka's play *The Lion and the Jewel*. The cast, many of whom had flown in from Nigeria, made me so very welcome and as the rhythm of this wonderful play beat through me I was inspired and my brain began to tick very quietly till Akin burst into my imagination and stayed there as I began to write *Storm Horse*.

Semsem, you are and always have been an inspiration to me.

A huge big thank you for helping me with the final formation of Akin goes to Dunni Akinola. Akinkunmi Ojo is of Nigerian Heritage of the Yoruba tribe. Akinkunmi means 'Valor fills me' which is the perfect name for this brave funny young boy who meets his challenges head on. Thank you for checking Akin and Mr and Mrs Ojo for me, educating me in Yoruba pronunciation and for your help, kindness, time and, most of all, for your encouragement that my instinct had put me on the right path in the creation of Akin.

For All Things Horse: Carol Bramhill from The British Racing School. I cannot thank you enough for your warm enthusiastic emails, giving me such delicious titbits, such as: some young people who want to be jockeys train on sofa arms. Gold dust! But also the appalling fact that the jockeys in the 1930s did not wear hard hats! I was inspired during my research by Khadijah Mellah from the Ebony Horse Club in Brixton who was the first British Muslim jockey who steered Haverland to victory in the Magnolia Cup.

Alia Cooper, bless you for all your time and help in the details and guiding me as I changed the Old Shed into a stable for Jammie Dodger. I have such respect for your vast horse knowledge. Thank you for advising on how Jammie Dodger would react in certain unusual situations like, how do you get a horse into a school hall with a packet of Jammie Dodger biscuits?

And to Winston, Alia's gentle giant of a horse who loves to lie down both in the field and in the stable – the images of him were inspirational to Keith Robinson and Michelle Brackenborough for the cover. Thinking of Winston in a field has been my happy place during this pandemic. Alia, I can't wait to come out and visit you and Winston again and promise to have lots of apples in my pockets!

As a child I always had a passion for horses and read pony books avidly, but I didn't have the opportunity to go riding. As an adult one of my favourite things was attending Sue Roberts' fascinating horse lectures at Ponsbourne. Thank you, Sue, for teaching me the rudiments. I miss those times so much.

For All Things Rescue Dog: Ira Moss, I am in awe of how you change so many dogs' and people's lives through all you do with your charity All Dogs Matter. Buster the Staffie, in his determined way, bounced on to the pages of *Storm Horse*. I have to say watching you and the late beautiful Abi the Staffie, Ambassador for All Dogs Matter, promoting this wonderful breed has touched us all. Abi is truly missed but her wonderful legacy lives on through those lives she touched. Ira, thank you for your thoughts and input and for taking the time to read extracts to ensure that the Beckham Animal Rescue Centre in *Storm Horse* was run as beautifully as All Dogs Matter!

For All Things Radio: My cousin Sally Randles was only the second woman ever to work as a television engineer for the BBC. Thank you for immersing me in the world of 1930s radio and explaining how the sound commentary would have worked. Also, thank you Tim Kennington for all your valuable advice about how Michael would have built his Beckham Estate Radio Station. A special thanks to Anna Webb for all your support and for all I have learned about our canine friends through BBC's Barking Hour. Emma Noakes and Jane Morgan, thank you for your contribution to my research of 1930s radio sound effects.

For All Things Library: Mrs Johnson is the inspirational librarian in *Moon Dog* and *Storm Horse*. A shoutout to all librarians, but particularly Annie Everall OBE, Zoe Rowley and Jo Clarke. I value your support so much.

For All Things Costume and Hair: Kate Butterworth, thank you for all your help and opening the fascinating door into the world of 1930s fashion for me. Katrina Baranyi, you are a talented hairdresser and a legend, thank you for keeping my own unruly mop under control and for all the advice you gave me for my characters' hair styles, in particular Michael's twists!

Now, for All Things Seabiscuit: never since the Great Depression has the time for Seabiscuit's story been more important. I did not know what was about to happen to the world when I started writing this book. Just as Seabiscuit gave hope to children in the Great Depression, I hope that his story brings hope to children who may be struggling today.

What better role model for a dyslexic child than John A. Pollard – or Red Pollard as he was known – Seabiscuit's book-loving, Shakespeare-quoting jockey. Red's pet name for Seabiscuit was Pops and as I did my research, my respect and awe for Red and his Pops and their amazing partnership grew and grew. Red, I salute you and I hope you are looking down and enjoying the fact that your story will now reach a new generation through *Storm Horse*. I also want to pay tribute to those that loved Seabiscuit. Charles Howard and Marcela Howard, Seabiscuit's owners, and George Woolf, who rode Seabiscuit to victory against War Admiral at Pimlico on 1st November 1938.

A special mention to Tom Smith, the trainer who saw potential in Seabiscuit when no one else could. All dyslexics need a Tom Smith in their lives to see their potential and bring out the gift of dyslexia. To me, Seabiscuit is a reflection of myself and so many dyslexics, winning against all odds.

This book would not have been written without Laura

Hillenbrand's book *Seabiscuit: An American Legend*. The research for this book astounded me. I lived and breathed it through the whole of my writing process and it helped me shape parts of my story. Barbara Howard's book *Letters to Seabiscuit* – a collection of letters that both adults and children wrote to Seabiscuit – was a fascinating read. Seabiscuit the celebrity who captured the hearts of a nation.

Christopher Ryan, thank you for all you did to aid me in my research, and for reaching out to your aunty Cherie Long, who worked at Windsor Raceway and once took a pilgrimage to Man o' War's grave in Kentucky. Cherie, I would like to thank you so much for all the fascinating information you sent in our direction about Seabiscuit and the racing world.

There are so many parallels between the Great Depression and the pandemic. During my research I found out that Eleanor Roosevelt did much to help writers during the Great Depression. I would like to thank the Society of Authors for all they have done for authors during the pandemic. This book could not have been written without an Authors' Foundation grant. I cannot thank you enough.

Eleanor Roosevelt did much to help the hungry children in her human rights work and I would like to shout out to Marcus Rashford for campaigning to keep our children fed and to all the people who work in foodbanks, the NHS and other frontline workers.

And finally . . . to All Things Friends and Family, who cheered me on and supported from afar whenever I was flagging in the race:

Marcia Mantack, thanks for all our fascinating chats about Jamaican and London beats and rhythms, word origins and all things Aunty Lou.

Mo O'Hara, Vikki Biram-Doig, Joseph Coelho, Naomi Jones, Susie Evans and Jennifer Killick – my writers' group, who believed in this book.

And as I get near the finishing post: those who cheered loudest!

Sharon D. Clarke MBE, Susie McKenna, Christopher William Hill, Patrice Lawrence, Kristina Stephenson, Steve Antony, Tracey Smith, Howard Grace, Paul Neaum, Christopher 'Sparkey' Hurley, Adrian Rammage, Phil Earle, Rhian Ivory, Lindsey Coulson, Curtis Ashton, Clare Calder, Nicky McCrae, Jenny Elson, Viv and Eric Beattie, Barbara Elson, Cris Penfold and Tameka Empson.

To dyslexics everywhere: keep believing.

And my final thank you goes to Seabiscuit himself, for giving a nation hope.

All Dogs Matter

Charity Registration 1132883

If you are considering adopting a dog and live in London and the surrounding areas, please consider adopting from All Dogs Matter.

All Dogs Matter is a dog rescue and rehoming charity working in and around London to transform the lives of unwanted and abandoned dogs. We also rehome dogs in need from overseas.

In 2019 All Dogs Matter rescued and rehomed over 370 dogs with new owners. We also found forever homes for 27 unwanted and abandoned dogs from China, Italy and Egypt.

AllDogsMatter.co.uk

○ ⅴ @AllDogsMatter

f All Dogs Matter

Photograph by Christopher Ryan

*In memory of
Abi the Staffie
Ambassador for
All Dogs Matter
2007-2020*

JANE ELSON

After performing as an actress and comedy improviser, Jane fell into writing stories and plays. Her books have won many awards, including Peters Book of the Year two years running. Her debut novel, *A Room Full of Chocolate*, was longlisted for the Branford Boase Award and Jane has twice been nominated for the Carnegie Medal.

Jane is loud and proud about her dyslexia and and over the years has mentored many neurodiverse young people, promoting the gift of alternative thinking. She was honoured to be named as one of the top 50 Influential Neurodivergent Women by Women Beyond The Box, a platform to amplify the voice of smart neurodiverse women.

Jane is an ambassador for the charity Nacoa and wrote *Lockdown Nell* – a free story resource for children affected by their parents' drinking during lockdown.

Jane is also an advocate for All Dogs Matter, a rescue charity close to her heart. She is pictured here with the late Abi the Staffie, Ambassador for the charity, who is sadly missed and for ever in our hearts.

www.aroomfullofwords.com  @jjelson35

ALSO AVAILABLE

Can a lost boy and a daring girl save the dog next door?

Moon DOG

JANE ELSON

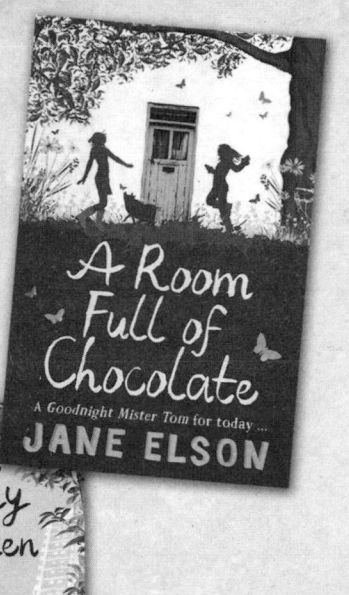

A Room Full of Chocolate

A Goodnight Mister Tom for today ...

JANE ELSON

How to Fly with Broken Wings

JANE ELSON

The tale of a boy who wants to make friends, and the girl who shows him how.

Swimming to the Moon

JANE·ELSON

The story of a promise and an unlikely friendship.

Will You Catch Me?

JANE ELSON

Sometimes the world looks better upside down ...